OUTLAW LAKE

More from Maisey Yates

Rustler Mountain

Anthologies

Santa's on His Way
The Two of Us
Small Town Hero

OUTLAW LAKE

MAISEY YATES

KENSINGTON PUBLISHING CORP.

kensingtonbooks.com

KENSINGTON BOOKS are published by

Kensington Publishing Corp.
900 Third Avenue
New York, NY 10022

Copyright © 2025 by Maisey Yates

All rights reserved. No part of this book may be reproduced in any form or by any means without the prior written consent of the Publisher, excepting brief quotes used in reviews.

Without limiting the author's and publisher's exclusive rights, any unauthorized use of this publication to train generative artificial intelligence (AI) technologies is expressly prohibited.

All Kensington titles, imprints, and distributed lines are available at special quantity discounts for bulk purchases for sales promotion, premiums, fund-raising, educational, or institutional use.

This book is a work of fiction. Names, characters, businesses, organizations, places, events, and incidents either are the product of the author's imagination or are used fictitiously. Any resemblance to actual persons, living or dead, events, or locales is entirely coincidental.

To the extent that the image or images on the cover of this book depict a person or persons, such person or persons are merely models, and are not intended to portray any character or characters featured in the book.

Special book excerpts or customized printings can also be created to fit specific needs. For details, write or phone the office of the Kensington Sales Manager: Kensington Publishing Corp., 900 Third Avenue, New York, NY 10022. Attn. Sales Department. Phone: 1-800-221-2647.

KENSINGTON and the K with book logo Reg. US Pat. & TM Off.

ISBN: 978-1-4967-5348-9
ISBN: 978-1-4967-5349-6 (ebook)

First Kensington Trade Paperback Printing: October 2025

10 9 8 7 6 5 4 3 2 1

Printed in the United States of America

The authorized representative in the EU for product safety and compliance is eucomply OU, Parnu mnt 139b-14, Apt 123
Tallinn, Berlin 11317, hello@eucompliancepartner.com

To the readers who love friends-to-lovers books as much as I do

Chapter 1

There is nothing left for me here. I'm going west.
   —Mae Tanner's Diary, June 15th, 1899

Perry Bramble loved Carson Wilder with all her heart.

It was just that her heart had been irrevocably broken into pieces when she was a child, along with any trust she might have had in the world, and Carson was an emotionally unavailable hot mess who had fallen in love with another woman.

As caveats went, those were pretty big ones.

It was why Carson was her best friend in the whole world, and nothing more. It was why she spent every evening with him, and many mornings, even though it wasn't convenient for either of them.

It was why they were attached—if not at the hip, then at the very least, the soul.

They had been best friends since she was seven years old, when her family had moved in next door to the Wilder Ranch.

Stay away from them, they're not the right kind of people.

That was what her dad had said, in his neat clothes with a bland expression on his face. And later he would turn into a monster and roll up those same sleeves while he hit her mother, and if that didn't satisfy his rage—Perry herself.

Perry lived with a villain. She hadn't understood that right away. What she did know was that . . . if her dad thought the Wilders were bad, she wanted to know about them.

She'd sneaked onto their property, and she could still remember plain as day, meeting a nine-year-old boy in overalls—nothing else—with skinny arms and a bony chest—who looked her square in the eye.

Do you want to play?

I do.

They'd spent the afternoon playing pirates, and when it was over they were best friends. As they had been ever since.

Not without trials, tribulations, and her dad trying to tear them apart, but Perry had learned one thing when she'd decided that Carson Wilder was her person: She was more than happy to be a rebel as long as she had a cause.

Her cause was Carson.

Though now she was thinking maybe—*maybe*—her cause needed to be herself.

She chewed the inside of her lip as she finished putting together her last arrangement of the day, which was due to be picked up just as she closed her shop, Bramble Flowers. Then she was going to Carson's for dinner.

Instead of going on a date with Stephen Lee, which was stupid. He'd asked her to dinner, and she would have said yes, but she had her standing plans with Carson. They were not firm or official and could easily be blown off, but she hadn't done it.

It was hard to want a new relationship when the one she had was so all-consuming.

And also she was wary of men.

Thanks, Dad.

She had once loved her dad with all her heart too.

It would have been easier if he had consistently been a fire-breathing dragon, but he hadn't been. It was why she rolled her eyes when young girls on the internet talked about red flags in men. As if there were clear and obvious signs that were visible to anyone and everyone from the first—and sure, there were men like that.

Those men didn't scare Perry.

It was the ones who smiled, who went to church every Sunday, and Wednesday besides.

The ones who built such a good facade that no one would believe they were monsters if you told them. And even if they did believe, they'd make excuses.

Why ruin a good man's life?

Her father had status, had friends in the community, and a good job. He smiled easily.

A smile that could quickly turn, changing the temperature of the room. A smile that trained everyone in the house to walk on eggshells to avoid the explosion that could come if anyone stepped wrong.

Perry was very good at taking careful steps. Ironically, given what an absolutely transparent mess he was, Carson never made her feel she had to watch her step.

If Perry thought back really hard, all the way back, to the last time she'd had someone who counted as a boyfriend, she could easily say why it worked so well.

She'd never cared about that guy more than he'd cared about her. She'd always known walking away would be easy.

She'd never wanted her whole life to be wrapped around a man, not the way her mother's had been.

The joke was on her, she supposed. She had thought that sort of obsession only came with romance.

But she chose not to think about Carson Wilder. Instead, she chose to think of the building in Medford—an hour away from Rustler Mountain—that had ivy climbing the sides and would be available in six months to house a new, larger florist shop.

The building that would require a heck of a down payment—one she could only realize by selling her house. Since she was renting this little building on Main Street, she wouldn't get anything from vacating it.

Her only asset was the Victorian house she'd inherited from her grandmother—which had issues that went well beyond the cosmetic. But if she sold it, she'd be able to buy the building in Medford and that would allow her to expand her business and her focus.

Most of which involved trying to grow a massive array of flowers for weddings. And maybe working nights at the twenty-four-hour drive-through coffee stand off the freeway—also over an hour away, but beggars couldn't be choosers.

She had a plan. For the first time in a long time.

She finished up her arrangement and waited for the customer to arrive. And once he'd left, she turned the sign, locked the door, and zeroed out her register.

She took a deep breath, and her lungs expanded, her heart lifting slightly. She always felt this way when it was time to see Carson.

Which was why she had to move forward.

It was also the reason for the broken date.

And the dry spell of the last several years.

Her general *girl treading water in circles around a man* aesthetic.

She loved Carson with all her messed-up, broken, crushed little heart, and that ended up looking a lot like codependence.

Or so a therapist she saw once eight months ago had said. She hadn't gone back because who wanted to hear that the most important relationship in their life was holding them back?

Not Perry.

But the worry had wormed its way into her brain like a weevil and had sat there, chewing and chewing and *chewing*.

She was devastated over what she was going to tell Carson tonight, yet she still felt so happy she was going to see him. As if she was racing toward the best part of her day even though tonight, it was going to be weird and difficult and maybe even *terrible*.

She was, perhaps, dramatizing.

It wasn't like she was moving to Canada. Or like she was moving *tomorrow*.

They'd lived farther apart before.

The last time that happened, he got married to someone else.

She had comforted herself for a number of years with the knowledge that Carson didn't seem to be interested in love. He was stoic and hard, her dearest friend. A man who was sometimes more like a well-guarded safe than a human being.

But he trusted Perry more than he did anyone else.

And in the absence of romantic affection, she'd been . . . happy with that. Sort of.

But he'd fallen in love with someone else. So the problem hadn't been him. It had been Perry all along that he couldn't love. That had been a wound she'd had a hard time healing.

She shoved that thought way, way, way out of her brain.

If she moved away, maybe she'd get married. Or not. She would move forward with starting a family because that was what she wanted, and she wasn't going to wait around for a man she might never meet to get the ball rolling.

Just as she was done waiting for a man who was never going to . . .

She was doing this . . . well, not because of him. It was because of her. And her need to get a life. A bigger life.

She told herself that as she drove down Rustler Mountain's quaint main street and looked at all the beautiful hanging baskets of pink petunias, smiling slightly at the new, updated plaques shining bright against the building facades.

Along with local wine and stunning mountain views, history was one of the big tourist draws in Rustler Mountain. As a gold-rush town eight miles from the California border, the romanticized American West was baked right into the red brick of the buildings.

The most notorious local legend was the death of notorious outlaw Austin Wilder right on the main street Perry was driving along now. An ancestor of her very dearest friend in all the world.

But Carson's brother Austin, named for the same man who was killed in these streets, had written a novel based on that event. His research had changed the long-held narrative in town, and since then there had been a lot of updates that gave folks a much deeper understanding of the history of town.

She'd miss this place.

That hollow thought reverberated through her as she drove on, out of town and along the road that would carry her to Outlaw Lake, Carson's part of the vast Wilder Ranch.

When she pulled up to the modern ranch house, Carson was

halfway out the door. Ready to greet her. She smiled and her heart squeezed.

She could remember him when he was a child. That skinny little boy in overalls. She had that picture so clear in her head, and she thought she probably always would.

But he was not that boy now.

Carson Wilder was well over six feet tall, with broad shoulders and the physique of a man who lifted tires and hay bales for fun. He had let his military haircut grow out over the last few years, his dark blond hair still short on the sides, but now longer on the top. It was rare to see him without his cowboy hat, but he'd clearly come in from working the ranch a while ago. His hat had been discarded, along with his boots. He was wearing a black T-shirt and jeans, his feet bare.

A common enough sight, and yet it also spoke to the level of intimacy in their relationship.

Intimacy was the wrong word. It was a nice word. But it made them sound like emotionally healthy human beings, and she had to remember that they were not.

She put her car in park, and Carson opened the door and held it, waiting for her. "Hey," he said, a smile on his handsome face.

His blue eyes were more intense than the sky.

She had to look away. "Hey, yourself."

She ducked under his arm and went into the house. It was military neat, just like always. He was terrifying that way. Perry herself was more . . . eclectic. She liked a clean dining table and a made bed. But there were also ribbons and odds and ends all over the place, and dried flowers hanging from every corner of her kitchen ceiling.

Carson's house had been as clean as if it was awaiting inspection until after his wife had suddenly died. Then it had been a mess, which was so unlike him it had been scary. A few weeks of untidiness had been one thing, but the ongoing mess had been a reflection of the pain inside him, pain he couldn't get a handle on.

Thankfully, right now it was clean. Which made her think he was doing well. Was more like himself.

"Pizza?" she asked.

"Yeah, I had to go into Medford earlier, so I got a take and bake."

"Ooooh."

She smiled, and for a minute things felt normal.

The oven timer went off and she followed Carson into the kitchen. It was such a pretty kitchen. A lot more stylish than anything Carson would have chosen on his own, but then, that was the whole house.

The white countertops and emerald green cabinets had been chosen by Alyssa, who'd died less than a year after the house had been finished.

And Carson still had to live in it.

She shrugged that thought off and looked at the white double oven with the gold door handles, watching as he pulled the pizza out.

"Thank you," she said.

"You cook for me often enough."

"I do, it's true."

One of them did, every night. They were never alone. They went out together; they spent their downtime together.

It was a lot.

And never enough.

This was so perfect. It was even more perfect when they sat at his dining table with pizza. And they'd do it again tomorrow, and the day after that and the day after that and they would never, ever change.

"I wanted to talk to you about something," she said, setting her uneaten pizza crust down on her plate—she didn't like crust.

He picked her crust up and started to eat it like a breadstick. "Oh yeah?"

She looked at those blue eyes, and emotion expanded in her chest, so big and bright it couldn't be contained. Carson Wilder was the love of her life.

And that was precisely why she had to leave him.

She let out a long, slow breath. "Carson . . . I'm moving."

Chapter 2

I feel like I should be sorrier to leave, but the truth is it's a relief. I could never be what everyone wanted me to be at home. I'll miss the ones I love, but I'd rather be who I am surrounded by strangers than keep on trying to be someone I'm not with friends.

—Mae Tanner's Diary, July 19th, 1899

Carson stared at Perry, whose face was as familiar to him as his own. Hell, more so, probably, since he didn't look in the mirror much. He never took a selfie, but he looked at her every day.

He'd have been tempted to make a joke if that familiar face, those bright green eyes and that mouth that pointed down slightly at the corners, didn't look so unhappy.

"What do you mean you're moving?" he asked, pushing his plate into the center of the table.

He'd eaten all of Perry's crust, so he didn't need the plate anymore.

"It's pretty self-explanatory."

"You're sitting still," he said, in spite of himself. If he and Perry couldn't make jokes even when it was clearly a bad time to joke, then everything was pointless.

"I'm leaving," she said, a small notch denting that space between her eyebrows.

He couldn't wrap his head around what she was saying. If someone else had been saying those words, he'd think it meant they were moving away. Leaving town. But Perry didn't mean that. She *couldn't* mean that.

She belonged here. Like the sun, the sky, the mountains. She couldn't up and leave any more than the trees could pull themselves up by their roots and run off.

But she was sitting there, looking at him like that. Saying that.

"You're moving out of your house?"

She spread her hands out flat on the table. "Yes." She seemed relieved.

"Down the street or . . . ?"

"To another town."

It was his turn to furrow his brow. "What?"

"I need to . . . I need . . . something?" She turned her hands over, palms up, spreading them wide. "I have been treading water for . . . for years, Carson, and I have to stop."

"You haven't been treading water. You've been sitting at my kitchen table." Her eyebrows moved up, just fractionally. She said nothing, and he found it annoying. "*Perry.*"

Her shoulders shook, as if she shivered. "I want to expand my shop," she said. "And I found a place in Medford. And I want . . ." She let out a long breath. "I want to have a baby. Someday. And how am I ever going to get that life sitting here every night?"

He felt like she'd punched him. In his guts. In his face.

"Excuse me?"

"I would like to have a baby, Carson. I am thirty-two years old, and it's time to do something . . . more."

"You don't have a boyfriend," he pointed out.

"I don't need a boyfriend to have a baby. All I need is sperm."

The word rolled around in his head for a minute, all alone.

Sperm.

It left him feeling . . . not good.

It was just distasteful to think about that word and Perry, together.

But not more distasteful than thinking of her leaving. Than thinking of her . . . having a baby. Moving on. From him.

He realized that was a thought that bordered on unhinged. But she was . . . his lifeline. *His* . . . God dammit, she was his person. In a way he couldn't have explained to another living soul. She wasn't just a friend. But she'd never been his lover. She wasn't a sister. It was deeper. More complicated. It was . . .

"We aren't good for each other," she said softly.

He looked up at her, then down at their empty plates, and back up at her. "What the fuck does that mean? And you're wrong. You don't like crust, and I just ate your crust."

She sighed heavily. "That's actually the issue, Carson. The crust. That I don't finish it, but you do. It's . . . codependence."

"I thought it was you being picky and me being raised with an old man who made me clean my plate?" It wasn't funny. He didn't laugh. Neither did she.

"It's . . . enabling."

"It's pizza crust, Per, not crack."

"For God's sake!" She slammed her palms down on the table. "You know what I mean."

He didn't, though. Or he didn't want to. Or maybe he did but he didn't see it as a problem and couldn't understand why she did.

"Perry," he said, his tone serious now because she was being ridiculous, and he wasn't fucking around. "You don't need to leave to have what you want."

He deliberately left the implications of everything she said she wanted out of his mind. He deliberately did not imagine her choosing random sperm. Being pregnant.

The image made him think of a desecrated saint. He couldn't cope with it.

She could get anything she wanted or needed here. She was being dramatic, and for some reason she was making him her bad object, which was a fine fucking thing.

He'd protected her, cared for her, for most of their lives.

For twenty-five years.

They'd hidden from her father in the old barn. Run feral out in the fields and played pirates at the lake.

Life moved on, relentlessly, horrendously, but Perry was like Neverland. His safe and never-changing haven.

He'd tried to be that for her.

Now she was leaving?

"You don't understand," she said, looking bleak.

"Obviously I don't."

"We can't keep doing this. It's not good for either of us. I could have been on a date tonight, but instead I'm sitting here in my childhood best friend's kitchen, letting him eat my pizza crust."

"You had a date?" he asked. Her dating life wasn't really the point of the conversation, but it snagged his thoughts all the same.

"Yes. I did. Stephen Lee asked me to dinner."

He frowned. He liked Stephen. Which actually kind of pissed him off. Stephen was good enough for Perry. He was an accountant, and he had his own tax firm. He and Austin both used him, in fact. He was successful and nice and honest and exactly the kind of man who could give Perry babies and a decent life.

He hated that such a great guy had asked Perry out and that she should have gone with him. Damn, he hated that a lot.

"You could have gone," Carson said.

"But I didn't because I knew you and I would have dinner if I didn't."

That made his chest glow with warmth. Perry chose him.

But she shouldn't have—that was the thing. Because all Perry was ever going to get from him was this. Him eating her pizza crust.

That wasn't true. He'd given Perry more than that.

He'd encouraged her to apply to the college she'd wanted to go to, and he'd been on the phone with her while she did her financial aid and scholarship applications. He'd offered to pay for her school if she didn't get enough money so that she would never have to ask her horrible father for anything—in the end, everything had been covered.

He'd promised himself he would always be her hero.

Her father had come to the house looking for her once, wild-eyed and furious, convinced that Carson was messing with his daughter. He'd been seventeen. Perry had been fifteen.

Carson had punched her father in his fucking face, and the man had had to wear a bruise on *his* face to his job as a mortgage broker. He'd had to sit there with the marks of violence on him in the pew at church.

Just as his wife and daughter had done for years. Though he'd never struck them where the bruises would show. His abuse wasn't caused by a temper he couldn't control, or anger management issues, it was systemic, controlled violence that wore a smiling face in public while inflicting pain in private.

Carson had never touched Perry in violence or as a sexual object.

He'd been determined—always—to be the man who protected her, not took from her.

But the last two years had been complicated.

If he was honest, the last four years had been.

When he'd moved back home with his bride, she and Perry had gotten along better than Carson and Alyssa had behind closed doors. Sometimes he'd felt as if Perry preferred his wife to him, which had been weird.

In the years before that, they'd written while he was on deployment. Actual letters. It had brought them closer, because he'd been able to put things in writing that he couldn't say in person.

But he'd locked some things away when Alyssa died. Just the same, Perry had relentlessly been there, open and honest as always and his sunshine when the day was so dark he couldn't breathe through the oppressive weight of it.

And now the only way she could imagine living differently was getting the fuck out of town?

Because apparently her relationship with him was a burden, not a bright spot.

"I'm fine," he said. "I mean, you don't have to babysit me every night."

"I'm not babysitting you. I'm choosing to be here but . . . I need to expand my life," she said. "I just do. I need . . . you know how it's always been with my dad."

Yeah. He did.

And he could still feel the man's cheekbone cracking under his fist.

He relished that memory.

"The day your dad dies, I'm sending a gift basket straight to hell so Satan will spend extra time on him."

"I'll add a card," she said.

She looked up at him with her wide blue eyes, her blond hair all disheveled, and he couldn't help but think of her as the little girl she'd been when they'd first met—a tiny little thing, only two years younger than he was. He'd seen her wander onto the property wearing a flowered dress and big rubber boots, and he'd thought to himself: *I'm going to keep her.*

Like she was a puppy.

But he *had* kept her, all this time.

"I'm going to do it like Mae," she said.

"Mae?"

"My five-times-great-grandmother who came out to Rustler Mountain as a mail-order bride."

"I missed the part of the story where some guy who works in car sales in Medford with an aftermarket spoiler on his Honda sent away to have you come to that mighty metropolis as his bride," Carson said, his tone dry.

She rolled her eyes. "That's not what I mean. I mean, she struck out on her own and she made her own life, and it's starting to be abundantly clear to me that that's what I need to do."

"You have a shop right on Main Street."

"And I live month to month because I can only afford one person to help me, and my job is so seasonal it's painful, and local people only send so many flowers, and and *and.*"

"So what's your plan, then?"

"I want to grow more flowers on my own. I want to be able to do more weddings and specialty events. But I need to be in a bigger hub to take that stuff on."

"Or you need a social media manager."

She gave him a very hard stink eye. "Are you offering?"

"Yeah, sure, I can post some pictures and put the little pound signs in afterward."

She put her face in her hands. "They're hashtags."

"What?"

"They're not pound signs. They're . . . never mind, you are entirely unserious."

"I'm not unserious. I'm just saying that I don't think you need to move to expand your business."

Silence settled between them, and he really hated silence in his house. More than anything, he hated the echo of his own thoughts. The unavoidable truths that he'd had to reckon with after Alyssa's death.

He'd never felt so starkly aware of his own limitations as he had then.

He was self-aware enough to know he'd been on a search for a twelve-step program to being a good man. He'd joined the military because it offered compulsory heroism. He'd gotten married because it provided a system, complete with paperwork.

Here I am, a finished man. A husband who has made vows he intends to keep.

Only to discover that neither institution had magically changed him at all.

He would always, always, always be a Wilder no matter what he did. No matter that he'd served in the military and protected his country. No matter that he'd found a good wife from a good family and settled down to live respectably.

There was a darkness he could never escape, and the universe made sure he knew it.

He grounded himself by looking at Perry. He stared across the table hard for a moment. At her. At her familiar face. Those beautiful eyes.

I'm going to keep her.

And that was when it hit him, really, that she wasn't looking for a reason to stay. She'd said it. She'd said that they were holding each other back. He'd heard the words, but he hadn't really begun to absorb them. He hadn't been able to.

"I don't want you to go," he said.

"I didn't ask you," she said, standing up from the table. "And I knew you were going to be mad about it, but haven't we had this fight once before?"

He didn't like to think about that day. When he'd met Perry under their favorite oak tree out at the far end of the property, he in a military uniform, to tell her he'd joined up and he was leaving town.

She'd been seventeen and he'd been nineteen. She'd sobbed her heart out as if he'd stabbed her.

"What, so I'm not allowed to have feelings about you leaving because I left for a while?" he asked.

"That seems fair to me. Doesn't it seem fair to you?"

"No. Because then you went off to college and you got your business degree, and it isn't like you didn't have experiences of your own out in the broader world too. It's not like you waited here holding a vigil for me."

"Yes, I did normal things when you went to go do your normal thing, because that is a normal thing for people to do," she said.

"I'm allowed to have an opinion about it," he said. "Because it's different now."

"I know!" She threw her hands in the air. "Like, that is literally what I'm telling you. I know it's different now, and I need my life to be different from this and frankly, so do you. I'm keeping you locked in your sad, single-man stasis."

"If I wanted to go on a date, I'd go on a date."

"I don't need you to want to go on a date, but you *do* need to not need me as your emotional support animal."

That made him wince, because he had just recalled thinking of her a bit like a stray puppy. But she made his view of her sound minimizing and unflattering, and to him it was anything but.

To him she'd always been important. Essential.

"That's not fair. You're my best friend," he said, the words ringing with conviction and sounding hollow all at the same time. Because that label did her a disservice too. She was more than his best friend. "And I have a right to be hurt and to be skeptical when you show up acting out of character."

"*Out of character* is me doing something you don't like? Good to know." She grabbed her purse off the back of his chair and started to stomp toward the door.

Were they fighting?

He and Perry never fought. Ever.

But then, Perry also never sat across from him and said he was bad for her.

Right now, she was saying everything he'd always feared hearing and never thought he'd hear from her.

One time he'd thought maybe he would.

When a man was born with bad blood in his veins and decided he wanted to live in defiance of his roots, he had to make choices. He couldn't afford to careen through life running into things and causing all manner of destruction.

There had been distinct moments in time when he'd had the chance to go in one direction, and he'd gone in the other.

One of those moments had been when Perry was fifteen, after he'd punched her dad in the face.

They'd been down at the lake, and Perry had been in a white dress that was translucent from the water, her cheeks sunburned, her hair a pale halo lit up in the light. She'd looked wild and wonderful. A mermaid. A pirate princess.

He'd thought then what it might be like to kiss her, the sudden riot of lust a shock to him. He wasn't a virgin then. Perry probably was.

It had felt like violence inside him, that sudden, dark need.

She must have seen it that way, because she'd looked at his face, and her eyes had gone wide, the color draining from her face beneath that sunburn. She slipped into the water like a selkie and swam to the other side of the shore.

She'd run from him.

He'd sworn to himself that he would never, ever scare Perry again.

Lust was common. Their connection wasn't.

One thing Carson was good at was drawing a line firmly underneath something and calling it done.

He'd drawn a thick line under Perry that day.

He'd done what he needed to do to protect her, and whenever he'd needed to reaffirm that decision, he'd done it.

She just didn't appreciate his determination.

"Out of character," he said, his voice low and angrier than he'd heard it in a long time, "is you blaming whatever bullshit you're going through on me. If you're pissed about your life, that's fine. But don't go heaping your unhappiness onto me as if I choose how you spend your evenings."

"That isn't what I said!"

"It damn well is, and you know it. If you're so miserable with me, get your ass back to town and make a dessert date with Stephen."

"Carson."

He walked past her to the front door and held it open. "Good night, Perry."

His tone was hard, definitive, and she looked up at him with hurt, shiny eyes, and he wanted to yell at her some more because what the hell? How dare she come in here and say he was bad for her and they were bad for each other and then act wounded when he gave her what she wanted?

"You want distance, take your distance."

"I said it was going to be in a little while!"

"You said a lot of shit. Now get out of my house."

Her mouth opened as if she was going to say something else, and then she just growled furiously and stomped out into the evening. "Fuck you, Carson, honestly!" she shouted as she got into her car and turned the engine on.

"Fuck you too," he muttered as he slammed the front door and paced back into his kitchen. He wore a groove in the floor, angrily walking back and forth. About the time he was wishing he had something to take the edge off his anger—something alcoholic—he grabbed his keys with the thought of driving to his brother's.

He wasn't going to start drinking. He'd gone down that slippery slope in the wake of Alyssa's death, trying to avoid clarity of thought, and he'd realized at some point that surrendering control to that substance was way too close to his dad's bullshit.

He'd quit cold turkey to spite his father's drunken ghost.

I'm a better man than you, even with all this!

Too bad the ghost hadn't answered.

But then, his dad had ignored his sons when he was alive—why would he bother to haunt them when he was dead?

Carson's life was actually weirdly devoid of ghosts considering all his losses.

Alyssa would never bother to haunt Rustler Mountain. No doubt she'd gone back home, and who could blame her?

He drove the short distance between his house and Austin's. They'd divided the property up when Carson had moved back home with his wife, and if he drove in a straight line across the fields, it was only two minutes from his door to his brother's.

Austin's house was older than Carson's, the original house on the property. It had that old log-cabin charm. Austin had always kept it meticulously, and now that he had a wife, it was even cleaner.

Out of habit, Carson walked right up the steps and into the front door, where he saw his sister-in-law leap up off Austin's lap into a standing position, her hair askew, her cheeks flushed.

"Do I have to hang a tie on the door?" Austin growled, looking over at him, and Carson had the good sense to arrange his expression into something vaguely shamed.

"I . . . sorry."

"What are we sorry about?"

His younger sister, Cassidy, slipped through the front door behind him, and he jumped. "Where did you come from?" Austin asked.

"I walked from the tiny house. I'm hungry and there's nothing in my fridge." She prowled past Carson into the kitchen.

"You have to be kidding," Austin groused. "Cass, I got you that tiny house so you'd stay in your own space!"

"But you love me!" she called back.

"What does that have to do with you needing to STAY IN

YOUR OWN SPACE?" He shouted that last bit louder than Carson thought was strictly necessary.

For her part, Millie had covered her mouth and was snickering into her hand. Carson closed the door behind him, but it didn't shut. Instead, it swung back open and their younger brother Flynn walked in.

"Are you having a party without me?" Flynn asked.

"We aren't," Austin said.

"Kind of," said Cassidy, leaning in the doorway holding a bag of corn chips and crunching on them noisily.

"*Plain* corn chips?" Flynn asked her, looking appalled.

"They're good," Cassidy said, talking with her mouth full like an outright heathen.

Flynn frowned. "Corn chips are a vehicle for salsa and refried beans. That's it. A necessary evil, one might say."

"They can also be nachos," Millie pointed out.

"Then they aren't corn chips anymore," Flynn said. "They've been transformed."

"You're insane," Cassidy said, shoving three more chips into her mouth.

"You're all in my house without warning," Austin said. He looked over at Flynn. "Did you strike out?"

Flynn smiled. "No, I didn't, big brother. I'm just done for the evening."

"Damn," said Cassidy. "Where can I send the lady my condolences?"

Flynn crossed the room and yanked the bag of chips out of Cassidy's hand. "Hey!" she shouted, walking after him into the kitchen, where they continued to bicker.

Millie looked at Carson, the softness and concern on his sister-in-law's face warming him for a second, until he realized he was also the only person Austin was being nice to. Which meant they knew he was here because he was on edge, and they pitied him. That they were right made it worse somehow. That he maybe needed their pity. Or support, as someone more evolved might call it.

Carson had evolved a lot in his life. Mostly without his consent.

But he was uncomfortable with certain things still. Needing support, or rather admitting it, was one of those things. But maybe that was part of what Perry had been getting at.

He took a lot of support from her while pretending that wasn't what it was. While pretending they were just hanging out, when especially in the aftermath of rock bottom, was not the case at all.

"What's up?" Austin asked.

"Oh, I . . . had a fight with Perry."

Both Austin and Millie looked shocked. Millie sat down next to Austin and looked up at him with concern. "About what?" she asked.

"She's . . . she wants to move away. Something about her business." He couldn't bring himself to tell Austin and Millie that she'd also said it was because of him.

"Where is she going?" Austin asked.

"Medford."

"It's only an hour away," Austin pointed out.

Carson had to stop himself from pointing out that except when he'd been in the military, he currently lived the farthest from Perry that he ever had in his life, at a whopping ten minutes' distance.

"Well, I got mad about it. And I yelled at her, and now I feel bad."

"You should go apologize to her," Millie said.

He wasn't sorry, though. He was sorry she was angry, he supposed, but he'd needed to say something about the bomb she'd lobbed into the middle of his dining table. And he was pissed, so didn't he have the right to say that?

"What's her plan?" Austin asked.

"I don't know," Carson said. "I didn't really ask."

"You didn't ask? You just got mad?"

"She said some things . . . she said some things I didn't really think were fair."

"Like?"

"It's private," he said.

Austin and Millie exchanged a glance.

"What?" Carson asked. "What does that mean?"

Austin shrugged and Carson almost punched him, he really did.

"She said she needs to get some distance from me and our relationship, okay?" His words throbbed in the air, with all his rage and all his hurt and all his everything.

Then Austin and Millie exchanged another glance. "Your . . . relationship?"

"What the hell is that expression about? Our friendship. Yes. She's . . . I don't know, she thinks we're too dependent on each other and it's keeping us from advancing in our lives." Indignation grew in his chest again, and he felt an extreme jolt of anger.

It just wasn't true. They supported each other. They . . .

She supported *him*.

Yes, there had been a time in their lives when the balance was different. Better. It had shifted though, after Alyssa died. He'd lost his perspective on everything, and Perry had been there the whole time to dig him out, to help him up.

She'd been his confidante, his cheerleader, his therapist.

Right then he realized the *real* issue was that she was right. About their relationship, mostly as it pertained to her.

He hadn't seen it because he was the one getting the most out of their friendship, and that was a really shitty revelation.

He *was* holding her back. She could have been out on a date with Stephen Lee, and God knew he was a fucking drain on her. She'd supported him, propped him up, cooked him dinner. Quite literally saved his goddamned life.

He'd left Rustler Mountain once upon a time, determined to make something of himself. If Perry wanted to do that, he needed to try to be supportive of her, but it felt as if somebody had kicked his crutch out from under his arm.

And that proved her point in ways that left him outraged.

"She's right," he said.

"Oh?" Austin asked.

"Yes, she . . ." He rubbed his hand over his face. "I haven't been a great friend to her."

"You've been her best friend for her entire life," Austin pointed out.

"She's been dragging me along for a couple of years now, Austin, and you know that."

"It's not dragging someone along when they've legitimately been through shit and have some healing to do. We all worry about you; we all care. No one else in our group has been through what you have. Yes, we've all been through stuff. But you're the only one who lost a wife."

He was the only one—until Austin—who'd ever been married. The only one who'd had enough hubris to fly too close to that particular sun.

He believed Austin and Millie would be happy. They'd worked through a significant amount of angst to get there, but Austin was . . .

In Carson's opinion, his older brother was an astonishing person. They'd been raised by their asshole father to be unconcerned with anyone's opinion, and to think as little as possible. They'd been raised by the town to see themselves as the bad guys, and Carson had responded in an extremely literal way.

He'd decided to go be a hero. What better way to do that than by joining the military? Everyone knew soldiers were a bunch of heroes, after all.

That wasn't Austin's way. He was a deep thinker. A cowboy and a philosopher. And a writer—his novel about their ancestor was still sitting on the *New York Times* bestseller list, which was a hell of a thing.

He wasn't competitive with his brother, and it was a good thing. No one was ever going to compete with Austin's success.

Though for all his deep thinking, Austin hadn't been immune to believing in the family curse. That the Wilder men lived fast and died young, and there was no kind of good living that would ever get the stain of *outlaw* off them.

Part of what he'd done with his book, which uncovered the true history of their family and the notorious outlaw Austin Wilder, their six-times-over great-grandfather, was to change the association of the family name.

In Carson's mind, Austin had redeemed himself.

The sad truth was, Carson had a problem that was a lot different from a belief in curses as old as the Wild West.

His problem was he'd been a hero. He'd been a husband.

It hadn't been enough.

Nothing he did was ever enough. The world was the same, his life was the same. Alyssa was dead and Perry was his last stand, really.

He was a man who genuinely prized action and hard work. When all his efforts turned into . . . nothing? That was some shit he didn't know what to do with. He'd settled in. He'd kept on working his land. Apparently, he'd leaned on his best friend a little bit too hard.

Apparently, he had failed her. Instead, he needed to keep being what he'd set out to be on that day at the lake, when he'd vowed he'd never ever frighten her again.

When he'd vowed to be her hero.

He had to change something.

It had to start with Perry. And not being an asshole. Supporting her instead of being angry.

He had an idea.

"You're right, Millie. I do need to go apologize to her."

"That would probably—"

"I'm going over right now."

Chapter 3

Mama thinks I've taken leave of my senses. Why would I marry a man all the way out west when I wouldn't consider any of the men here? It's because I can't stand the thought of being a wife in Boston, in a town house, married to a banker, being stuck in this city. I want adventure.

—*Mae Tanner's Diary, July 20th, 1899*

The truth was, she'd considered calling Stephen. Just thinking about it made her feel guilty, because she would only be going out with him because she was mad at Carson, and that wasn't fair. Stephen was a nice guy. He didn't deserve to be put in the middle of her issues with her best friend.

If he was even her best friend anymore.

She curled up into a tight ball on her couch, and for a moment, she let herself just feel miserable.

Of course he was still her best friend.

You couldn't know somebody as long as she'd known Carson, you couldn't care for someone in the ways that she had, and just stop being friends over one fight.

But it was quite a fight. The worst one she could remember, and given the amount of time they'd known each other, that was saying something.

Well, what had she expected really?

She had said some pretty strong things to him. And it wasn't really a shock that he was mad. Her announcement had come out maybe a little bit more harshly than she had intended.

Which wasn't really fair. The decision to leave Rustler Mountain was about her. It wasn't about him. Well, it was kind of about him. But it was complicated.

She'd gone through some of her grandmother's things recently, and she'd found Mae Tanner's diary.

In the last few weeks, she'd read the diary religiously, following Mae's first six months in Oregon. It always made her sad there were no entries after that.

Mae had gone west to marry Jedediah Tanner, a widower with two small daughters, Sarah and Elizabeth.

It had been a hard experience and a harder relationship. He was remote and distant, attached to the ghost of a woman long gone (Perry related to that more than she would like), and Mae had fought to get him to forge a relationship with his children.

Perry wondered how things were between husband and mail-order bride.

All she had to go on were sepia-toned portraits in which everyone looked serious and formal.

Only the diary showed her another side of Mae. The brave, plucky part of her that Perry wanted to emulate.

Perry didn't feel brave, honestly.

She felt soft and cautious, and oftentimes sad.

When she heard the sound of tires and a truck engine pulling up close to her house, she immediately turned and looked out the window. There was Carson's truck. And the man himself. He got out of his truck and paused. She looked at him through the slats of the blinds, and she wasn't entirely sure whether he could see her. She watched as he paused, looked up at the sky, and seemed to curse a little bit before walking toward her front door. Her heart twisted in her chest. Because of course he had come to apologize.

She knew that. She could see guilt written all over his face. She scrambled up off the couch and went to the door. And waited. She didn't know how long it was going to take Carson to actually make his way over to her. She thought she would give it a good chunk of time. And then he knocked. She opened the door before he could get a second round in.

"What are you doing here?"

"You know what I'm doing here," he grumbled, walking inside.

Her house was a large Victorian she'd inherited from her grandmother—on her mom's side—and selling it was one of the hardest parts of her decision to leave.

That was a lie—there were so many hard parts. Her beautiful little shop on Main Street, with its cheery red bricks and beautiful hand-painted wooden sign that Carson had made for her. Carson himself.

But her home held a substantial part of her heart, along with memories of the most functional adult in Perry's life. She'd spent a lot of time with her grandma when she was young, up until her death when Perry was nineteen. By then the house had been showing signs of wear, and at this point it was bordering on ramshackle.

There were rooms Perry didn't even go in because spots in the floor were too soft and the wallpaper was bubbling from water damage. She used the kitchen, the sitting room, the bathroom nearest the kitchen, and her bedroom. The end.

The house needed an overhaul but Perry didn't have the money. On the bright side, if she sold it, whatever she got would be money in her pocket since her grandma had owned the place outright.

She was a little sad she'd never be able to restore the house to its former glory.

When Lydia Tanner had left the rambling old house to Perry, she'd been very clear. It was to be a home or a financial asset, but never a millstone.

I don't want you to keep it forever if it's holding you back. Remember, Mae Tanner would never have let the flowers grow beneath her feet. She went off and planted her own.

Flowers were a theme in her family. Her grandmother had grown the most beautiful flowers in town. She'd been Rustler Mountain's unofficial florist for years, offering up her personal garden for weddings and baby showers.

Her mother had always liked flowers.

Perry's name was, in fact, short for Periwinkle.

You're the only flower your father ever gave me.

That statement made Perry so sad. It had then, it still did.

Her parents were still together, living off in Wolf Creek, more than an hour away. Her mother continued to live with her cold, abusive father, and Perry was out of breath from telling her she needed to leave.

She just didn't talk to her mom much anymore. She didn't talk to her dad at all.

She could not understand why her mother's affinity for flowers had suggested the name Periwinkle; there were any number of names she could have been given that wouldn't have been half so unconventional. But flowers had become special to Perry over time.

She'd lived in a home with a man who had been so controlling. So spiteful in so many ways. And there had been a real lack of control in most of her life. One thing that had always fascinated her was nature. The way it persisted even as people imposed themselves upon it. A field of wildflowers, so beautiful and resilient, had always felt like a metaphor for the kind of person she wanted to become. She had considered a lot of different jobs in different naturalist fields, but she'd kept on coming back to flowers.

So she'd majored in business with a minor in horticulture.

She had always thought horticulture was a lot of work when flowers themselves just decided to grow on the sides of highways, byways, and mountaintops. Those flowers were also a metaphor. Because people could do the same. *You can grow where you are planted.* She had spent a lifetime doing that.

But if you really wanted to thrive . . . you had to do more than just grow where you were planted. You had to fight to grow sometimes. And you had to learn to lean on yourself, instead of surrendering your power.

In that way, her mom had given her a gift.

"Let's hear it," she said.

"I'm sorry," he said. "What I said was way harsher than was merited."

"Agreed."

"I've taken a hell of a lot more from you than I've given over the last couple of years. And I'm sorry. I . . . I want to help you. I didn't really listen to you when you came over—I just got mad. Because I took your decision personally."

Well. It had been personal. There was no getting away from that.

She didn't voice her thought, though. Because he was here saying nice things and she didn't want to be churlish.

Because she didn't want Carson out of her life. She just needed to change their arrangement. And she wasn't expecting to leave immediately; the last thing she wanted was to get into a situation where they weren't speaking.

She was just trying to . . .

Get enough distance that she could actually accomplish the things she really wanted to. Actually start creating the life she needed.

"Thank you."

"Aren't you going to apologize to me?"

"No. You were mean."

"Okay. But some of what you said felt a little bit mean too," he said, stuffing his hands into his pockets.

"I'm sorry. I wasn't trying to be mean. How about that?" she asked.

"I accept. What do you need to do to get your move in order?"

"What?"

"I hear you, Perry. You want more for your life. And you don't feel you're going to get it here. You're right. I can understand that. I had to leave to join the military. To meet Alyssa."

She felt as if he had just stabbed her. Which was fine. She was used to it. It was also pointless and petty to be this upset about his marrying Alyssa when the woman was dead.

She had been a nice woman too. That was the worst part.

Perry had hated that Alyssa was nice. That Carson had met someone who had been amazing enough for him to change his whole life. That he'd met someone he wanted to make vows to, vows about forever, when he'd been hers forever before that.

And no, she and Carson had never been romantic, not once. Not even close. But how could he give his heart to somebody else when he'd had hers from the beginning?

Before he met Alyssa, they'd been writing letters. And she'd been convinced that special corner of Carson was reserved only for her. That maybe when he came home, things would be different.

They were different. Just not the way she'd hoped.

When that last letter she'd written returned, unopened and undeliverable because Carson had left the barracks already, when he'd come home with Alyssa on his arm, Perry had wanted to burn the world down.

She had spent sleepless nights grappling with the right thing to do. Alyssa loved Carson; Carson loved Alyssa. And what it came right down to was: how could she resent the love he'd found?

She could. In the quiet of her own heart. But she couldn't resent *him*.

He was more than her unrequited feelings for him.

It turned out that he could be close to more than one woman. How great for him.

She pushed that recollection aside. He was trying to be nice. He was trying to be understanding. And she was making it about something that just didn't matter anymore. Something that was long since over. She had even sort of been friends with Alyssa, for the brief time she'd known her.

When she thought of Alyssa, she didn't feel pain because of her relationship with Carson. It was just hearing Carson talk about having to leave home to find love. Because obviously for him it wasn't here.

"If you feel like you need to get out of here to do the things that you need to do, I want to support you. So what has to happen?"

"I have to save money so I can put a down payment on this building when it becomes available. The current lease ends in two months. I can sell my house and take what money I have to use on a down payment, but I'm not going to have all the flowers I'll need to get started. What I really need is about six months to get my own shop growing, and . . ."

He was looking at her, his eyes intense.

"You need to be able to sell your house soon, but it's not ideal if you also have to open the business right away."

"Yes. I'll have to move as soon as I sell the house, because I'll need a place to stay, and I have to work so I have some income. If I go to Medford, I'm going to have to close the store here right away, because commuting between the two would be nearly impossible. But without flowers growing, I can't really start up the new business . . ."

"What if you could sell your house and stay here running the store, put in the offer on the new building when it comes up for sale, make your down payment, and maybe even have time to get your flowers growing before you open the new business?"

"Yes," she said. "That would be ideal. But also not possible. If it was, then that's just what I would do."

"I get that. But, Perry, it's really very simple. You move over to the ranch."

"What?"

"Yeah. You can bring your greenhouse, and I can designate some additional land for you to grow flowers on. Hell, we could probably fit a couple greenhouses out there. You could start cultivating exactly the way you want, and you can stay there for free."

"Carson," she said, about to turn down the best offer she was going to get. "This is sort of . . . not really helping with the codependency stuff."

"No," he said, his voice certain. "This isn't codependent. This is friendship. Perry, you have given me absolutely everything. You drove me home from the hospital when I had to leave without my wife. That wasn't codependence, that was the best example of friendship I've ever experienced."

Guilt stabbed her like a blade. Was she being a bad friend, moving away? A bad person? She didn't want to abandon him. She loved this stupid, infuriating, wonderful man.

But where did staying at the ranch leave her?

Chained to a house that was never going to be her home.

"That's not true, Carson. We spend a lot of time together, and it's mutually enjoyable. It's just . . . we have a dynamic. And that dynamic doesn't leave room for a lot of other things, or other people."

He nodded. And she wished he would say something. About how maybe there didn't need to be other people.

But he didn't. He just breezed right by the opportunity.

That was why she had to leave. It really was. It really, really was, because as much she told herself that although she loved Carson Wilder, she wasn't foolish enough to be in love with him, a huge part of herself knew that wasn't true.

Because she could never get over how beautiful he was. Because there was never another man who had measured up. Because when a wonderful man asked her on a date, all she could do was—it wasn't even comparing him to Carson, it was just the knowledge that she would rather eat pizza with Carson knowing he didn't desire her than be with a man who wanted to have sex with her. Kiss her. Be romantic with her, maybe even marry her someday.

The fact that she would choose pizza every night with Carson Wilder over dinner out with a date meant that she had a problem. She had to change it.

In order to change her behavior, she had to change the pattern. It was just the truth.

But he was offering her a pathway forward. And the truth was, the biggest part of her didn't actually want to leave him.

Quitting Carson cold turkey would be like giving up heroin without tapering off. It might very well kill her. Maybe what she needed was this time with him. Maybe she could sort some things out, knowing there was an exit strategy.

She had never planned to give Carson up entirely. But she wanted him not so wrapped around her day-to-day. As long as that was still the plan, what he was offering made some sense.

"Let me help you," he said.

"You just suddenly want to help me." Her tone was skeptical.

"I suddenly saw myself. I . . . I realized that I haven't been a very good friend, and that a lot of the support between us flows from one direction. I don't know how to respond to some of the things that you said to me, but I can understand your needing a life outside of this place. This town."

The truth was, she loved Rustler Mountain. She loved her little shop. But she had a feeling of incompletion, and she was never going to be able to fill the void with the love she had wanted from the time she was a child.

She didn't want to be a sad woman who hadn't gotten any of the things she wanted in life because she had been sitting around waiting for something that wasn't going to happen. She had told herself she wasn't doing that. She'd told herself she was living life and being realistic. She'd had romantic relationships. Relationships that she'd had relatively serious intentions about. She wasn't sitting around waiting for Carson Wilder.

Or at least, that's what she'd convinced herself. For a whole lot of years. He'd gotten married, and what was she supposed to do with that? It had been a great opportunity to truly let go.

So she'd believed.

Not of their friendship, of course. But of any sneaky, weasely romantic feelings that existed inside of her.

Alas.

The trouble was, Carson was her standard.

When he'd been a boy, she'd thought he was the most beautiful thing she'd ever seen. Then he'd become a teenager, rangy and tall, his jawline dangerous, his blue eyes a registered health hazard.

Gradually, that boy had become a man. He'd filled out, his shoulders and chest becoming broader, the mischievous glint in his eyes taking on a harder look.

She had thought he was the standard of male beauty at every single age.

He was a formative experience for her, one of those early childhood development milestones you couldn't just unlearn.

She had reasoned with herself a lot over the years regarding her attraction to Carson. She liked to think of it like ice cream.

Yes, everybody had a favorite flavor of ice cream, but they could eat other flavors. She thought other men were attractive.

Carson might be her favorite flavor, but he wasn't sold in her local grocery store, so to speak. Still, there was no reason to swear off treats altogether.

Of course, when you were really craving one thing and settled for another, it was usually disappointing. You maybe even ate a little bit too much of it because it didn't really satisfy.

That had nothing to do with whether or not she should move to Outlaw Lake.

Even the name of Carson's ranch made her stomach go tight. He had bought his own section of the family ranch, including the lake, right after he married Alyssa. He'd built their house mostly with his own two gorgeous hands. Carson making that place for Alyssa recalled a very dark part of Perry's life.

"And where am I going to stay?"

"The cabin."

She knew the cabin. It had once been their pirate hideout. It had been more or less abandoned when they were kids, and in the years since, it had been fixed up a little bit, with different members of the family cycling through when other construction projects displaced them.

It was small, but nice, nestled right at the base of Rustler Mountain itself—the mountain not the town—and on the shores of Outlaw Lake.

"Well. That wouldn't be so bad."

She would have a lot of space. It wasn't as if she'd be moving in with him.

"And," he said, "if you want, we can set up a greenhouse out there, we can start growing flowers. We can do flowers outdoors too, but you know it's going to be a mission to get a deer fence up."

"Yes. Well. Deer are a nemesis of mine."

Arguably her *biggest* nemesis. Moles, voles, gophers, and digger squirrels, they caused their own problems, but deer were relentless. She had watched them jump over the fence around her yard more times than she could count, and outright behead beautiful flowers with no compunction.

"I guess . . . I guess it makes sense."

"Good. But now I have to ask you, where's the codependency thing coming from?"

"I'm sorry I said that," she replied, mostly because she wanted to avoid that conversation. She couldn't blame Carson for her own problems. He wasn't responsible for her feelings. He had been a good friend all this time.

He hadn't done anything to make her think that they were destined to be more than friends. He had always treated her like . . . she would say a little sister, but he did not treat his little sister as nicely as he treated her. Like a cherished little sister, she supposed.

"Sometimes I feel that . . . we keep each other alive." She winced. "I don't mean it like that."

"No. I can understand why you might feel that way. But I'm not in such a dark place anymore. I promise you I'm not."

"I know that. But I think maybe what I'm trying to say is we fill such a substantial role for each other that it keeps us from having other relationships. It keeps us from doing other things."

He regarded her closely. He nodded. "I'm sorry. I'm sorry I did that to you, Perry. I really am."

"You didn't do anything to me."

"No. I think I did. And I'm damn sorry."

She felt awful. But if he thought he understood, she wasn't going to correct his thinking. She wasn't going to say . . . *The problem is, Carson, in spite of my best efforts, I think I might be in love with you.*

No. She wasn't going to say that.

"I love you, Perry. I'm going to do whatever you need me to."

He said those words to her frequently enough. They hurt. They always did. Because they meant a great deal. They meant so much. But they never meant everything.

She couldn't say them back, because if she did, they would mean something very different. And that would be a hell of a mess.

"Well. I guess I'll call Marissa Rivera and get my house listed. She's the agent who'll be handling the sale."

Historic Victorian, for sale, as is.

"Great," he said. "You can move in to the cabin as soon as possible."

"All right."

She had gone and radicalized him. She could see the light in his eye. That was the thing about Carson. He had spark to him. A desire to change things—himself, the world, things around him. But he'd lost it in the last few years, and the loss had been one of the most terrifying things she'd ever seen.

When he said he wasn't in that dark space anymore, she believed him.

But at moments like these, she missed that Carson.

She supposed she ought to be grateful she could see that old spark now. Maybe it was a sign she was doing the right thing. Maybe it was evidence that they were both going to be better off. He had a mission now, even if it was just the mission of getting her moved in.

His enthusiasm was still linked to her, but she wasn't going to examine that too deeply.

"Thank you," she said.

He smiled, and it was as if the sun came out from behind the clouds. "You're welcome, Perry."

Chapter 4

He is matter-of-fact in his letters. There is no warmth there, but no malice either. I refuse to tell Mother I worry about my decision. I will hold fast, and I will see it through.

—Mae Tanner's Diary, July 25th, 1899

Carson was feeling pretty damned good after his apology to Perry. So good that he decided to meet his brother and sister down at the Watering Hole, their favorite outlaw bar at the end of Main Street the following evening.

Flynn was a lot. And there were some days Carson struggled to engage fully with the Flynn Wilder Experience, but also, sometimes it was nice.

Cassidy was a spitfire and a half, but he enjoyed her feistiness.

Flynn's friend Dalton Wade had also joined them for the evening, and Carson was beginning to regret not asking Perry.

But he had promised that he was going to give Perry a little bit of space. She was working on getting her house listed, and they'd made a plan to move her belongings on Sunday, when the florist shop was closed.

So here he was, not monopolizing her time. Not being codependent. Hanging out with other people. One of whom he wasn't even related to.

He ordered a Coke and sipped it slowly.

"I know everybody in here," Cassidy said, grousing. "I mean, everybody in my age group."

"You say that like it's a bad thing," Dalton said.

"It *is* a bad thing. I'm not interested in any of these goobers.

I remember when they used to shout *LeBron* and try to throw crumpled-up paper in the trash can from across the classroom." Cassidy wrinkled her nose. "A huge spoiler alert: none of them are LeBron."

Dalton laughed. "Well, I remember when you loosened my saddle when you were a twelve-year-old asshole—"

"You didn't really do that, did you, Cassidy?" Flynn asked.

Cassidy had the decency to look chagrined, her cheeks turning pink. But then she quickly recovered and shrugged. "I was attention seeking," she said, looking innocent as could be. "Because of my trauma."

"Get in line," Flynn said. "We all have parental abandonment drama. And seek attention accordingly." Flynn finished that last bit as he scanned the room, obviously looking for women who might want to give him some attention.

"At least Dad was alive when you got abandoned. I had to be raised by you."

Carson grunted. Everyone looked at him. "Was that a laugh?" Flynn asked.

"I guess so." The truth was, they'd had their share of losses. Hardships. Some would say more than their fair share, and some would say it was fair play for a family of outlaws.

That was the tricky thing about Rustler Mountain.

Austin was too stubborn to leave it. He always had been. Their family history had been as wild as the West itself, as wild as the name suggested, and Austin had decided that he was too damn stubborn to leave, even though he hadn't liked the family's reputation.

Flynn, for his part, embraced it. As did Cassidy. They had their own baggage and their own reasons, different mothers from each other, and different mothers from the one that Austin and Carson shared.

He couldn't claim to know the exact way their issues had shaped them.

For his part, Flynn had family in town, on his mother's side. In fact, the property he lived on came from her people. But he never got any credit for being associated with a respectable family, and Carson wondered if that was part of why Flynn embraced the outlaw angle so enthusiastically.

A big *fuck you* to the family who didn't really acknowledge him.

Inheritance was one thing, but it wasn't actually having people who cared about you.

Carson had a different reaction to their outlaw heritage. He didn't need to stick around, he didn't need to carve a place out for himself, and he didn't really relish being tarred with the same brush.

That was why he got out and decided to be a hero.

For all the good it had done.

Still, sometimes he felt like a little bit of a shithead for winning the trauma Olympics.

He had won. That was the truth.

No, he couldn't speak to exactly how their experiences had affected them, but he had seriously fucked-up stuff in his head from his time in the military, and his wife was dead.

He was the winner of a competition he hadn't even asked to play.

Lucky him.

"So," Flynn began as he leaned against the bar top, resting his elbows on it, then grimacing. He lifted them, and Carson heard a distinct sticky sound. "This place is disgusting," Flynn said, instead of whatever he'd been about to say.

"Fits the clientele."

They all looked across the way, to see Jessie Jane Hancock, descendent of Butch Hancock, the traitor, the member of their ancestors' gang who had betrayed the Wilder family.

Jessie Jane had it in for Flynn. Carson wasn't entirely sure why. If this were the playground, he would assume it was because she liked him. Pulling his pigtails and all that.

But it wasn't the playground. So he couldn't rightly figure out why she felt the need to needle his brother all the time.

"You're here too, Jess," said Flynn, raising his beer bottle to his lips.

She responded with a raised middle finger.

"Anyway," said Flynn. "Before the queen of the trailer park over there saw fit to interrupt, you were about to tell me what the fuck is going on with Perry."

"I was *not* about to tell you that," Carson said.

"You were. Because I was going to ask, and you were going to tell me."

"You're in a fight with Perry?" Cassidy asked.

"I'm not in a fight with Perry," he said.

"I thought that was what I overheard at Austin's last night."

"Well, we had a little bit of a disagreement. But we are not in a fight. She's been my best friend since I was nine years old, it's not like we're ever going to have a real serious conflict."

He ignored the strange, hollowed-out feeling in his stomach that made him question whether or not he was lying.

He wondered if what had happened between them was a little bit more serious than he was letting himself realize.

No. They were fine. Yes, she'd said some things. Yes, she was planning to move away in a few months, but he wasn't going to think about that. He was going to put one foot in front of the other one. That was how he'd survived the last couple of years; it was how he was going to survive the next few.

He wasn't going to think six months to a year down the road. Because there was no way she was actually going to leave in two months. Nobody's plans came together seamlessly like that. A big move, figuring everything out with her new storefront, none of that was going to happen instantaneously. She was going to end up needing his help for quite some time.

"What about?"

"She's talking about moving. To Medford. Opening up a bigger florist shop."

"Oh," Dalton, Flynn, and Cassidy all three reacted at the same time.

"It's reasonable. This is a very small town. Her shop is cute, but outside of tourist season, and wedding season, I think it's difficult to drum up enough business to keep the business going."

"Yeah," Flynn said, rubbing his chin. "I bet you're not happy about that, though."

"What I want or don't want has nothing to do with what Perry ought to do."

They were all looking at each other, their expressions almost comical. Like meerkats popping out of a burrow.

"Just say it," he said.

"She's like your emotional support critter," Dalton said.

"I ought to punch you in the mouth for that, Dalton," he said, even though privately, he had to agree a little bit. And he didn't like it. It was an unflattering characterization of their relationship. And it spoke to exactly what Perry had been talking about. It made him feel like an ass, and maybe he ought to feel like an ass.

"Hey, I'm not a Wilder. I'm not getting in the middle of all that." Dalton held his hands up. "But it'll be a big change for you."

"I'm not . . ." *Damaged?* Was that what he was going to say? He was a goddamned mess and everybody knew it.

"You must've gotten pretty mad at her when she said she was leaving," Cassidy said, looking furious herself.

"A little," he said. He wasn't going to get into exactly why she had made him mad. The truth was, when she had talked about codependency, he'd thought it was ridiculous. But when she'd looked at him last night, tried to explain . . .

She was worried she was holding him back, and that was so profoundly unfair to her he couldn't even begin to process it. He couldn't do that to her.

She knew his darkest secret, the darkest part of himself. She knew that he'd lost hope, that he thought not being here was the only option for him, for his family, for his friends. And she still felt worried about him, whatever she might say. Perry had put her life on hold because he was a mess. He had put her through that hell; now he had to support her going out and finding whatever life she wanted.

He wasn't going to get into all that with Flynn and Cassidy, though, not here in the bar, maybe not ever.

"I think it's shitty," Cassidy said. "You've already lost too much. You can't lose your best friend."

"That's not fair, Cass," he said. "She doesn't have to live her whole life in service to me. And that's what I was having to process last night. Because apparently, I am a little bit more emotionally stunted than I would like to believe. She's my best friend. And that means that I have to want what's best for her. Otherwise, I'm a terrible friend."

He was pretty sure he *had* been a terrible friend. For a while now. He didn't want to be terrible.

He wanted to be better.

He'd never wanted to be Perry's burden. Not ever.

"I'm going to have her move onto the property while she gets things in order."

"I don't understand," Flynn said. "She's got a pretty decent business."

"I don't know. She's talking about starting life over, having a baby . . ." Even saying the words just about killed him.

"Having a baby?" Cassidy said, looking agog. "Does she even have a boyfriend?"

"No. But you know, there are a lot of ways to have a family."

"Hear me out," Flynn said. "*You* could have a baby with her."

Carson had never wished that he was still drinking more than he did at that moment. Him? Have a baby with Perry. His Perry. His sweet, perfect Perry?

He was the furthest thing from sweet, the furthest thing from perfect, and the furthest thing from what she needed.

"What? *No.* I am not . . . No way."

"You seem to like each other well enough," Dalton said.

"Yeah. I do. I like her. I have, since we were kids. That's not . . ."

"Why not?" Cassidy asked.

"Because that's not how life works, squirt."

"I was under the impression that when you were an adult, you got to choose how life works," Cassidy said.

"I would think you might recognize that I am exhibit A, proving you have no fucking control over how your life works, no matter how old you are."

Cassidy winced. "Sorry. I didn't mean . . . I mean, I guess I get it. You were so in love with Alyssa, and now you probably can't imagine . . ."

She let her sentence trail off. And he let his own guilt on that subject die off with it. He wasn't going to get into his marriage, least of all with his little sister.

Hell no.

"So," said Flynn. "Perry is moving away, and . . . what are you going to do?"

"For now, I'm going to help her get ready. I'm her friend. And I've been . . . not a great one."

"That's not true," Cassidy said.

His sister's loyalty warmed his heart. It really did. She was a sweet kid, and the truth was, having been raised by Austin, Flynn, and himself, it was kind of a miracle.

"That isn't what I meant," said Flynn. "I meant what are you going to do with your life. Because . . . Perry is kind of your life."

And that was the rub. That was where it came right back down to what Perry had said about codependence.

"I guess . . . do the same things I always do. Just without her. Work the ranch, eat dinner."

"You've never even gotten your ranch going," Flynn pointed out.

"Do you want to run Austin's place by yourself?"

"I sure as hell do not. I'm only saying that there's a lot you could do."

He *liked* ranching. He had sought to expand the Wilder outfit when he bought his own property. It had seemed like the right thing to do when he had a wife. It seemed like a reasonable, decent thing to do when he'd been thinking about building something. About what it took to be a real man. The man of the house. Something their father had never been.

Alyssa had come from a great, functional family. And he hadn't known anything about that sort of life.

But she had been happy to put a little distance between herself and her parents, and most especially the shitty guy she'd been dating before him, who had proved to be a total loser. Carson had promised to be the good man she needed. She had wanted freedom. She had been happy to get a couple of states away from everyone. It had seemed healthy to him. But then, she had never seemed quite as happy here as he had hoped she would be.

"When are you going to start dating?" Flynn asked.

Carson nearly spit out his Coke. "Dating. Hell. I don't want to date."

"Why not?"

"Because I never want to get married again."

"So," Flynn said. "I don't want to get married either."

"I don't understand the point of dating, then."

"Put it this way," said Flynn, taking a drink of his beer. "Do you want to spend the rest of your life celibate? I find that very hard to believe."

"I don't need you to believe anything about the state of my sex life."

"Your dead sex life," Cassidy said, looking up at him.

"My *wife* is dead, Cassidy. That was a very insensitive thing to say."

He felt mean scolding her, because he knew his sister didn't mean it that way, and it was unkind of him to make her feel bad.

Especially because...

Well. Hell.

Because things were different from what he let everyone believe.

Pain was pain, though. Maybe.

"Don't do that to her," said Flynn. "You're not offended. My point is, your best friend is going to move to another town, your older brother is married, they're going to have a baby. And you're just going to . . . what? Spend every evening at home?"

"I'm not home now."

"You don't even drink alcohol anymore, Carson. Don't think I haven't noticed."

"You say that like it's a bad thing."

"It's not a bad thing," said Cassidy. "Not for you."

"Yeah. I know. That's why I stopped drinking."

"Also as a middle finger to Dad, I suppose," Flynn said, and Carson was shocked by how unerring his brother's observation was.

"I figure if I do things differently from Dad, I'm halfway to being a good man."

Flynn chuckled. "Maybe."

"Was he so bad?" Cassidy asked.

He felt guilty then. Because Cassidy hadn't known their father at all, and he hadn't been the worst. When compared with Perry's dad, he'd been a pretty decent guy. Uninterested in his kids sometimes, sure. But pretty decent.

He'd gotten them motorcycles and they'd terrorized the town on them. They'd had dirt bikes and four-wheelers and rifles. Oftentimes not a full pantry of food, but that had been their dad's problem.

He'd been a big, cheerful narcissist.

He'd delighted in everything that felt good, everything temporary, everything wild and free. Carson had always hated that attitude. He'd tried to be a real man.

But look at him now. Spending all his days working his brother's ranch, spending his evenings on what? He wasn't hurting anything, but he wasn't helping either.

Maybe that was part of the point Perry was making.

They were both sort of treading water. Not advancing their lives. And they were in their thirties. It felt wrong. Because he had spent a lot of his young adult years trying. Joining the military. Marrying Alyssa.

He felt pretty damned justified in sitting down and stopping for a little while. But now he supposed it was time to start trying again. He didn't want to make the same mistakes over again. Didn't want to go over the same decisions.

"You should download dating apps," Flynn said.

"God Almighty," said Carson. "Do I really have to do that?"

"I don't think you do," said Cassidy. "Mostly because I don't really care what you do or don't do as far as all that goes. I don't think that's the key to happiness. Look around town. Half the people are miserable because of sex, not because of the lack of it."

"Not wrong," said Carson.

"A little wrong," said Flynn. "They're miserable because they're chasing the high of sex, little sister, and it's taking them down dark alleyways. I thought you were old enough to understand that by now."

Cassidy blanched. "Gross. Don't talk to me about such things."

"We're all grown," said Flynn.

"That doesn't mean I want insight into your psyche, Flynn Wilder."

"I'm not giving you insight into my psyche. I'm just talking philosophically."

"Well, maybe I don't want to hear your philosophy."

"Your loss."

Cassidy stuck her tongue out.

"Give her a break," said Carson. "She had the bad luck to be raised by us. That means she deserves niceness."

"Says the man who just poked at her."

"A reminder for myself too," said Carson.

"I don't need you to baby me, Carson," said Cassidy.

"Somebody ought to, Cassidy."

He did believe that. Firmly. Not that anybody had ever really . . . babied any of them. Maybe that was the problem now. He just struggled to see the point of things. Because . . . he didn't believe in happiness. Or at least, it was hard for him. Austin and Millie were happy.

It did him a lot of good to see his brother so happy. If Austin had a different set of experiences, it might give the rest of them hope.

Maybe that was his problem. He was always trying to look down the road to find some kind of happiness. The mythical nuclear family that he had never truly experienced.

A feeling of being settled. Of having all the difficult things in life be complete so he could just rest. Enjoy.

Maybe he needed to look at things a little bit more the way Flynn did. Flynn liked to feel good for a moment. Carson could remember being that way when he'd been in high school, but after their father had died, something in him had changed. Everything just felt pointless. Silly. He felt he was wasting his life. He was just sort of floating along now, though he'd never chosen that lifestyle. Maybe he needed to make the decision. To approach pleasure the way Flynn did. And as far as the ranch . . .

He wasn't sure ranching was what he wanted. Not really. He wanted to keep his property, yes. But he wasn't sure cattle were his future.

Hell, he knew what he loved to do. Woodworking. Restoration. Now that there was some funding for the Historical Society, he had been thinking about offering his services.

That would be a hell of a thing.

He'd gotten into restoring old things when he and Austin had worked to reinvigorate a Conestoga wagon that had been in their family for generations. The Historical Society used it now for reenactments, and Cassidy often drove it through town.

A regular Oregon Trail covered wagon. It was a great draw.

Then, of course, there was the Wilder house. The one on Main Street that his family still owned, that the original Austin Wilder—his six-times great-grandfather, and his older brother's namesake—had built for his wife.

It was a project part of him had always wanted to take on. He hadn't, though, because there had always been other priorities.

Other things that he was supposed to be working on. Other things he was supposed to be striving for.

A part of him had always found peace in restoration work. Making something old into something new. Gee. He wondered why that was.

Maybe that was the problem. He hadn't pursued that dream even a little bit. Instead, he had grabbed on to the sweetest thing from his past.

Perry Bramble.

And he had held them both back while doing it.

"If I do this, I'm going to blame you," he said, looking directly at Flynn.

"Blame me. Credit me. I don't care. It's all the same to me." He grinned in that shameless way of his. And Carson knew what he'd said was true.

His thoughts turned to Perry's old Victorian. He needed to fix the place up. That's what he needed to do. He could help her get the most money possible out of it.

And keep it all original, which he knew was a really big deal when it came to historic homes.

That's what I need to do.

He needed to make old things new.

He was committed to that idea. It felt like progress. And it felt better than he could've imagined.

So out of what had been a pretty terrible week, he suddenly had a revelation.

There was a point and purpose to everything if he could get a handle on what it meant to be a better man. Maybe he couldn't do it the way he had before, but he could help Perry, and in the process, he could help himself.

It was as if the clouds had parted and he could see.

Perry had thrown him for a loop when she'd said she was moving.

Alyssa's death had knocked the wind out of him, left him uncertain of so many things and stewing in his own failure.

But there was still hope for him to come out of this life a hero, and dammit, he was going to meet that challenge no matter what.

Chapter 5

Today I arrived in Medford, and he was there at the depot. He is much taller than I imagined. His mouth is firm, as if he has never smiled once. We went by wagon to Jacksonville, where he paid for me to have my own room. We are to be married in the morning.

—Mae Tanner's Diary, August 28th, 1899

Perry felt awful.

Last night's discussion with Carson played over and over in her mind. She couldn't let it go. She was like a wolf with a bone.

He had offered to let her move in with him. Which was great. Honestly, it solved a lot of problems. And okay, she wasn't moving in with him moving in with him. Just going to live on his property. He was giving up acreage for her to plant on. It was great. Except it wasn't. Except she felt terrible about their fight, and she felt bad that he felt bad.

She wondered if this was a side effect of all that intensity she wanted to escape. She suspected it was.

She wanted to fix him. Every time he had a bad mood, she wanted to lift it. She never wanted to be the cause of any of his suffering, and the fact that she had oppressed her spirits.

Normally, working on a romantic flower arrangement—something for an anniversary or Valentine's Day, or any sort of special event—made her feel warm and happy. But she couldn't focus on the lovely softness of the hydrangeas because she was so wrapped up in the Carson of it all. And there was her issue.

So when he walked into the flower shop, and her heart scurried up her throat and nearly exited her mouth, she shouldn't have been all that surprised. Just the standard Carson response.

Why was it like this? They'd been best friends for most of their lives.

True, their relationship had shifted. Because there had been a point in time when she had thought he was beautiful, but had never considered that she might want to see him naked.

She knew full well that she wanted to see him naked *now*.

It was the kind of thought that could consume her if she let it. She knew him. But she didn't know how he did . . . the most intimate things.

She wiped her mind clean so that she could make eye contact with him. "What are you doing here?"

"I came to say hello," he said.

"Oh. Hello."

"To you too. I had an idea."

"You had an idea?"

She felt a deep concern just then. Carson often had ideas when they were younger. They were generally harebrained. She couldn't really say the ideas he came up with as an adult were much better.

"What kind of idea?"

"I want to help with your house. I know that you want to sell it quickly, but honestly, I think that if I help you restore it, you're going to be able to sell it for a hell of a lot more."

That was so . . . not what she'd been expecting. Of course, he'd been surprising her ever since he'd come storming over to her house to apologize and demand she move in with him.

Suddenly he wanted to do everything, carry it all on his back. It was the way he used to be, but she hadn't seen him like this in the last few years.

"Oh, there's no way I can afford to have you do that."

"You, you're my oldest friend in the entire world. I'm not going to charge you for my time. I'm not going to charge you for anything."

"You can't go around doing work for people for free," Perry said.

"Perry, I can do whatever the hell I want. Especially when it comes to you."

"Carson . . ."

"Perry," he repeated. "Let me do this for you. I went out to the bar with Flynn last night."

"God save us."

"And while I was there, he asked me a question. And I won't bore you with the details, because it's Flynn, so you know, it was . . . Flynn. But I have to have something. Something that I care about."

His blue eyes burned into hers, and it was damn near painful. He wanted something to care about.

Well. Too bad she already did, and it was him.

"I'm a cowboy. Ranching is in my blood. But when I really think about setting up a spread on my ranch, my heart's not in it. I love helping Austin. But it's not everything to me. The different restoration projects I've done, that's . . . more. More me. I have plenty of money. I've got a home, and I don't need much. If I can restore your place, then the old Wilder place in town, I'll have a basis for a business. I can redo antique furniture and historic homes."

"That seems like a good, lofty goal," she said.

She meant it. Because he needed to care about something. That was great. His wanting more than to sit in that empty house was great. Truly, it was great for her too because she wouldn't have to imagine herself abandoning him while he was at loose ends. He was looking to tie up an end. And he made beautiful things. He didn't only do restoration; he built fantastic original furniture as well.

He had actually made all the cabinets in the house he'd built for Alyssa.

The idea of him working on her house? The one she was about to move out of so that she could leave town and him forever? That was a hell of a double-edged sword.

"I want to do this," he said. It was so hard to argue with Carson. Maybe it was because he was extraordinary, charismatic in a certain kind of way. Or maybe it was just because she loved him. She would never really know the answer one way or another.

"Of course that would be amazing," she said.

Even as she said it, she felt a tug of regret. Because . . . it would've been nice to live in that revamped Victorian home. It would have been nice to keep it, but she had made her decision. How ironic that she was getting more ensnared in Carson just as she was trying to leave him.

"Well, when you close up shop here, let's go to your place and have a look. Of course, you can't live there while I'm doing major renovation."

"You're not going to be doing electrical and things like that."

"No," he said slowly. "But there's going to be sawdust all over the place. That old floor of yours is trashed in spots. I think I can resurface and restore some of it, but I can also cut new subflooring, new planks. There are some built-ins that definitely need a little bit of work. And anyway, it'll be easier to do with all your stuff moved out."

"That's just . . . that's so nice of you."

"I'm not being nice. I'm your friend and I haven't been what you needed the past couple of years. Our conversation really drove that home."

"I really need to say this to you, and I need you to hear me. My decision to move isn't about you or the way you've been over the last couple of years. Your wife died. You're grieving. You weren't being a bad friend—you're a great friend."

"I appreciate that. But I feel like I haven't shown up for you, and I want to. Also, you're right."

"Well, I do like to hear that."

"I haven't been moving forward like I should. I didn't even realize I needed to."

She couldn't help but wonder what that meant to him. She loved that he was thinking about a new business, something that aligned with his interests. His creativity.

She remembered when he'd carved her a little wooden box with a pocketknife and a piece of madrone. She still had it. In that box, she kept a dried flower he'd given her when they were teenagers, a necklace he'd given her one year for Christmas, and a note he'd written her in middle school that said: *Will u go to the woods w/me after school? Y or N circle.*

He should do things like that. Creative things. He'd ignored that part of himself but she knew it was a substantial piece of who he was.

She finished up the arrangement and put it in the cooler. It would be picked up first thing in the morning. She had already zeroed out her cash register, and she went to lock the front door, turning off the lights. "I'm parked out back," she said.

"I'll walk you," he said.

He went behind the counter with her, and they both opened the back door to the gravel lot behind the cute little brick building.

"Are you parked out front?"

"Yeah," he said.

"Should I give you a ride?"

He chuckled. "Around the block?"

"Yeah."

"Okay."

He got into the passenger seat of her car, having to fold himself immediately. He was way too tall for her little sedan. Being enclosed like this with him made her lose her breath in a fun way. It was addict behavior; that's what it was. The way she both loved and hated being with him.

"So, what did Flynn say to you?" she asked, starting the engine.

"He asked if I was really going to be celibate for the rest of my life."

She hit the gas just a little too hard, and then braked abruptly as she came flying backward out of her spot. "Oh?"

"Yeah, and it's not like . . . I'm thinking about that all the time. But he got me thinking about things in the long term."

Well. She had, in fact, talked to Carson many times about what he might do with his life, and what he wanted for the future, but apparently what had sunk in was Flynn mentioning sex. Because men were going to be men.

She couldn't get her bristles down. She'd been hoping Flynn had said something more along the lines of . . . learn to carve beavers with a chain saw or something.

"Then I started thinking about the ranch, about restoration. About . . . hell, Perry. You said that you wanted to have a baby. We both need to get out there, apparently."

"We . . . we *do*," she said, suppressing a growl.

"We should download some dating apps."

"Dating apps."

"Yeah. Increase the likelihood of meeting people."

"Don't you men just go to the Watering Hole and approach the first woman who gets separated from the herd?"

"You're thinking of Flynn. I've never been much for that."

She sniffed loudly. "I don't need apps."

"I just think . . . how long has it been since you've been in a relationship?"

It was too hot in the car. She wanted to peel her skin off. She turned toward the next block and saw his beat-up blue pickup truck parked against the curb. "I can't remember."

"Then it's been too long."

"Wait, are you actually asking me when I last had sex?" She watched as he went straight. His face twitched as if his nose had literally gone out of joint. She had never seen anything like it. She decided to push him. "I know that's not what you said, but I get the feeling that's actually what you're asking."

He looked perturbed by that. "It is *not* what I'm asking."

"Because I remember when *that* was," she said, feeling ornery.

"I don't need you to break your diary out, Per."

"I could, though."

"I'm *good*. It was more a hypothetical question."

"I wouldn't need to get my diary out, Carson. It hasn't been that long."

She was a liar. But she didn't care. Because it wasn't his business. He wanted nothing to do with her sex life. Not a single thing. So why should she give him any information at all? Any.

"Good for you," he said.

But he didn't sound as if he thought it was very good. She didn't care. They'd known each other long enough that no subject was taboo, but there were certain things they didn't discuss in a lot of detail, that was for sure.

"Anyway. There's your truck."

"I'll just follow you over to your place."

"Okay," she said.

He got out of the car, and she tightened her hands around the steering wheel. Before he even climbed into his truck, she took off. He knew how to get to her place, after all. It wasn't like she had to lead the way.

Dating.

Carson was going to download dating apps.

That was fine. She ought to go on a date with Stephen Lee.

But then, she could also download apps. She could date some men in Medford. That made more sense. She shouldn't get involved with anyone who lived here, because she was leaving. She needed to actually commit to her plan.

She pulled into her driveway and got out of the car. She was in the process of unlocking the front door when Carson parked his truck behind her.

He got out, and for one long moment she lost herself. She watched him as he put his cowboy hat firmly on his head. As he brushed his hands across his battered jeans.

And then walked toward her, a strange sort of intensity in his blue eyes.

She cleared her throat, finished unlocking the door, and pushed it open.

He followed her in.

"So," she said. "Dating apps. To what end, Carson?"

"I don't know. But that's the goal: to not consider the end. I've never tried that before."

Well. There was some truth to that. He was always just a little bit too serious.

He was always trying to do something to redeem his family's reputation.

To make himself into something of a hero.

"I want to focus on what's right here in front of me. Because when I look too far into the future, I feel defeated. I feel . . . you have no idea what it's like, Perry. To feel as if everything you do means nothing."

Well. He was wrong there. Sometimes she really did feel the things she did were akin to dumping a Dixie cup of water into an ocean. When it came to him, when it came to . . . everything.

She wasn't persuasive enough to inspire her mother to leave her father. She wasn't the kind of daughter who transformed an abusive father into a loving one.

She just felt insignificant sometimes. And of course that feeling had intensified when Carson married someone else. It was unavoidable. Even if she should be over it by now, even if she should grow up and stop taking it so personally. She couldn't.

"Right," she said.

She wasn't getting into it right now.

"I think maybe I want too much. Maybe if I can just focus on today, I'll find something. Something that makes me feel . . ."

"What are you looking for?"

"Maybe I don't need to matter. Maybe I don't need to single-handedly redeem the Wilder family—Austin has done a good enough job of that anyway. I'm not going to let life knock me on my ass and keep me there, Per. I've never been that man. I'm not my father. I refuse to be."

There was a near religious fervor in his eyes as he said that. She knew, better than most, how important it was to Carson to rise above his name.

He hadn't always been that way. Being his friend when they were younger was like being on a roller coaster ride. He'd always been good to her, but he'd been wild. Impetuous. He'd gone speeding around on his motorcycle raising hell.

She'd asked him one time if she could ride on the back, and he'd said no. She'd asked why and he'd said it wasn't safe.

So then why do you do it?

He'd had no answer for her. Later, he'd said: *It's just my job to protect you.*

She'd found the declaration sweet at the time. Over the years she'd started to wonder more and more why he thought he had to protect her.

It didn't seem like an equal friendship to her.

Just the same, she should be a good friend, not a jealous shrew. She was about to cut the cord. Sever this thing with him.

Not their friendship. Not entirely. But their relationship would cool with distance.

She wouldn't hang on to it as she had when he'd been deployed. She wouldn't write four-page letters by hand, telling him her every thought and feeling.

They would gradually start seeing each other less and less, and that would make phone calls and texts less frequent. Eventually, maybe they would go out on each other's birthdays. If she found a boyfriend, maybe they wouldn't go out at all.

It felt sad right now. Just thinking about it made her ache. But it wouldn't always feel sad. She would get used to it. When her grandmother had died, she'd thought she would never smile again. She'd felt as if she'd lost absolutely everything. And it was like that when Carson was deployed, living halfway across the world.

That had felt awful. But she'd had to pick herself up by her bootstraps and be enough for herself. Her mother had been too fragile to support her. Carson had been as supportive as he could be from another time zone. She knew from firsthand experience that she could be more independent than she was now. They had slipped into this codependence over the last two years. They could make their relationship into something different. And it wouldn't kill her. Whatever she might think right now.

"So you aren't looking to get married again."

"Hell no," he said.

He said it so definitively. And it was stupid for her to be upset. She felt like a small, terrible person for feeling jealous of a dead woman. Alyssa deserved to be loved this much. Perry wanted to cry. But for a variety of reasons, and that was the complicated part.

"So it's just . . ."

He shrugged. "Making some connections. Having a little bit of fun."

Perry wrinkled her nose. "I don't know that I would call dating around fun."

"I used to share that opinion."

She liked him even more for saying that. For not making some flippant, lewd comment about hookups. That just wasn't Carson's way.

"But my life has changed," he said. "It's going to change even more." His voice got gruff. "I'm going to have to change with it. If you don't evolve you die."

"Or at least flounder around."

"True, and neither of us is a fish. Well, show me around the place. I never walk around the whole house."

"Neither do I," she said. She was happy to get onto the subject of the house. "Because it's kind of a disaster. It needs so many repairs, and I don't know where to begin."

"I know there are certain things you're not allowed to change because it's on a historic registry."

"Yes. Since this is a historic district."

"Right. Okay. I can work with that. I've done a lot of reading on the subject."

"Has Austin infected you with his library bug?"

"I'm not anywhere near as well-read as Austin is, but I fell down a huge rabbit hole when I restored the cabin that you're going to live in. I've always been interested in history. The places that people live, their furniture, their vehicles, like the Conestoga wagon, all those things say so much about a time and a place. About the way people relate to each other. You know, there's an interesting theory that people were more social before technology. I'm not sure I agree.

They may have been in some ways, but look at the way that houses have been built now for quite a while. With all these big common rooms."

"Right," she said.

Carson walked from the entryway into the sitting room. He flicked the lights on, and Perry grimaced as she looked at one of the loose pieces of wallpaper. "With these houses," he said, "there were lots of small rooms. And that was so families could get away from each other. They could sit and read in different rooms. The women could cross-stitch in one space, while the men talked in the other. People always did want their privacy. It just says a lot."

"That is interesting," said Perry.

"Yeah. I think so. I like looking at the things personal possessions tell you. Hope chests, for example, used to be really important. Women would travel with them, even though they were large and heavy. For hundreds of miles."

"Mae Tanner had a hope chest," Perry said.

Mae had been the original owner of this house, along with her husband, Jedediah Tanner. When Mae had come out west from Boston, the hope chest was essentially the only thing she had brought.

It had been her hope for a better life.

"Do you have it still?" he asked.

"Yes," she said. "It's in one of the guest rooms. It's cracked on the top and faded. I wish it had been kept in better condition, but it was sitting in the sun for years, and the wood got damaged."

"I can probably do something with it."

"Really?"

"Yeah. I mean, if you don't mind me replacing some of the wood. But I'm pretty good at stain matching and all of that."

"That would be amazing. I mean, I would love to have the chest. To keep it."

"It could be the hope chest that you take with you to your new life, Perry. A gift from me."

"You're already giving me a lot of gifts."

"Well, you deserve them. You really do."

"You're so good to me." She meant that. In spite of the tension between them recently, she wanted him to know that. She wanted him to feel it. "Carson, I really do appreciate your doing this."

"Well. It's going to be a pretty big job. We are definitely going to have to take the drywall off in this room. There are companies that sell wallpaper reproductions. We should be able to get some period-appropriate stuff. A lot of this trim looks great, it just needs to be restained."

She was impressed by Carson's expertise. She supposed these topics didn't come up in conversation and she'd never known the depth of his knowledge. She felt a little bit in awe.

He had a plan for everything—for the banister, the stairs, the floor. The way he talked about the house painted a beautiful picture for her.

"I think this probably used to be a deeper cherry color," he said, his hands moving along the banister, and an answering heat began to burn in the center of her body.

His hands.

She could remember very vividly the first time she'd wished he would touch her with those hands.

She tried to push that thought away now.

"I love it. I . . . I really feel like this is too much."

He clasped her shoulders. She swallowed hard, her throat getting tight. Where he touched her burned. She felt as if she was on fire with his hands resting on her.

"Thank you," she said, moving away from him.

"I love you, Perry."

She closed her eyes. He said it so easily.

"Thank you."

"I feel like I haven't done a very good job of showing it."

"No. Don't. Please don't take this all on yourself. You're way too comfortable with that."

"What's wrong with taking responsibility?"

"It's not being a hero, it's being a martyr. Burning yourself at the stake isn't valuable to me."

He chuckled. "I guess not."

"So," he continued. "When do you want to start?"

"I guess that depends on when I can move into the cabin."

"Any time."

"I rented a storage unit down in Medford. I figure I'm going to need it, and it makes sense to bring the stuff down there."

"Great," he said.

"So, I can start moving things down there."

"I assume you'll need my truck."

"Oh, I need more than your truck. I need your truck and trailer, and your muscles."

"My muscles are yours," he said.

She fought against the slight bit of discomfort that statement created within her.

Maybe discomfort was the wrong word. Maybe it was . . .

She was such a tragic case.

"I will accept any and all help."

"Do you actually have the storage unit set up?"

"Yes."

"We can do it all Monday, since the florist shop is closed."

"Okay. That sounds good."

"Then it's settled. We move on Monday."

"Yeah."

Carson stayed for a few more minutes after that, and then he left.

And Perry was left with nothing more than the strange sensation that she had seen a boulder sitting at the top of a hill and had pushed it without fully thinking through the consequences.

Now it was rolling, and there was nothing she could do to stop it.

"It's for the best," she said out loud. "Because I don't need to stop it. I need to see this through."

She could only hope that was true.

Chapter 6

The wedding was not romantic. I didn't expect it to be. I did expect he might take my hand.

—Mae Tanner's Diary, August 29th, 1899

Carson was at Perry's place bright and early on Sunday morning with a horse trailer. Because horse trailers weren't only good for moving horses.

She was bringing her personal items to the cabin, but bigger things like furniture were going to the storage unit.

Flynn and Austin had come along to help load everything in, and when he was winded less than halfway through, he was grateful for their help.

He hadn't appreciated the sheer amount of old wooden furniture in the Victorian. But then, it was easy to forget how big the place was, because Perry really did only occupy three rooms. When he had done his walk-through, he could see why. There was a lot of water damage, and the house was rough around the edges.

But it had a lot of promise. The place was gorgeous. Exactly the kind of project he was looking forward to sinking himself into.

"I'm going to be a little bit scarce over the next couple of months," he said as he and Austin lifted a giant hutch up onto a dolly, and then began to guide it through the house.

"Oh yeah?"

"Yes," he said.

"Why is that?"

"I'm going to be working on fixing up Perry's house."

"You seem to be doing an awful lot for her," Austin said, looking past Carson, which Carson assumed was him keeping watch for Perry so she didn't overhear him saying something like that.

"Well. She deserves an awful lot."

"I'm not implying that she doesn't."

With great care, they got the hutch down the steps and began to take it toward the trailer. "I had a conversation with Flynn and . . . the truth is, while I enjoy working the ranch with you, I don't actually think I want to be a full-time rancher."

"Really?"

"Yeah. Really. I want to do woodworking. Specialized construction stuff. Restoration."

"How long have you been thinking on that?"

"Not that long, really. But the minute that I thought of it, I couldn't let it go."

Austin frowned. "And a conversation with Flynn put you on this path?"

"Actually, it started as a conversation about sex."

He heard a small noise, and turned to see Perry standing there, at the back of the truck. "I'm just recapping the conversation we already had," he said. He didn't know why he felt weird or uncomfortable that she had heard some of his explanation.

"Right," she said. "Restoration."

"Yeah."

She did *not* say anything about sex.

He felt a strange sort of discomfort settle over his skin.

The breeze rippled, and the leaves of the trees parted, allowing a shaft of light to fall across Perry's face. To illuminate her curly blond hair and cast a golden glow onto her skin before she disappeared back into the house.

She was beautiful, was Perry.

He had made a decision about Perry really early on.

Her beauty had to stay out of reach. Because the men in his family had a tendency to break the things they took in hand.

Perry's dad had already broken her enough, and Carson could

never forget her reaction to seeing a look of attraction on his face. Well, he'd never know for sure what she'd seen, but he could tell it had frightened her enough to slip away from him.

That wasn't who he was supposed to be to her.

So he'd decided that Perry was too far above him to touch.

Once made, the decision had been surprisingly easy to keep. Something he didn't have to think about overly much.

He was grateful for that. Because he needed Perry in a very specific way, and he always had.

He had never wanted to ruin what they had by ruining her.

But sometimes he would look at her and he would forget. Right along with forgetting how to breathe. Forgetting how to speak.

This was one of those moments.

He chose to let it pass.

He never let it go further than this. He never let it get deeper than appreciating how pretty she was—that he could excuse as just being observant.

Responsibility was something else he had learned early on. A man had to take control of his thoughts, because his actions followed. It was weak men who wouldn't be held accountable for what they thought, and therefore what they did.

"Anyway," he said, looking away from Perry and toward his brother. And sanity. "Yeah, I'm going to be focusing on this restoration. If it goes well . . . who knows? There's the Wilder house."

"That place is probably a wreck," said Austin.

"I know. It probably is. But it would be great if it could be in walk-through shape for the community."

Austin rubbed his chin. "My wife would love that."

"I know. Hell, so would your readers, Austin."

Austin looked deeply uncomfortable at that comment. He didn't know quite what to do with being the *New York Times* bestselling author of a hit book that was now going to be a TV series. Flynn, Cassidy, and Carson loved to harass him about it.

"It's a great idea," said Perry. "It would be a huge draw for Rustler Mountain."

"And a chance to put more Wilder history front and center."

"Something to take away from Butch Hancock's Wild West Show."

Austin grimaced. "Come on now. Something that amounts to basically a museum is never going to compete with a show like theirs. What they do is pure entertainment, and that's why it's appealing."

"Sure. But we can get the schoolchildren and the old people," Carson said.

"Listen, it's a very good idea."

"I know it," he said. "And makes the most of my specific talents, which you have to admit are not really fixing fences."

"Is anyone *gifted* at fixing fences, or do we just have to do it?"

"I'm not stepping out on you altogether. Just let me see how this goes."

"Dammit. I like seeing you invested in something too much to say no."

"Excellent," said Carson.

They finished loading everything into the horse trailer, and Austin looked at all the furniture stacked inside. "Are you going to be able to get this into the storage unit without help?"

"Yeah, I should be able to. There aren't going to be stairs like there were here. And I should be able to pull right up to the entrance."

"All right. As long as you're set. Millie has a doctor's appointment in a couple of hours." Austin cleared his throat. "We should be finding out whether we're having a boy or a girl."

"That's amazing," said Carson.

It was still strange, watching his brother about to become a father when Carson had been certain that he would be one by now. When things had been going well, he and Alyssa had really wanted to start a family. For all that he had issues with his own father, Carson had wanted children. It was part of wanting to be a better man.

Maybe you should have a baby with Perry . . .

Flynn's words echoed in his head.

He pushed them aside.

He had been a different person then. When he'd married Alyssa, he'd believed that the world was still fixable in a way he didn't think it was now. That *he* was fixable in a way he didn't think he was.

Yes, he'd had a good set of dreams Once Upon a Time.

Part of him still yearned for them.

But he knew better.

"Text me as soon as you know," he said.

"Will do."

He watched as Austin and Flynn pulled away, heading back toward the ranch.

Perry came out of the house, dressed in faded blue jeans and a yellow button-up shirt tucked in. She looked cheerful and put together; he probably looked like a mess after lifting all that furniture.

"Are you ready?" she asked.

"Yep. Ready to take the grueling drive down the mountain."

"Thank you again," she said.

He waved his hand and got into his truck. "See you down there."

He did the tricky maneuver of pulling the truck and trailer out onto the narrow street and then began the drive down to the closest large town around. He wasn't going to call it a city.

The winding two-lane road took them past Applegate Lake, and on impulse, he pulled the truck and trailer off the road when he reached the viewpoint that looked out over the deep blue water.

It was warm, but the mountain in the distance was still covered in snow.

Perry pulled in behind him and got out of the car.

"I always think this place is so beautiful," she said, putting her hands on her hips. "It doesn't matter that we drive past it so often."

"What I like best about this road is that not much has changed on it in the last thirty years. Some new houses. No major developments. This viewpoint is the same, and so is the boat ramp down there."

"Yeah. My dad always used to talk about the town that's underwater now. The town of Copper."

"Yeah. My dad too. But the dam was put in before we were born, so . . . I guess that would've been the last major change."

"It would be so different to have another town out here. Instead of having to drive so far to the next community."

"Well. It still wouldn't have had any major stores or restaurants."

"True."

"We can go crazy tonight. We can go to Applebee's. Get real fancy."

She laughed. "Actually, that sounds like fun."

She walked in front of him to the picnic table and the guardrail that kept people from tumbling down the cliffside into the water. Then she pulled up her phone and took a few photos.

"Right. Ready?" she asked.

"Ready," he said.

Yeah. He was ready. Ready to send Perry off into her new life. And he had . . .

"What if we skip Applebee's? What if we download those dating apps and see where the night takes us."

Perry looked up at him, her eyes round, and he had a weird feeling that he'd said the wrong thing.

"Sure," she said. "That sounds like a great idea."

She said it with an edge that made him feel she didn't actually think that. But hadn't they agreed they should begin dating?

Well. She'd agreed. And she wasn't his wife, so he didn't have to look at the subtext beneath her words.

"Great. As soon as we get down where there's cell service, I'm downloading one of those apps."

"Same," she said.

Then she got into her car and sped off before he was able to climb back into his truck.

Chapter 7

When we arrived at the house, he introduced me to the children and showed me to my room. We had not discussed this—how do you speak to a man of intimacy in letters? But it is clear he doesn't expect me to be anything other than his governess.

—Mae Tanner's Diary, August 30th, 1899

Perry stewed the entire way to Medford. But by the time they got there, she felt she was experiencing a moment of clarity. An odd thing to feel as one pulled into a storage locker facility, but there it was.

It was a good thing he'd suggested the dating apps, because he was pushing her further and further away from him, and closer to her goal.

Carson had decided he wanted to fuck his grief out of his system, apparently. Good for him.

Good for him.

He was making changes. Honestly, she couldn't say that wasn't good.

She recognized that stagnation was a bad thing for him. It was just . . . she hadn't imagined that he was going to get back into all this stuff quite so quickly. She had thought that maybe he would take on one challenge at a time. But no. Apparently he was going to be restoring old houses and picking up women, impressing them with his knowledge of historic homes.

How good. How great.

But she had already decided that she wanted to do some dating too, so she would start tonight.

Maybe she would meet an eligible bachelor out at . . . Rocky Tonk. It was possible.

While Carson started to unload the heaviest furniture and move it into the unit, Perry stood leaning against the truck, downloading different apps.

It was signing up and making a profile that was the hard part.

But she looked cute today, if she said so herself, and she took a few selfies to use as her profile pictures.

She wasn't sure quite what to say in the write-up. That she was hoping to start a new life and looking for serious candidates who wanted to have children and get married?

Probably not.

Quickly enough, she had one profile completed, and she started looking through her potential matches.

A lot of men in polos. A lot of men in real estate.

But that wasn't necessarily a bad thing. That was the kind of man she should be looking for. A professional. One who matched her energy. And stuff.

"What are you doing?" Carson asked, swiping his forearm across his brow. And she realized that she had taken no hand at all in moving her own furniture.

"Oh, I was signing up for the dating apps."

"The dating apps? Which ones?"

"All of them. Pretty much."

"Well. I wouldn't want you to break a nail, but maybe you could help out."

"Maybe," she said.

She went to the horse trailer and picked up a small box, then carted it down into the already full shed. "Ta-da."

"Adorable, Perry."

"I *am* adorable," she said.

"Austin texted," Carson said.

Perry turned to look at him, her heart pounding. She didn't know why this announcement felt emotional. Significant. She cared about Austin. She really liked Millie. She was so glad that they had found each other. But there was something about their pregnancy that felt . . . this was what she wanted.

A shared life. Love.

She wanted a family.

She wasn't going to be able to have a family exactly the way she wanted. But she didn't want to become one of those people who let her dreams be sidelined because she was too specific about how they were realized.

"Well," she said. "What is it?"

"A girl," he said, looking a bit in awe. "I kind of love it. I mean, we had Cassidy growing up, but she came late. And you know, none of our mothers stuck around. It will be nice. To have another girl in the family."

She couldn't be envious, then. She could only be happy. It was such a gift. For Austin to know love like this.

"I'm going to have to buy them something pink."

She realized that she would be moving around the time the baby was born. And that made her feel sad. But it was part of the change she needed. She wouldn't be around these people all the time. That was the point. She had to start having her own life. She had to.

"All right," Carson said, clearing his throat. "What app should I download?"

She cleared the cobwebs out of her mind. "Try these three."

He pulled his phone out and scowled at it. If he was in charge of downloading the apps, this was never going to get done.

"Let me do it for you," she said, grabbing hold of the phone.

She went to his apps and started to download the same ones she had selected for herself.

"You have to create profiles, you know," Perry said.

"God. How am I supposed to do that?" He looked mortified, and it was actually kind of funny.

"I mean, say you're a widower, for a start."

"Why?"

"Because women think that's hot."

"Why?" he asked again, narrowing his eyes.

"Because you're sad and lonely. It will make them want to touch you."

Her own jealousy was trying to strangle her and she did her best to shove the beast away. No. She was making positive moves *away* from this man. She didn't need to . . .

She didn't need to do this.

He looked appalled. "I don't want pity sex."

"What does it matter? You don't want to seriously date anybody. Why not use pity?"

"Because it's distasteful. To use my . . . my . . . my wife to get sex."

She grimaced. "Okay. That's fair. I really wasn't thinking of it that way."

Silence settled between them. "I'm bad at all this," he said.

"You're really not, though," she said.

"Maybe I wasn't, once upon a time. But . . . I never wanted to have to do it again."

"I know," she said, suddenly feeling contrite. She was upset about things that weren't his fault. It was so easy for her to get mired in her own feelings, and that made it too easy to minimize his.

The truth was, there was part of her that was angry at him. For not loving her. She'd thought she was over it until the possibility that he might want her existed again.

She had struggled mightily with her conflict, especially in the last year. Because when he'd gotten married, she'd thought that she had let go of that hope forever.

Then genuine, actual tragedy struck that she would never have wished on him or Alyssa, or anybody, and it felt awful.

Alyssa's death had also brought up all this . . . stuff. All these hopes and dreams and things that she had thought long buried. They were not that buried, it turned out.

"Do you really want to do this?" she asked.

"Yeah," he said. "I mean, it was my idea, mostly."

"Yeah," she said. "Mostly. But kinda Flynn's."

"Yeah. Kind of Flynn. And kind of you."

"How me?"

"Because. You're changing your life, and it makes me want to change mine. I know. Maybe we *are* too connected. Maybe everything is too much the two of us. But you're inspiring me to do something better with myself, or at least something different."

"Well. That's good." She cleared her throat and looked up at him. "Let me take your profile picture."

"I probably have something already."

"No. You can't be trusted."

She pulled up the camera app and centered him in the frame. He crossed his arms over his chest, and she knew that he was basically just giving her his most steely gaze, but he looked gorgeous. His jaw was sculpted, his shoulders broad, his blue eyes extra bright in the sunlight.

He was everything.

At least to her.

She snapped the photo and then turned the phone screen to face him. "Here," she said. "What do you think?"

He looked uncomfortable. "I don't know."

"Well. Trust me. You look great."

"Thanks."

"Put that you're a cowboy in your bio."

"A cowboy. I'm not putting that in my bio."

"You *should*. You're going to have to trust me about what's hot. That's hot."

He frowned. "Is it?"

"Yes."

"It just sounds cheesy."

"Fine. Rancher and veteran."

"Okay. That I can do. Of course, then they're going to think I want to talk about the military."

"I thought the whole point of this was that you didn't want to talk."

She should be getting frustrated with him. The situation felt fraught, and she felt sweaty. This was not uncharted territory for her and Carson. They had dated other people in each other's vicinity before. It was just that although she had declared she was going to date, she wasn't really prepared to deal with it. She certainly wasn't prepared for him to start dating.

Selfishly, she realized that she was hoping to find a relationship, even have a baby before he got around to doing anything.

She was hoping to be settled in her new life so she wouldn't have to witness him falling in love again.

Still, she looked his bio over when he was finished typing, and she clicked Save.

"There. Now we are ready to go."

"I guess. So, like, we just go to a place, and we turn the app on, and theoretically we find somebody to match with?"

"I think we can do it from here," she said.

They both opened their apps, and she watched as he stared at his phone intently.

"Who are you being matched with?"

"I don't know," he said.

"Come on, Carson."

"Women." He frowned. "Some of them look a little young."

Perry scowled. "Well, then you should swipe away. Nobody likes a creepy old man."

"I'm thirty-four, Perry."

"Yeah. Well. It stands."

"I should not swipe on this twenty-one-year-old."

"Carson," she said. "No."

Then she really looked at his face and saw that he was absolutely trolling her.

"You seem upset, Periwinkle."

"Not at all. Do you think I should swipe right on this twenty-one-year-old?" She flashed her phone toward him, because she was serious. There was a legitimate twenty-one-year-old in a backward baseball cap with a polo shirt who had matched with her. "Braden."

"Oh, please no," Carson said. "Is this what we've come to?"

"I don't know. I don't think it's a bad thing. We have options. And none of this has to be serious."

She did mean that. She had never been a big casual dater herself.

But she had also never really been all the way into a relationship. For complicated reasons. Well. Many of them standing right before her.

"Fine."

He turned his phone toward her. "She's pretty."

She felt like he'd taken a knife and slipped it effortlessly beneath her skin. "Yes, Carson," she said, looking at the brunette staring back at her. "She *is* pretty."

"I'll match with her." He picked the brunette while Perry kept scrolling furiously through her phone. She didn't like any of her options so far. Not really. But then she saw a man in a blue button-up shirt with a tie, who had a little bit of gray at his temples; he was closer to forty than thirty, but she wasn't opposed.

"How about this guy?" she asked.

Carson made a very similar face to the one he'd made the other day when she had brought up the last time she had sex.

"Yeah. Why not."

"Great."

"I'm going to tell him that I want to meet at Rocky Tonk."

"I don't know where that is, but it sounds fine."

"It's just downtown."

"All right. I'll let Vanessa know that also."

"*Vanessa.*"

"What?"

"Nothing. I just wanted to say her name. Because it's a nice name." She was a liar, and not a very good one. She needed to get better at it. Not just to Carson, but to herself. She didn't like that her running internal monologue was this honest.

"Great."

"If you want to, we can leave the trailer here instead of trying to park it downtown."

"Yeah. That seems like a good idea."

"You just pull it into the lot, and I'll bring my car around."

She realized belatedly, as they went to their respective vehicles, that the two of them pulling up together was likely to be a little bit confusing to their respective dates. But this was just a trial run.

That's all it was. Carson wasn't going to go home with Vanessa. Surely not.

He parked his car and trailer across two spaces, and then got into the passenger seat of her vehicle. She drove out on West Main, heading toward the bar.

It was relatively early to get started on a going-out kind of evening, but again, it was just a trial run. They had a little bit of time before they were supposed to meet their dates, so they stopped and got Taco Bell. And then continued on.

She found a parking spot against the curb, and the two of them crossed the street, heading toward the upstairs bar.

It wasn't crowded at all at this hour, and they took a booth in the corner, while she opened up the app and decided to message Ryan, her date for the evening.

Be there in five.

She took a breath and tried to still the jitters in her chest.

It was Vanessa who got there first. And she looked beautiful in a yellow dress, which was both too close to the color that Perry was wearing, and too much nicer for Perry to feel anything but insecure.

She gritted her teeth and tried to focus as Carson got up from the booth and went over to greet Vanessa. They didn't discuss what they were going to do next. She looked up at them and saw him gesture toward her. She assumed he was explaining the relationship. Perry lifted a hand and waved, and Vanessa waved back.

Regrettably, she seemed both sweet and pretty.

Perry drummed her fingers on the table.

A few minutes later, Ryan walked in wearing the exact color blue shirt he wore in his profile picture. A coincidence? Intentional? She wasn't sure she would ever know. She decided that it would be better if she made him come to her. She waved when she saw him, and he smiled and nodded and then made his way across the room.

Ever so slowly, the bar was beginning to fill up, and she hoped that the crowd would make her less conscious of Carson and Vanessa.

"Hi," she said as Ryan sat down at the booth.

"Hi."

"Glad that I caught you. Because I was just getting off work."

"Great. Perfect timing."

She knew that he worked as the manager of the tech department at one of the big-box electronics stores. Because it was in his app profile. "So, tell me about your job."

"Oh. I mainly manage the intake of broken computers all day. Same stuff all the time."

"Right."

"You're a florist?"

She nodded. She found her gaze slipping over to Carson. She had forgotten how much she didn't like this. Having to get to know somebody. It didn't happen quite this way when she was dating in Rustler Mountain, because everyone had a common background there.

So many of them had been in high school together. Or even went back further, with parents and grandparents who knew each other. Everybody knew that she owned the flower shop on Main Street, and usually, she had some idea about her dates. That meant they got to skip some of the small talk, and sometimes they could even come together to gossip about people that they both vaguely new.

That was the perk of small-town living.

Medford was also a small town, in fairness, even if it was much larger than her town, but it wasn't her town.

And because of that, she didn't know the local lore.

"Yes," she said. "I own my own shop in Rustler Mountain."

He frowned. "Where's that?"

"Do you know where Jacksonville is?"

"No."

It never ceased to amaze her how many people had no concept of the small outlying towns in the area. If they didn't go to them, they didn't know.

"Oh. Well . . . it's around twenty miles out of Medford."

"Wow. That's quite a drive."

"Yes," she said. "But I'm probably moving here in a few months.

I just brought a bunch of stuff to the storage unit, which is why I thought I would start trying to get to know people here."

"Oh," he said. "Interesting."

She couldn't tell if he really thought it was interesting or not. The problem was, she already knew that she wasn't interested. And it wasn't anything he had done specifically, it was just that . . .

She looked over at Vanessa and Carson. The brunette was clearly more into Carson than Perry was into Ryan. Vanessa was leaning in and touching Carson's chest every time she spoke and smiling broadly every time he said something.

She was obviously totally charmed by him, and who wouldn't be? He was the most gorgeous man in the room.

"I could use a drink," said Perry.

"Sure," said Ryan.

He didn't seem to think anything of getting up from the table and going over to the bar. Definitely he was going to pay, but he hadn't asked her what she wanted. She decided to let that go. He brought her a mojito. She noticed that a few minutes later that Carson had a drink too, but it appeared to be soda.

She was glad he was sticking to a nonalcoholic drink. But she also knew his choice might invite questions from Vanessa. Or maybe not. Maybe she wouldn't pry. Maybe she would think he was a Mormon.

"There's just a lot of corporate politics."

She turned her head and realized that Ryan had been talking the whole time, and that she hadn't been listening. Which was really crappy of her, because if he had done that to her, she would be furious. Thankfully, he didn't seem to notice her distraction.

"Really. I wouldn't have thought so."

"Oh yeah," he said. "Honestly, a lot of the managers here float around all the different retail stores. The same thing is true of the CEOs. There's only so many businesses in the area. A lot of them are medical."

She nodded. She did not tell him that she knew that. Because while he might be ignorant of Rustler Mountain, she was not ignorant of Medford. Folks spent a lot of time there buying supplies, or utilizing the medical facilities.

"You want to dance?"

She hadn't really noticed, but the music had been turned up, and it was currently thumping pretty loud. People were out on the dance floor, seemingly having fun, though she was having a difficult time imagining herself enjoying dancing at the moment. But then Vanessa seemed to ask Carson the same question, and at that moment, Carson turned and looked at Perry.

Their eyes locked. She turned back to Ryan. "Yeah. I'd love to."

He reached his hand out, and she took it. She did her best not to marinate on the fact that letting a stranger hold your hand was actually an exceedingly weird thing.

She wasn't attracted to him. That wasn't really fair. Because he was a pleasant-looking man. It was just that there wasn't that extra *thing*. Remembering the ice cream analogy, she preferred praline pecan.

So *sometimes* she could settle for caramel ribbon crunch.

But this man was cotton candy ice cream. Which was way too far removed from what she actually wanted.

It made sense in her head.

Still, she let him pull her close, and she danced with him through an entire song. But then she made the mistake of looking over at Carson and Vanessa. Vanessa had her arms looped around Carson's neck.

And Perry did something that she would be ashamed of later when she looked back on it. Maybe.

She pretended that her phone was buzzing. She took it out and frowned at the screen. "Oh. Oh no. My grandmother is having a medical emergency. I need to go."

"Oh," said Ryan. "That's too bad. I was having a nice time."

"I know. I'm sorry. I forgot to mention. I have a grandmother, and she's not very well. We live together, actually. I have such a long drive to get back home. So. So."

She pulled up her texts and pretended to be responding about her grandmother but was actually texting Carson.

Carson jolted when his phone buzzed, and then he looked over at her. He took the phone out and looked down at the text. She could see him making apologies to Vanessa.

Perry reached into her purse and took out five dollars. "To tip the bartender. Thank you. For the evening. Maybe we'll run into each other again when I'm actually living here."

"Yeah," he said. "Maybe."

She had a feeling that he knew she was making an excuse, and she felt guilty.

She hadn't said anything about Carson, so if Carson followed her too soon, it was going to look weird. She hustled herself out of the bar and down the stairs without looking at Carson.

When she ended up on the street corner, she wrapped her arms around herself. And waited.

The door opened, and the cowboy himself was out there on the sidewalk with her. "What was that about?"

"I'm sorry, I was not feeling that guy."

"Why not?"

"I don't know. I just wasn't. Like there was nothing actually wrong with him, but it just . . ."

"Yeah. It's fine. I was ready to go anyway."

"Really? You seemed to like her."

"You thought that I liked her, and you still made up a dying grandma excuse?"

"Yes." She looked at him cautiously. "I thought I was getting to be the selfish one for a little bit."

"You are." He sighed. "She was nice, but I think she was more into it than I was."

Perry wrinkled her nose. "She was definitely into it."

"I'm sorry that was weird."

"It *was* weird."

She sighed heavily and started to walk back toward the spot where she'd parked the car.

"What exactly are you looking for in a guy, Perry?"

Perry was immobilized by his question. "I . . . I don't know.

Because I grew up in a dysfunctional home surrounded by dysfunctional people. I want something different."

"I can understand that."

"What were *you* looking for? I mean, when you met Alyssa."

She had never asked him this. It hurt to do it.

"It's hard to explain," he said as she unlocked the car, and he sank into the passenger seat. "You know, I was living on base at the time, and Rustler Mountain felt so far away. The person I'd always been felt so far away. I'd already been on deployment, what . . . three times? And hell, I don't know. I was getting close to thirty, and I thought . . . this is the missing piece. I thought I didn't want to be like all the men in my family before me. Austin Wilder loved his wife by all accounts. He was a good father and a good husband. He was bad at everything else. He got himself killed because he didn't know how to stay on the right side of the law. I never wanted that to be me. Then there was my father, who managed to keep his ass out of jail more often than not, but he was just shit with women. He really was. He made my mother's life hell—he chased her off with his infidelity. But he was charming. You know, Flynn reminds me a lot of our dad."

"Oh," she said. "I don't know that I would have said that."

"No?"

"Well, I barely ever saw your dad. He was around, but not around."

"Yeah. That describes him pretty well. Around but not fucking around."

"But Alyssa . . ."

"I was hanging out in town and met her at a bar. We started talking. She wanted the same things that I did. She was ready to get married. Start a family. She said that would probably scare me away. I said I was looking for the same. It just felt possible then."

He wasn't talking about fireworks or love at first sight or any of the kinds of things she would've expected. But it was still a statement of some kind of connection. They had met at the exact right place, at the exact right time, wanting exactly the right things.

"So, you're saying if I meet a guy, I should just tell him . . ."

"Say you want to get married and have a baby. If he runs, he's not the guy. You don't want to be in a relationship just to be in one."

She scowled, mainly because she was mad that he was acting as if he had any idea what she thought or felt. "I don't know. Maybe I do for a little bit."

"I don't think you do."

"Maybe you don't know everything about me."

"I know that you used to love popsicles. What flavor were they? It was like pineapple and cherry or something. Bright red and yellow swirled together. I know that you pretend to be brave, but whenever you see so much as a garter snake, you want to run for the hills, even though you keep your feet planted because you'll never show anybody that you're afraid. I know that you hate spiders, but like mice, which I find contradictory. I know that when you smile, you get just the smallest dimple on the left side of your face."

Perry felt as if each and every word was baptizing her in warmth. Cleansing her of some kind of pain that she'd been carrying around for such a long time.

"Hell, Perry. I'd say that I know you pretty well."

She cleared her throat and started the car, pulling out into the street. "Yeah. I guess so."

"That guy was boring," said Carson.

"I don't know that he was boring. He just wasn't special." Perry let silence lapse between them. "Honestly, Vanessa seemed pretty special." She was being so fair and so good and so damned giving right now.

"Maybe the problem is me," he said.

"Well, when you met Alyssa, you didn't have to think about it."

"I'm not looking for marriage again. I think that's the problem. I don't know how to fundamentally change . . ." He shook his head. "The man I was when I wanted that future, he's gone. I can't see my way into the future anymore."

"You just loved her so much."

The only sound was the tires on the asphalt.

"Perry, I . . . I don't know that I did."

Perry felt all the blood drain from her face. "What?"

"I did love her. I would never have . . . married her if I didn't. But it's not . . . I had this idea of what was going to work. Had an idea of who I would be happy with. She fit the mold. She ticked the boxes. I don't know that I was the right husband for her."

"But she loved you," Perry said. "I hung out with her sometimes. She only had nice things to say about you."

"I'm your friend. What was she ever going to say to you?"

That had never occurred to Perry. That Alyssa would have known she was Team Carson, no matter what. She was still trying to untangle what he had just said.

"I thought . . . I thought the pain you're dealing with right now is because she was the love of your life and . . ."

"It's not that simple. That's all."

Perry couldn't process his admission. Because she had assumed that when Carson had come home with another woman and introduced her as his fiancée, she was the absolute unequivocal love of his life.

She had never once imagined that their marriage was based on anything less.

In fact she'd been . . . lanced with jealousy, nearly killed, honestly. When he'd come home to Rustler Mountain with Alyssa and that ring on her hand, Perry had been forced to reckon with the fact that he had fallen deeply in love with someone else.

That the love, the connection, the trust she shared with him wasn't special because he could give it to someone else *plus* sex and romance.

She'd felt sidelined, she'd felt *maimed*.

He hadn't loved Alyssa?

"I don't know what to say to that," she said.

"I don't know what to do with it," he said, his voice raw now. "The truth rattles around my head all day every day." He paused. "I think you might have grieved her, her presence, more than I did, and I can't shake my guilt."

Perry thought she might be sick. "I don't think that's true."

"Maybe not. I cared for Alyssa but . . . it's the guilt that makes going on feel impossible. I just thought I would become something different, something better when I got married, and I didn't. I wasn't what she wanted or needed. I'm not the man I thought I was."

Silence settled between them.

"This is hindsight stuff," he said. "It's not like I thought . . . it's not like I thought I didn't have strong enough feelings for her when I married her, Perry. And I feel . . . awful about it. The whole thing. I feel like I brought this woman into my sphere, and I did nothing but mess her life up. I did nothing but ruin things for her."

"She wasn't ruined," Perry choked out.

"She's dead, Perry."

"You can't blame yourself for that," she said. Except she had a feeling that he did. It was the most Carson thing she could imagine. To think that somehow he was responsible for the health issue of another person. As if associating with him, the legacy of his family, had caused this poor woman to die.

"There is no curse on your name," she said.

"It feels like it," he said, his voice rough. "I know it doesn't make any sense. But Austin felt like he was destined to die before he turned thirty-five, and I have that feeling too. The feeling that everything I touch turns to poison."

"It's not true, though," Perry said.

They could excavate his feelings later, or maybe they didn't need to. Maybe it didn't matter.

Though there was a burning feeling right at the center of her chest that suggested it did.

"Remember when you restored that wagon?" He didn't say anything. "It's beautiful. The work you did is beautiful. And work that you do on the ranch—you create life. You plant seeds, you tend herds of cattle. You restored that cabin and built your house. Your hands have life in them, not poison. Alyssa died, and it was a terrible, awful tragedy. But she would have had a brain aneurysm if she was living in New York City in an apartment by herself, or on an island somewhere with a different man. You don't control the world."

"But I want to," he said.

"Worse," she said. "You think you do. But only the bad parts."

They arrived at the storage unit, and she entered the code to open up the gate. She drove in silence up to the side of his truck.

"I'm just going to head straight home," he said.

"Right," she said.

They had stepped neck deep into a very emotional conversation, and of course he wanted to avoid it. That was par for the course.

Not just with him. With anybody.

She could understand it, but she wanted to keep . . . keep digging.

"Good night, Perry," he said, getting out of the car. She wrapped her fingers more tightly around the steering wheel and waited until he started his truck. Then she turned around and drove out of the facility.

His words echoed in her mind, and she tried to turn them over, decode them. Get to the bottom of what they meant and why they felt so significant to her.

It was going to take her time to process this.

Alternatively, you could just not. Because it doesn't matter. Who and how Carson loves doesn't matter to you.

That was true. It was why she was changing her life.

But his name echoed in her mind. The sound of his voice, the angles of his face.

Everything he had said about popsicles and garter snakes and knowing her.

A tear slid down her face, and for one, heartrending second, all her plans felt like the world's most hopeless endeavor.

What she really needed was to figure out how to fall out of love with Carson Wilder.

She wasn't sure it was possible.

But failing that, she could establish distance. She could find somebody better than Ryan. Maybe she did need to do something fun. Before she jumped into serious. Maybe you couldn't go from a lifetime of being in love with your best friend to finding a man you could marry and have babies with.

Maybe she needed to just have a fling.

She didn't find the thought particularly comforting. She didn't feel an instant sense of resolve.

She didn't feel hopeless either.

Right now, Perry would take that.

Chapter 8

I made my choices, and I accept them. But the ghosts in this house loom large. Not only his late wife's spirit. He is the living ghost that haunts these halls. Neither I nor his own children can reach him.

—Mae Tanner's Diary, October 14th, 1899

Carson was doing his level best not to reflect on the conversation he'd had with Perry the other night.

It had never been his intention to tell her about his marriage. In fact, he had fully intended to keep all that to himself. Those were the jagged, late-night thoughts that kept him up. The terrible alligators that swam beneath the surface of his internal swamp.

Nothing that needed to be said out loud.

Because there was no untangling the problem. There was no making it better. There was certainly no point trying to go over what had happened. Not when the other person involved was gone. He could never make it right.

He'd brought Alyssa here, married her, and realized too late he didn't understand what the fuck love even was. Let alone how to give it to another person. The more she'd tried to dig into him, the more he'd locked himself up.

He'd started to resent her. She wanted vulnerability from him; he didn't even know how to give that to himself.

What makes you cry, Carson?

Nothing. What's the point of tears?

That conversation, when she'd asked him that question in an exasperated tone, lived in his head. Now he wished he could tell her: losing you made me cry.

That was true, at least. But talk about too little, too late.

He hadn't meant to suck at being married. He'd been so sure he knew the basic rules. Don't drink too much, don't cheat ever. Give her babies if she wants them, take care of those babies. He'd felt ready for that.

You'd be a terrible father! How could you ever give kids what they need? I live alone in this house with your body in it!

She'd felt distance because there had been distance. He couldn't deny what she'd said. He couldn't even be angry about it.

There were other things too, things he hadn't told Perry. The last fight he'd had with Alyssa had been such a blowout that the next day he'd gone out on the ranch without talking to her. Then come home and found her on the bathroom floor.

He didn't know what love was. He knew that losing her hurt, though. He knew that he was filled with regret, what-ifs, rage. Because whatever would have happened to their marriage, even if they'd become just one in the long line of broken Wilder marriages, she'd deserved a longer life. A happier one.

Did he not love her, or did he just not love anyone enough?

Did he just not know what love was?

Was it easier to turn his marriage over in a new light now that he wasn't actually living in it than it was to live with having lost some deep, great love?

All he knew was that everything inside him felt dark, dirty, and awful. And had for far too long.

He had to get Perry moved into the cabin today. She couldn't live in a mostly empty house. That was the biggest item on his agenda.

He had texted her this morning, just about the move.

He didn't want to get into everything else.

He had gone over to Austin's and done all the chores that needed doing, and now he was in town picking up some things for dinner and waiting for Perry to close up shop.

The town was vibrant today. The weather was nice, the sky blue, and the air clear. It was early enough in the summer that there wasn't any threat of wildfire yet. Wildflowers were blooming everywhere, small yellow dots in bright green fields, poppies on the side of the road, Oregon grape in bunches, and purple shooting stars curving elegantly around the bases of trees.

There were tourists pouring in and out of the different boutiques on Main Street, iced coffees in hand, sunglasses in place to shield their eyes from the emerging Pacific Northwestern sun, and smiles plastered on their faces.

Maybe if he were a different sort of man, it would lift his heart to see people enjoying this place he loved.

Instead, he felt as if he was standing on the other side of a plate glass window, staring at something he couldn't afford.

It wasn't a feeling he could break down easily and examine.

Because he'd always had that feeling. It wasn't new. Wasn't unique to the experience of having been married and lost a potential future with his wife. There had always been a distance between himself and groups of happy people.

That was one thing he valued about Perry.

You should have married her. She's the only person you actually seem to care about.

The words Alyssa had hurled at him during that last fight were sharp, as sharp as always.

But with Perry it wasn't necessary to share feelings, and Alyssa hadn't understood that. Perry had been there for him. She'd watched his life unfold. She understood without any words.

Perhaps because neither of them had been given the gift of a happy family.

It was sort of terrible to be bonded by dysfunction, he supposed. And to be grateful for the bond. But neither of them had chosen to grow up the way they had. He wouldn't have. It just was. You couldn't fight reality. At a certain point, you just had to accept it.

So he'd accepted that he felt distant from other people. It had been harder for his wife to accept, and that felt like his own failure. His blind spot. He hadn't realized that holding something back could hurt someone. It felt like protecting her.

He felt grateful he had at least one person who wasn't a member of his own dysfunctional family who seemed to get it too.

What he did not feel distant from was the iced coffee. He decided to head into the coffee place on the corner to get one for himself. And just as he crossed the crosswalk and put his foot on the sidewalk, none other than Jessie Jane Hancock walked out of one of the knickknack stores on Main and nearly collided with him.

Her eyes widened, and she pushed her dark hair off her face, her arm full of bracelets jingling with the motion.

"Carson," she said. "I see you so rarely without Flynn. We never talk."

They didn't. Flynn did not like Jessie Jane. Jessie Jane didn't seem to be a big fan of Flynn's either.

Though he didn't know why that would prevent her from talking to Carson, or why she would want to.

Jessie Jane smiled and put her hands in her back pockets, thrusting her breasts forward. He suddenly had a small worry about why she might want to talk to him.

"Can I do something for you?"

He wished he had asked a less loaded question. But Jessie Jane just laughed and took one hand out of her pocket, waving it in the air, creating a chorus of singing bracelets with the motion. "Actually, yes. It has come to my attention that it was you and Austin who restored that Conestoga wagon that Cassidy has been driving around town."

"It was," he said.

"My family has one. It's been in the family for generations, I assume like yours. My dad has a hankering to restore it for the Wild West Show."

Interest rose up in him, along with a healthy dose of reluctance. Helping the Hancocks out with anything was forbidden in their family. Butch Hancock was the traitor responsible for the death of the original Austin Wilder.

Some families kept a Holy Bible with their written lineage inside. Others passed down furniture, porcelain figurines, or beloved toys. Their family passed down grudges as deep and bitter as they came.

The Hancock family was nothing but trash as far as the Wilders were concerned.

He had often thought as a boy that it was a funny thing they hadn't bonded together. Seeing as the whole town saw them as the same sort of trash. Outlaws with a tradition of bad behavior that was as old as the town itself.

But no.

That was not the case. The Wilders held a grudge against that whole family, always and forever, because Butch had given false testimony to Sheriff Lee Talbot, which had ended in three of the Wilders being executed for murders they didn't commit.

Logically, though, Carson knew that Jessie Jane had nothing to do with that. Any more than he and his siblings should bear responsibility for the crimes committed by their ancestors.

Nonetheless, Austin definitely hated the Wild West shows. They were historically inaccurate, and that bothered the hell out of Carson's older brother.

"And?"

"I couldn't ask Austin about restoration," Jessie Jane said. "He hates us."

Carson couldn't argue with that.

"You want me to restore the wagon?"

"Yeah. I wouldn't mind. I mean, we'll pay you for it, of course. Maybe we'll even dedicate it to you. The Carson Wilder Covered Wagon Spectacular." She fanned her hands out like she was doing a jazz routine.

"I don't need that," Carson said. "But I would definitely consider restoring the wagon."

"Great. I can get it up on the flatbed and bring it over to your place if you want."

"Yeah," he said, feeling somewhat hesitant. "I could do that."

The thing was, this was exactly what he wanted to do. He wanted to take on more jobs like this. He wanted to involve himself in restoration. He had loved doing the work that they did on his family's wagon. Getting the chance to work on another one for a different family felt like a pretty incredible opportunity. It was his version of restoring history.

He was never going to write a book like Austin.

Your hands contain life.

Perry's words echoed in his mind.

He . . . he wanted that to be true. He wanted to build more things than he broke down. Maybe that was why this project felt important. Maybe it was why he felt so drawn to Jessie Jane's proposal.

"Yeah. Bring it by the ranch any time in the next few days. If I'm not up there, I'll take a look at it when I am, and I can let you know how much work I think it will take."

"Great. I'll just give you my number."

Jessie Jane grinned, and reached into her pocket, taking out a business card for Butch Hancock's Wild West Show with her name on it.

Manager and performer. Blacksmith.

He nodded and took out his wallet, shoving the card inside. This was business. And he wasn't going to overthink her giving him her number.

"Talk to you later," she said.

She practically winked at him before she walked away. All right. He really hoped there was nothing underlying her flirtatious manner. That was the kind of entanglement he wanted absolutely nothing to do with.

He continued down to the coffee shop and got a drink for Perry and for himself before he crossed the street again to Bramble Flowers.

Right before he walked through the robin's egg blue door, his heart turned to stone. Perry was leaving. This little shop wouldn't be here. It would be filled with someone else's things. More importantly, it would be filled with someone else. She wouldn't be here.

Medford's not that far. It's not that big a deal.

It felt like it. Right then, it felt like death all over again, and he just couldn't face it.

But he knew what happened when he didn't face his own issues head-on. So instead of freezing, instead of walking away, he pushed the door open.

Perry looked up from behind the counter and smiled. It was as if his heart came back to life. As if the stone cracked and fell away, and suddenly he could breathe again. She was such a powerful force in his life.

Always had been.

Their connection felt especially important right now. As he stood there with two iced coffees in his hands. Everything in her little shop was immaculate. He could remember helping her set it up. Installing the coolers, which contained flowers and bouquets that had already been assembled. He could remember mounting shelves, installing the new hardwood floors.

"Is one of those for me?" she asked.

"Of course it is," he said, pulling himself out of his reflective state and walking toward the counter. He handed Perry her coffee—which was sweet and full of cream—and then took a drink of his own much more bitter concoction.

Perry smiled and clutched her drink to her chest. "That is so nice of you."

He grinned, but then suddenly they both seemed to feel the elation drain out of them. These moments would be rare once she left.

He promised himself then and there that he was going to bring her drinks sometimes. Even when she was more than an hour away.

Because he wasn't going to let moments like this become a thing of the past. He just couldn't bear that.

"I hope you have most of your things together," he said.

"I'm all packed."

"Great. So tonight, you get to spend your first night in the cabin."

He didn't think she had ever seen it, not since he had redone it.

They had played in it often when they were little, but it had been a dust trap back then, primarily a home for mice and spiders, and certainly not for Perrys.

"Are we going to move my bed?"

She took a sip of her drink, and he watched her lips close around the straw. He thought about her bed for too long. Just a second too long. He couldn't quite move his mind on from the shape of it. His reaction was half formed, like the feeling of standing behind a pane of glass. He didn't give it a name, or any more than the fuzziest of impressions in his thoughts.

"I can if you want. But there is a bed at the place."

"I like my bed," she said, giving him wide, doe eyes that made it impossible for him to turn her down.

"I'll pick your bed up," he said. "We can put everything in the back of my truck."

"You're very good to me," she said.

"Well, I'm trying," he said.

She tapped her hands on the counter.

"Can I help you close up, Perry?" he asked.

"Oh, I'll never turn help down," she said.

He locked the door and started turning lights off. Perry turned her focus to the cash register. In no time at all, it was closed, and they were caravaning back to her place, where he helped Perry load up her personal belongings. Then he lifted her mattress up, while Perry held the corner, and they carried it downstairs and put it in the back of his truck.

Then he disassembled the bedframe; as he methodically unthreaded each and every screw his brain continued to remind him that he was holding pieces of Perry's bed.

He turned his mind back to Jessie Jane. And the possibility that she might've been flirting with him.

Jessie Jane just didn't interest him. That was the problem.

He stared at a long metal screw in his palm. This piece of Perry's bed was more interesting. He wasn't going to look into that truth too closely. Instead, he packed up all the hardware and began to take the pieces down in as few trips as possible.

He waved at Perry and got into his truck, and the two of them began driving out of town.

It was easy for him to space out on his way to his place. Up the long dirt driveway that went past his brother's house, past the house he had built for himself and Alyssa, toward Outlaw Lake and the little cabin where he and Perry had once spent hours of their childhood.

It had been a safe space. Away from the toxicity of her home, the drama at his. It had been their pirate ship. And Outlaw Lake had been their ocean. She had been his anchor.

She still was.

The road made a tunnel through pine trees, and when they came around the bend, a clearing opened up. He could see the little cabin, with its cheerful smokestack and the wide expanse of blue lake beyond.

A strange settled feeling came over him as he pulled the truck right up to the front of the cabin.

She belonged here.

No. He wasn't going to get into all that. He was just supporting her plan to move.

He gritted his teeth and turned the engine off. Then he got out of the truck and stood there resting against the driver's side, his arms crossed as he watched her pull up next to him.

She looked through the window and grinned.

He did his best to smile back.

She turned her engine off and got out. Then he saw her rummaging around in the backseat, emerging with a box. "Come on," she said.

She was practically chirping as she walked up to the front of the cabin.

"You're going to need the keys," he said.

"Oh right. I sort of thought you didn't lock your doors up here."

"Of course I do. I don't trust anything."

"I forgot about your deep and abiding cynicism."

"How could you forget about that? It has been a defining characteristic ever since I was a child."

She laughed, though it didn't sound particularly joyous. He moved up beside her and unlocked the door, pushing it open. He found himself holding his breath, just for a moment, as she looked around. "It's so different from when we used to play here."

"Yeah. Well. It was falling apart."

"It wasn't that bad. Or maybe it just seemed not that bad to me. It was quiet, peaceful."

"It was not quiet or peaceful when we were sword fighting with sticks."

"Hiding in here with loaves of bread and pretending that we had run away."

"And that we were sailing the high seas."

"Obviously," Perry said, setting the box down on the floor as she looked around. He didn't often take time to be proud of his handiwork. But as he watched her survey the space, he felt a small rush of pride. He had restored all the wood. He had polished the floors, redone the stonework around the fireplace. It was small, but it was cozy. The countertops were polished concrete, warm and natural. He had added modern conveniences.

This was where he and Alyssa had stayed while their other house was being built. Perry hadn't really come over to visit during that period. Which was strange, because she and Alyssa had become good friends later.

"Have you ever actually been here since I fixed it up?"

She looked at him, and something about her expression reminded him of when she had been little, caught doing something she wasn't supposed to. "Oh. I mean, I'm not sure. I must have."

"I don't think you have."

"Well. Maybe not. You didn't stay here all that long."

"No. I guess not."

They began to move in unison, not making much conversation as they brought in boxes and the pieces of her bed.

And then, unexpectedly, he heard a big growling engine and tires on the gravel.

He walked outside and saw Jessie Jane Hancock in a flatbed truck, with a giant wagon strapped on the back.

Great. This was unexpected and terrible timing.

"Hey, Wilder," she said, waving her arm out the window.

Perry came out of the cabin and looked over at him.

"Long story truncated, I *did* tell Jessie Jane that I would fix her family's wagon."

"That's weird," Perry said.

"Life is weird, Perry."

Their eyes caught and held, and something passed between them on some kind of psychic wavelength—the unknowable truth of just how weird *everything* was. But he couldn't quite find the thread so he could unravel it.

And then Jessie turned the engine off and got out of the truck. "Hi, there. Perry, right?" Jessie Jane asked in that bold way of hers.

"Yes," said Perry. "Jessie Jane."

"The very one. Thanks for offering to take a look at this, Wilder," Jessie Jane said.

"Yeah. I'll just . . ." He walked up to the flatbed, and then hoisted himself up on it, looking at the wagon, which was primarily an axle and a whole lot of rotted wood.

"It's a little rough," said Jessie Jane.

"Yeah," he agreed. "A little."

"Do you think there's anything you can do with it?"

"Yeah. I can do a lot with it."

"Anything that's going to keep some of the original parts?"

"It might end up being the Hancock wagon in spirit more than it is in actual construction."

"Whatever works," said Jessie Jane.

"I might just have you drive this down to my shop."

"Yeah. I know I passed your house, but there wasn't a great place to turn around . . ."

"You can do it here."

"I'll go back down," she said.

She climbed back into the truck and started up the engine.

"When did this occur?" Perry asked.

"Oh, right before I got to the shop today. I did not think she was going to come up with the wagon so quickly."

"Flynn might skin you alive," Perry said.

"If Austin doesn't cook me over an open flame."

"Actually, those two things feel compatible."

"Yes. I am aware that doing anything with the Hancock family is liable to create drama in my family. But I wanted the opportunity to restore the wagon."

"Right."

"It won't take away from what I'm doing at your house."

Perry blinked. "I wasn't worried about that."

"Oh. I thought you might be."

"No. You'd better follow her."

He nodded. "Right. Well. I'll be back up to see how you're doing. I'll bring some dinner."

"Okay," said Perry.

And he left her standing there, even though it felt wrong. He wasn't sure what was shifting underneath their feet right now. But he could feel it all the same.

Carson Wilder didn't like the ground to move.

He couldn't seem to get it to hold still at the moment, though.

A damned fine reminder of the fact he didn't control the world.

At least he could fix things with his hands, even if he couldn't fix the more indefinable, internal things.

That would have to do.

Perry was rattled by several thoughts, and she wasn't sure how to prioritize them. So they were just sliding around in her brain while she unpacked her things.

She hadn't come to the cabin when Alyssa and Carson had lived in it, because she had been upset and jealous. By the time the main house was finished, she had gotten it together. Carson didn't know that. And apparently hadn't really noticed until today.

He was helping Jessie Jane fix that wagon, and Jessie Jane was beautiful. She would probably be happy to give Carson sex, whether pity or otherwise.

This place was the site of so many of their childhood adventures. Then it had become the place he had lived with his wife. Now it was her last stop before she left town.

Jealousy. Goodbyes.

The same themes seemed to play out in her life over and over again.

She did not assemble her own bed. She waited for Carson to return. When he did, he came with a giant bowl of spaghetti and meatballs, and a green salad. They ate at the small, square dinner table in the cozy little kitchen on blue-and-white-speckled camping plates, and she tried not to think about the last time they'd sat down to dinner together, when she had imploded the familiarity of their lives.

"I'd better put the bedframe together for you," he said when they finished eating.

They hadn't really talked about anything substantial since his return.

"You're going to fix that wagon?" she asked, leaning against her bedroom doorframe as Carson knelt down, screwdriver in hand. "I mean, you came to an agreement about that?"

"Yes," he said.

"Oh good. I mean, I think it will probably be a great thing for you to do."

"Yeah. She also said we ought to come by the Wild West show and see what it's about instead of being so against it for no earthly reason."

"Mm." The single syllable sound said a lot with a little.

"You annoyed by that, Perry?"

"She might be flirting with you," she pointed out.

He paused, then looked up at her. "I wondered about that."

Perry sniffed. "I see. And how do you feel about it?"

"I don't know."

She sort of liked his answer. Because if he didn't really know what he thought about beautiful, busty Jessie Jane flirting with him, then it couldn't be all that serious, could it?

How much interest could he possibly have if he felt so uncertain?

"I mean, it would create a huge scandal," she said.

"Well, I wouldn't have to tell anybody."

Except her. She would know, because they'd talked about it. She wasn't sure how she felt about being classified as nobody in this context.

She knew what he meant. But still.

"You're twitching, Perry," he commented, before turning his focus back to the bedframe.

"I am not," she said.

"Yes, you are."

"Well, you said you wouldn't tell anybody, like I'm not anybody."

"You know what I mean. You know . . . if somebody says don't tell anybody, I say okay, but I never mean you. You don't count, because you're like part of me. I wouldn't know how to keep something from you if I tried."

That wasn't true, though, because he had just dropped that strange bomb on her last night about Alyssa, and how he wasn't entirely certain that he had been desperately in love with her.

"I don't keep things from you," he said.

He could read her mind sometimes. But never when she wanted him to.

"I know I told you some stuff last night that made it seem like I have. I know that I went to a really dark place a year ago, and you didn't know what I was thinking. But neither did I. There is this stuff inside me. This kind of pain. But it doesn't have a name, and it doesn't have words. I didn't know it was going to take the shape that it did a year ago. Since then, I've been able to put some words to it.

Hopelessness. And doubt. The doubt is part of what I told you last night. About Alyssa and how I feel. I'm not keeping it from you. I'm sharing as soon as I figure it out myself."

She had just been wishing that her own internal monologue wasn't quite so clear. Looking at Carson, she realized confusion wasn't ideal either.

She also felt terrible, because he was claiming a kind of transparency with her that she couldn't actually claim with him. He didn't know everything that was going on inside her. She had hidden certain truths out of a sense of protection. Both for herself and for him. For their relationship.

But that was the status quo. And had been for a very long time. There was no point feeling bad about it now.

He stood up, and her breath froze in her chest. He stopped about a foot in front of her, his eyes intent on hers. "I don't know what my life looks like without you in it," he said.

She took one step forward, and before she could think it through, she reached out toward him, and pressed her palm to his, then curved her fingers around the back of his hand and squeezed. "Neither do I."

They didn't move. He just let her hold him, his skin like sandpaper beneath her fingertips, rough from all the hard work he did. Restoring wagons and building houses. Renovating old cabins. Taking apart her bedframe and putting it back together. She hadn't just been making him feel better when she'd said his hands weren't poison. They had built so much. It broke her heart that he couldn't see that.

He took a deep breath, and it changed the air around them. Everything went silent, still. As if the room drew closer around the two of them. As if the space between them shrank with it. Her heart gave one great thump. Then another.

She tried to breathe.

She found she couldn't. As if that great gust of a breath he had taken had used up the last of the air.

The place where she was connected to him began to burn, her skin like fire pressed to his.

Like touching a hot stove. Except she didn't draw her hand back instantly. She let it stay. Let it catch fire.

Their eyes met, the blue of his suddenly like the center of a flame. It was all just burning now.

And that was when she dropped his hand. Took a step back. Her throat was dry, her heart beating so hard she was dizzy with it.

She turned around and walked out of the room, wrapping her arms around her midsection. Then pressing her hands to the top of the counter as she tried to normalize her breathing.

Carson didn't follow her. She began to put the dishes in the sink, filling it up with water, soap. Slowly cleaning while she waited to see what would happen next.

He emerged just as she was drying the plates.

"Bed is assembled," he said.

He looked like himself. The air felt normal. Had that moment been all in her head? Had it been one breath, one second? It had felt like a shift. Like something significant. And now he was acting as if it hadn't happened at all.

"Thank you," she said.

He nodded. "Yeah. No problem."

"I'm tired," she said.

"I bet."

"I'm going to . . . I might just go to bed."

"Sure. Hey, Austin texted me and said that Millie wants to have a little get-together tomorrow night. Something to welcome you to the homestead."

"Oh. Well." She gripped her upper arms as if she was giving herself a hug. "They don't have to do that. It's not like I've never been here before. It isn't like I am not here all the time."

"I know. But you've never lived here."

It was true. She hadn't.

"Great. Well. That will be nice. Can I bring anything?"

"No. Millie wants to put together a big feast for you. But I assume that Austin will be doing most of the cooking."

"Usually, I do a lot of the cooking," Perry said.

"I know. But we are throwing a party for you. So you're not lifting a finger."

"Okay," she said.

He took a step back and gave her a half wave. "See you tomorrow."

She watched him walk out the door. And kept on watching the door even after it had closed, and she couldn't see him anymore.

She had nearly lost her mind for a second there.

She was only glad that Carson hadn't seemed to notice it at all. Her inclination was to avoid dinner tomorrow. But she wasn't going to. This was her last bender. Before she cut herself off.

She should just immerse and enjoy it.

Though as she touched her fingertips where they had just been burned, she thought *enjoyment* might not be the right word.

Chapter 9

I fought with him today, and it was the first time I've seen his mouth in anything other than that grim line. Poor Sarah wants her father, and he will not hold her. She's lost her mother and her father, and my heart can't take the tragedy of it. I perhaps should not have screamed this at him. But how else am I to reach him? I yelled, and so did he. But in the end, there was a spark in his eyes I had not seen before.

—Mae Tanner's Diary, November 18th, 1899

Carson was plagued by dreams that night. The kind that left him sweat-slicked and shaking. The kind he couldn't recall having since he was in his early twenties.

And once in his late twenties, right before he'd decided to go and find a wife before he returned to Rustler Mountain.

He woke up hard, and he woke up mad.

He let the ghost of the woman in his dreams fade away. So he couldn't see her face.

By the time he had his coffee, the dream was well and truly gone, and he couldn't have recalled the details of it if he tried.

But what he could recall was last night at the cabin.

When Perry had touched his hand.

She didn't touch him that often. It was an unusual thing. He hadn't realized how soft her skin was.

He didn't let himself think about that again the whole time he did his ranch work. Or while he rode his horse up along the ridge above Outlaw Lake, just to clear his mind, and not for any particular useful purpose.

Then he went down to the barn to evaluate the Hancock wagon again. But abandoned that project in favor of Perry's hope chest.

It wouldn't take a lot of work. In fact, other than letting the stain dry, it would only be an afternoon's worth of labor.

He replaced the cracked panel, sanded the rough edges. He found a stain match and went over the whole thing.

By the time he was done, sweat was dripping down his brow, and it was past time for him to head to dinner. He looked at his phone and saw four texts from his brother, two from his sister, one from Jessie Jane, and none from Perry.

He didn't respond to his family, but he did look at Jessie's text.

Wild West Show tomorrow?

Maybe. I'll see if I can get the family on board.

You're never going to get Flynn to set foot on Hancock land.

Probably not. I'll let you know.

He shoved the phone in his pocket, shut the lights off in the barn, and left the hope chest to dry.

Then he drove over to Austin's place. When he arrived, Perry's car was in the driveway.

He walked straight into his brother's house without knocking; he wasn't worried about interrupting Austin and Millie in a private moment just now.

When he entered, Millie was opening a present while Perry stood by with an expectant look on her face.

There were pink socks in the bag, and a little dress, pink cowboy boots, and the cutest little Western fringe vest he had ever seen.

"Perry," said Millie. "This is too nice. This night was supposed to be for you."

"But I'm very excited about the baby," said Perry. "And really happy for you."

Perry picked up the little pink cowboy boots and Carson felt a strange shift in his brain. It was easy to picture Perry with a gently rounded belly, looking at boots that were meant for her baby.

Something gripped him. Something low and visceral. Something that felt like Neanderthal-level possessiveness.

It didn't feel heroic. It felt dangerous.

He shoved the feeling back hard. "Hey," he said, walking into the room.

"Where have you been?" Austin asked.

"Working," Carson said. "I have some projects going."

There was a funny look on Perry's face when he said that. Well, she would find out soon enough what he had been working on.

She could buy herself little pink cowboy boots. They could go in that hope chest. That's what it was for, after all. Perry was hoping for a new life. A life away from here. A life away from him.

He didn't know where his irritation had come from. Yes, there had been a little bit of it here and there, but not quite like this.

His phone buzzed and he took it out of his pocket. Jessie Jane again. He could see Perry's gaze skim over his phone screen and something flared in her eyes then.

"Working on the wagon?" she asked.

Oh no.

"I . . ."

"Wagon?"

Flynn came into the room from the kitchen, holding a bowl of chips. Cassidy and Dalton were behind him, and just like that, he had a whole-ass audience for this moment.

"No," he said. "I wasn't working on the wagon."

"What wagon?" Flynn asked.

"He's restoring a wagon for Jessie Jane Hancock," Perry said.

Perry had chosen violence. He had no idea why.

"Yeah. Well, I was going to mention that. At some point," he said.

"You're restoring a wagon for that . . . weasel?" Flynn asked.

"*Weasel*," Carson said. "She's never done a damn thing to you."

"She's . . . she's a problem," said Flynn.

He looked over at Austin, whom he expected to be annoyed. But his brother didn't seem annoyed at all.

Flynn also noticed. "Aren't you irritated by this?" he asked his older brother.

"No," said Austin. "I am absolutely for the preservation and restoration of history. No matter whose it is."

"Agreed," said Millie.

"Yeah, no offense," Flynn said, "but maybe the man who married a Talbot, and the Talbot herself, aren't really the right ones to be weighing in on Carson's fraternizing with the enemy."

"I'm not fraternizing," he said. "I'm fixing a wagon. I want to do it. It's giving me something to care about."

"I see," said Perry.

He didn't know what to make of that. "Anyway. I was going to say. It only came up yesterday, and I just finished figuring out what I could even do to fix the thing. It's in way worse shape than ours was. But thankfully, I have the benefit of having fixed one before."

"I'd love to take a look at it," said Austin.

"You're a bunch of nerds," Flynn said.

"No one's ever called me that before," said Austin, looking awed. "I kind of like it."

"Disgusting," said Flynn.

"Honestly, what is your deal with Jessie Jane?" Dalton asked. "Because it feels like . . ."

"I don't have a deal with her. Except, you've seen for yourself what a pain in the ass she is. She's always busting my chops, I can't go into the Watering Hole without her trying to embroil me in a betting scheme, or just generally harassing me. Also, she's a Hancock."

"I get all that," said Carson. "I'm not helping her because she's a Hancock. I'm helping me. Because I want to take the project on. That's all."

"Well, aren't you glad you're moving onto the ranch, Perry?" Cassidy asked. "It's very peaceful."

"She started it," Carson said. "She threw me under the wagon."

Perry shrugged. "I didn't realize you hadn't told everybody."

She was lying. He could see that. Little pirate.

"Jessie Jane wants everyone to come to the Wild West Show."

That earned an extremely loud and mixed response from the group.

"No way," Austin said.

"*That's* your line in the sand?" Flynn asked, giving his brother side-eye.

"I don't like junk history."

"She said she wanted our family to see the show so that maybe we'd have a different point of view on her family."

"Doubtful," Cassidy said.

"She's offering free tickets, and she said she'll put us on the list up front."

Flynn's gaze went sharp. "You've got to be kidding me," he said, looking appalled.

"I'm not kidding. Maybe we should go. We're doing our best to put all this feud stuff to rest," Carson said.

"Not 'we,'" Flynn said. "I have no investment in any feuds ending."

"I do," said Austin, looking thoughtful. "I don't want all of us to be defined by the way our ancestors were seen in the past. Why do we want the Hancocks to be defined by it?"

"Because I don't care what people think about them," said Flynn. "Hell, I'm not even bothered by what people think about us. That's your all's personal issue, not mine."

"Maybe," Carson said, deciding to appeal directly to his older brother, "if we actually involve ourselves in the Wild West Show we can convince them to start adding some actual history."

"No," said Flynn.

"You just have a beef with Jessie Jane," Carson said.

"And you're, what . . . trying to hook up with her?" Flynn asked.

"No," Carson snorted.

Perry, who was examining her nails, looked up at him out of the corner of her eye.

"You started this, you little brat," he said to Perry. "You have to come to the Wild West Show with me."

"Do I?" she asked, her eyes glittering.

"Yes. I think you should."

"I think I want to go," said Austin.

"Regrettably, I'm curious," said Cassidy.

"Sorry," said Dalton, looking at Flynn. "I want to know."

"I love community events," said Millie.

"Yes," said Carson. "Let's go to the Wild West Show."

Perry looked hesitant. Flynn looked ready to start a mutiny. Carson ignored his brother.

"Periwinkle Bramble," Carson said, looking her directly in the eye. "Are you a pirate or a mouse?"

"I'm a pirate," she said, squaring off with him. His heart kicked in his chest.

"Good then. Be piratical and come to the Wild West Show."

She looked up at him and something about the challenge in her eyes made his heart lift in his chest.

"I'll be there," she said. "With spurs on."

Chapter 10

He held Sarah in his lap tonight. The fight was worth it.

—Mae Tanner's Diary, November 20th, 1899

The venue for Butch Hancock's Wild West Show was at the Hancock ranch, fourteen miles out of Rustler Mountain. There was a billboard off the interstate, some forty miles away from town, and a big sign on the winding highway that led there. It was white and red with a drawing of an outlaw figure holding two pistols. And there was a woman who was drawn overly curvy, holding a whip.

Perry, in Carson's passenger seat, squinted skeptically at that sign, as they approached the show.

"I hope they have concessions," she said.

"Jessie Jane said they do. She said it's practically like a day out at the ballpark. But with cooler stuff."

"It is funny how you never go to such things when you live next to them," Perry said. "Of course, also it would've been a great betrayal of our friendship, and yet you're the one dragging me here."

"I'm not dragging you."

She was admittedly being a little bit ridiculous about Jessie Jane. Carson had never shown any interest in her. And even if he had . . .

This was the problem. Her poor heart had been back and forth so many times over the years. She didn't endlessly pine. Yes, she'd had a crush on him as a teenage girl. Then she'd gotten a boyfriend. Carson had a girlfriend, sort of.

He went into the military, Perry went to college. They'd talked on the phone, but didn't see each other very much. She slept with boys who didn't call her back and let them hurt her feelings for a while. Then she came home to Rustler Mountain, where she didn't have the mystique that she had at school.

She and Carson were there at the same time for a while, and she got drawn back into longing. Back and forth. The seesaw of it.

He'd been deployed and they'd started writing. The writing had taken on a different tone than texting, calls, or in-person conversations.

Her own longing to be with him again made its way onto the page, along with his feelings of missing home, of being uncertain what he was doing, what he was accomplishing. The tarnished idea of heroism.

Carson had always been a rock of a man. Her protector. The one who'd punched her dad in the face. He was a god among men, untouchable in many ways.

He'd revealed something more, something deeper in those letters.

If she'd ever been able to tell herself that what she felt was a crush on a friend, attraction to a man she'd imprinted on when she was too young to know better, that year of writing had destroyed the illusion.

She'd fallen in love.

She'd thought maybe he had too.

She hadn't expected him to come back from the military engaged. But he had.

She could still remember trying to fake a smile until she thought her face might break. That had been one of the worst experiences of her life. And it had showed her that even though she thought she had come to terms with her and Carson only being friends, it really wasn't what she wanted deep down.

Then she'd gone through a whole different kind of accepting and grieving. She'd made friends with Alyssa as best she could. It had been a strange, perverse need in her. She wanted to like the woman Carson was marrying, because how could her friend be married to someone Perry hated?

That would never work. So she'd gotten to know Alyssa.

She'd gone to dinner with her, gone shopping with her.

She'd done the flowers for their wedding. She'd wept the night before while she'd assembled the bridal bouquet and told herself it was because she was emotional, not heartbroken.

One of his groomsmen had been an Army buddy. She'd gotten his number. They'd gone on a couple of trips together, but she had broken up with him when he'd started trying to get more serious. It had made Perry claustrophobic, and the sex had been mediocre at best.

And always, there was that piece of her that felt hopelessly devoted to Carson.

There was a big sign that arched over the entrance to the Wild West Show, and a large gravel parking lot. It was surprisingly full for a weeknight. There were more shows during the summer, but she was still shocked at the turnout.

"Pretty impressive," Carson said.

"I guess," Perry said, realizing she sounded uncharacteristically churlish.

"What event are you most looking forward to?" he asked, grinning.

Perry got out of his truck, and that was when the rest of Carson's family arrived. Cassidy, Flynn, Austin, and Millie. And Dalton for good measure.

She could smell snacks. Popcorn and hot dogs. Her stomach growled. There was a carnival atmosphere, with country music blasting over the speakers. It was full-on twangy country, and there were men in cowboy hats, and women in short denim skirts all around.

When they got up to the ticket booth, they could see that it wasn't just a concession stand. There were actually food trucks. And while Flynn got their free tickets from the booth, she went and examined the menu.

"It's on me," Carson said, when he came back over to her.

"It better be. I didn't choose to come out tonight."

"You're so petty," he said.

He really had no idea how not petty she was sometimes.

"I want street corn," she said.

"How about street corn and a burger from the shack over there?"

"Yes please," she said, feeling buoyed in the moment.

They got the ears of corn, covered in all the good stuff, and then they meandered over to another stand, where he ordered a burger exactly the way she liked it. Because he knew just how. This was why she had made a bargain a long time ago that she was going to preserve their friendship.

Because it was so comforting, when you lived with parents who couldn't be bothered to care, to have a person who just knew her.

Who cared.

He was foundational in that way.

Basically the first person who had ever cared about her in a way that seemed to go beyond his own needs.

That was why it had been so easy to get wrapped around him.

Sometimes, when she could rationalize her feelings like that, she felt a little bit better. For a while.

They walked into the stadium area, and she was honestly surprised by the size of the venue. The large dirt arena was surrounded by tiered seating all the way around.

Flynn was standing right in the aisle when they walked in, and he handed them tickets with their seat numbers. "Up this way," he said.

They were in a decent spot, not in the front, but near enough that they would have a good view.

Flynn seemed determined to avoid a positive attitude of any kind, while Millie and Austin seemed to be examining their surroundings with the sort of interest history nerds like them often had. As if they were cataloguing the reactions of the people around them, and every detail of the venue.

Dalton seemed to be cataloguing the attributes of the women in attendance. Cassidy was focused on her corndog.

She and Carson took their seats in the stands, and she attacked her corn with vigor. When the show started, it was pure spectacle.

A parade of horses with bedazzled riders streamed in, waving American flags. Followed by the national anthem. It was like a rodeo in more ways than she had realized. William Hancock, patriarch of the Hancock family and leader of the show, took to the stage, making a grandiose presentation, talking about the age of the Wild West, outlaws, and those who had tried to tame them.

What followed was a stunt show that was more spectacular than Perry could have anticipated. Jessie Jane did trick riding standing on the back of a horse, flinging herself down alongside the horse while it ran before hauling herself back up. There was sharpshooting with pellet guns, all of which culminated in the famous shoot-out reenactment that Austin had been so angry about all this time.

An actor playing Austin Wilder, the original, squared off with one posing as Sheriff Lee Talbot, Millie's ancestor, in the middle of the arena.

She looked at Austin out of the corner of her eye and saw that he was watching with skepticism.

And when it was all over, Perry couldn't deny that she felt a rush of adrenaline. It had been an amazing show.

The whole crowd was on their feet, stomping and clapping.

She could see why it was such a popular attraction that people came from out of town to see it.

But the performance didn't really make her feel any less weird about Jessie Jane and her sudden preoccupation with Carson. In fact, watching her be a badass on the back of that horse, doing her sharpshooting and all her tricks made Perry feel soft and incredibly uninteresting.

Alyssa was pretty in an immaculate way that Perry had never been. Perry was frizzy, while Alyssa's brunette hair had always been sleek. Her makeup was always done in a way that Perry felt was impossible on her own very pale features. Anything too bold made her look alarmingly like a circus clown, and definitely not a sophisticate.

Jessie Jane was pretty in a different way. She was curvy and edgy. Not necessarily done up but bedazzled in that way cowgirls often were. And she was strong. Athletic. Her arms were cut from both the trick riding and the blacksmithing. Perry fought the urge to pinch her own insipid upper arm.

Carson tapped her shoulder. "One second."

Then he walked away from her and went to where Jessie Jane was standing, chatting with a crowd of people. Perry looked away. She didn't want to watch. Was that ridiculous of her? Maybe. Well. She knew that it was. She had watched him go on a date with that Vanessa woman from the app. It was just irritating . . . it was irritating that he was now talking to a woman from town. It felt personal. Like a particular sort of slight. She didn't like it.

Of course, she hadn't liked it when he had brought back Alyssa after the two of them had been writing letters. When the two of them had . . .

Everything was so complicated.

"Well, hello there."

She turned, shocked to see that one of the men from the show had approached her. He was tall. Gorgeous. A tight black T-shirt stretched across his muscular chest. It took her a second, but then she realized who it was. West Hancock. Jessie Jane's older brother.

Wild West. That was what they used to call him in school. Because for all that the Wilder boys were hell-raisers, and earned the word *wild* in their name, West had been something else.

He had broken into liquor stores all through his teen years. His arms were tattooed, and there was a scar on his otherwise flawless face.

"Hi," she said, still a little bit surprised that he was talking to her.

"You're the florist, right?"

She nodded. "Perry. And you're West."

"My reputation precedes me."

He smiled ruefully at that.

"A little bit."

"Does that put you off, or would you be willing to take my phone number?"

Without meaning to, she whipped her head over to look at Carson and Jessie Jane. Then she looked back at West. West was nothing like the men she normally dated. She didn't gravitate toward dangerous. And West was danger personified. He wore his credentials on his sleeve. Literally in ink.

Men like her father hid everything. They relied upon the good assumptions of the people around them, and hid in the shadows of all those good thoughts, because they seemed professional and affable and important.

Not that men like West couldn't be a problem, it was just their wrongdoing was likely to be less buried, and therefore didn't worry her in quite the same way.

Still, she had gravitated toward men who were more middle-of-the-road. What would Carson think if she went out with West? Well, it would put up the hackles of the entire Wilder family, for sure. But Carson was already talking to Jessie Jane. Why shouldn't she take West's number?

"I'll take it," she said. "But I don't know when I'll use it."

"You said when," he said, handing her a card for the Wild West Show that had his name on it. "Not if."

"I guess I did."

Then he tipped his cowboy hat and turned away from her, leaving her feeling charged up and a little bit triumphant. When Carson returned to her side, she decided not to say anything about the exchange.

"What was that about?" she asked as they headed out of the venue with the rest of the family a few paces ahead of them.

"Just telling Jessie Jane I enjoyed the show. Giving her a little bit of a timeframe on the wagon. I'm going to have to order some things."

"Right."

"Austin says that everyone can come over for dessert."

"Like we didn't just stuff ourselves full?"

"I guess Cassidy made something."

She nodded. "Oh. Well. Okay."

"I'm going to drop you off at Austin's. I just have to get something from the house."

For some reason, the whole way back she wondered about what that was. She let herself start to believe that maybe he was actually going to call Jessie Jane. Or text her. After she had outed him for texting her the other night, she doubted that he was going to do it in front of her again.

She thought about West's phone number.

Would she use it?

When she ended up at Austin's house without Carson and ten minutes of waiting for him turned into twenty, she decided that she damn well would.

Chapter 11

We went for a walk today as a family, and he was very nearly a gentleman. He felt, in some ways, like my husband. Not my employer. I feel such deep confusion when I look at him. My heart beats too fast and my stomach feels wrong. I want him to come closer, and yet I don't know what would happen if he did.

—Mae Tanner's Diary, January 15th, 1900

Carson got the hope chest loaded into his truck and then traded a few texts with Jessie Jane, promising to begin on the wagon once all of his commitments to Perry were squared away.

Your girl comes first.

He didn't know what to say to that since Perry *was* his girl in many ways. But also wasn't.

Yeah.

Then he drove over to his brother's house, ready to present Perry with the chest. But first, he had to get through Cassidy's dessert.

"It's a no-bake cake," Cassidy said, as he slipped into the kitchen and sat down next to Perry. "I made it with pudding mix. You can't mess it up."

"I'm sure it's fantastic," said Perry, overly kindly.

He noticed that Cassidy didn't respond to Perry.

Perry didn't acknowledge his arrival, and he found himself distracted by her coolness.

They had been victimized by Cassidy's attempts at baking before. Poor Cassidy. She had always been missing that maternal touch. And she seemed to want a little bit of softness sometimes, to bring some of those traditionally feminine skills into play. She was determined, he would give her that. But not naturally skilled.

But she was right about the no-bake cake. Which seemed to

consist of lemon pudding, Cool Whip, and graham crackers. It was damned good.

"This is great, Cassidy," said Dalton.

And he caught a pleased expression on his sister's face when Flynn's friend complimented her. Carson wasn't sure he liked that at all.

But the look was gone as quickly as it had appeared, and there was really nothing left for him to ponder.

He was still kind of annoyed at Perry, and the way she had brought up the wagon, but he was still going to give her the gift. For some reason, he didn't want to do it in front of everybody.

"Hey, Perry," he said, elbowing her. "I want to show you something."

"Fine," she said.

He stood up, and she followed him into the living room, through the immaculately clean house—which was all Austin, not Millie—and out the door.

"What? Are you enlisting me to go help you practice a monologue for your upcoming date with Jessie Jane?"

"I was working on something for you," he said.

He kept on walking down the porch stairs, but he realized that Perry wasn't following him.

"What?" He turned and saw her standing there, looking . . . Small somehow. The porch light was shining on her face, and he could see something wounded and painful there.

"I'm sorry. That was really bitchy of me. All of this. From mentioning your interest in working on the Hancocks' wagon to . . . my reaction just now."

"Kind of," he said.

"She rubs me the wrong way," she said, finally walking down the stairs and coming to stand beside him. "I'm sorry. I . . . I don't want it to be her, Carson. If you sleep with somebody . . . I just don't want it to be Jessie Jane."

The words hooked him in the stomach, kept him standing there, rooted to the spot. "Why?"

"I don't know. I don't like her; I don't trust her."

"Why don't you like her? You have no part in our family history."

"Okay. Maybe that's not fair. It's not fair that I don't like her. Because it would be for the same reasons that people don't like you. But . . . honestly, Flynn would be mad."

"I know," he said. "Because he hates her."

"He's attracted to her," Perry said.

That jolted him. And he . . . well. Hell. That was true.

"Oh. How did I . . ."

"I mean, come on. He protests so much."

"I guess he does."

"He'll never do anything about it. Because she's a Hancock, and I really do believe that bothers him."

"Yeah. It does."

"Anyway. Just . . ."

"I don't want to sleep with her," Carson said.

"You don't?"

"No. I really do just want to fix her wagon. It's not a euphemism. I'm not interested in her. She has never turned my head. I've lived here in this town all my life with that woman, and I have never once been tempted by her. Why would I start to be tempted now?"

Perry looked poleaxed, but didn't say anything.

He walked around to the back of the truck and lowered the tailgate. Perry came around beside him. "What is it?"

"The stain is a little bit wet, so I don't want you grabbing hold of it. But I'll drive it over to the cabin."

"You fixed it," she said. She climbed up into the bed of the truck and hovered over the hope chest.

"The crack is gone."

"Yes. The crack is gone. I . . . thank you," she said.

"Well. You're packing up and you're leaving your life behind. Moving on. It just seemed . . . it seemed right."

He got up into the back of the truck with her and sat down on the edge of the bed. Perry did the same, clinging tightly to the side.

"I'm sorry," she said. "I was being mean. I think it's . . . all the change."

He scooted a little closer to her and nudged her with his shoulder. "You're the one that changed things."

"This time," she said, looking up at him.

He remembered his dream. He remembered the face of the woman in it. He remembered Perry's hand touching his. Right then, everything was clear. Far too clear. Perry's bed. Perry's hands. Perry right now.

Seventeen years of good intentions evaporated. He felt as if all the good he'd ever done was dissolving then and there. It was the very worst thing.

Because she was looking up at him, face upturned, eyes glowing in the moonlight, her lips parted softly.

And it was like that moment when the wind had come up and caught her hair, when the sunbeam had bathed her in that warm glow. Sunlight, moonlight. They revealed all those secrets he didn't want to know. How beautiful Perry was being chief among them.

He wanted to kiss her.

The thought was as strong as it was horrifying. He wondered how soft her lips were. If she would get softer beneath him if he pressed his mouth to hers.

Or if she would get stiff and fierce and angry and smack him in the shoulder. That's what she should do.

Carson was very good at catching a feeling when it was still a seed. When it hadn't yet grown into a coherent thought, into a fully realized fantasy.

He had done that with Perry since they were teenagers. With what could've been attraction to her. He had caught it and choked it before it could ever become anything quite so clear as wanting to kiss her.

Sometimes there were sweat-slicked dreams, but he blamed his subconscious for that. Dreams that had grown in intensity when he was deployed and Perry represented everything he missed. She was home to him. And he'd dreamed of her every night.

He'd also realized he needed to make some changes.

He'd never thought about kissing her when he was right next to her.

Somehow, though, he'd missed a stray thought. It had gotten away.

He had missed it just now. Or maybe he had missed it last night. Maybe he'd lost his grip on it when he was sleeping. But somewhere along the line things had broken down, and now he was thinking, bright and clear, that he wanted to kiss Perry Bramble.

He didn't move. Because if he did move—if he freaked out and pulled away, or if he leaned in—bad things were going to happen. So he acted like this wasn't happening. Like he could take this sprout and shove it back into the seed.

God damn.

He tried to erase the words from his mind, tried to take that clarity and make it fuzzy. But nothing took away the longing. The way his chest ached, the way his body was on high alert.

This was something new. This feeling. Attraction like this. He didn't recognize it. He didn't know it. He didn't know himself. And fuck all that.

He didn't want this. Not with her. Not with anybody. He didn't want any emotion so intense, so strong.

He knew what it looked like when everything around him was reduced to rubble.

No. He didn't. Actually, the really terrifying thing was that he didn't know what it was like when everything around him was reduced to rubble. Because Perry had always been there. Standing strong, being her. She was always there.

And that was why this was a risk he was never going to take. Not ever.

He wanted to be her hero. Not . . .

This.

He moved away from her slowly. "I'll drive it over to your place. After."

"Okay." Her voice sounded subdued.

"Why don't you . . . why don't you head on back in. I mean . . . They're probably playing cards."

"You aren't coming?"

"I will in a second."

Perry got out of the truck bed, and so did he.

Then he rounded the side of the truck and opened up the passenger door. He dug around in the glove box, saying a prayer that his last remaining occasional vice was still there.

He'd given up alcohol. So this seemed like a reasonable occasional indulgence. There was a pack of cigarettes there with two left inside, and a lighter. Once he finished this packet, he wouldn't buy any more. Maybe.

He leaned against the side of the truck, put one cigarette in his mouth, and lit it.

He closed his eyes, leaned his head back against the door of the truck, and took a deep inhale.

Tonight reminded him of high school. Of tearing around Rustler Mountain on a motorcycle. And then he remembered him and Perry running around like heathens, her blond hair a tangle. Looking so pretty. Her bottom lip always had teeth marks in it. It was always a little red. He wondered if it was from holding things back. When her father would say awful things to her mother, had Perry been forced to bite her lip and keep it all back?

He had never wondered then. He did now.

And then he suddenly thought of him being the one to bite it. He nearly dropped that cigarette.

"What the fuck are you doing?"

He startled, and he felt as if teenage Perry had just appeared to scold him for his inappropriate thoughts. Except it was Perry right now, and it was about the cigarette.

"Just taking a break," he said. "I thought you went back inside."

"I worry about you when you're weird and moody."

"*I'm* weird and moody?" he asked, gesturing with the cigarette.

"I didn't say I *wasn't*."

"You decided to leave Rustler Mountain, and now you're having an emotional reaction to your own choices. That's not really my problem."

She scowled. "I'm your friend, so what I want and feel *is* your problem."

"You want us to be less each other's problem. That was a *you* thing, not a *me* thing."

"I also would like you to not destroy your health." She gestured to the cigarette.

"I don't need a lecture. I'm just going to finish the cigarette and go back inside."

"They're bad for you," she said.

"Sure. Though they're not an enemy bullet, so I feel like I can take the risk."

She reached out and plucked the cigarette from between his fingers. "I wish you wouldn't."

She was standing in such a familiar position. Holding his cigarette, looking up at him, mad. It reminded him again of being teenagers. And it made him think of wrapping his arm around her waist and pulling her up against him. What would she do?

What would she have done then?

He pushed those thoughts aside.

He did not need to be thinking about that.

"Perry . . ." he said, beseeching because he wanted the fucking cigarette.

"Just a slow way to kill yourself."

He growled. Took the cigarette back and tossed it on the ground, grinding it under his boot. "I'm not trying to kill myself. I'm just trying to catch my breath."

"Weird way to try to catch your breath."

Then don't make me feel like my chest is being torn open.

But he didn't say any of those things, because he didn't even know quite why he was thinking them.

Everything just felt like a mess. That was the honest truth.

"Thank you for the PSA," he said.

"Come on," she said. "Let's not fight."

"It feels like we are. It feels like we've been fighting since Jessie Jane showed up last night." If he were honest, it kind of felt like they had been fighting since that first night she'd told him she was moving.

"I'm sorry," she said. "I had a weird reaction to her."

There was a pause. Then she turned to look at him. "I think changing the way we are with each other is actually going to be a little bit more work than I realized."

"You thought it was going to be so much work that you figured you'd move away."

"It's not the only reason I'm moving away."

Except right then, he had the feeling it was the biggest reason. Not her business. And that felt bad. Very bad.

"I'm glad you like the hope chest."

"I do. I love it."

She looked as if she wanted to say something else. "What?"

"I would really like to say that you can sleep with Jessie Jane if you want to, and that I don't care. But it would be a lie."

"I already told you," he said. "I don't want to."

He didn't want to have this conversation. Because everything inside him felt tangled up. He felt tangled up.

"Hey, tomorrow why don't I go by your old place, and we'll take total inventory of all the stuff that needs to be done."

"Oh," she said, looking like she had whiplash. Fair enough. He was giving himself whiplash, but he wanted to get out of this murky valley they'd found themselves in. He wanted to get back on solid ground.

He didn't like the shifting. He didn't like it at all.

"Yeah. That sounds great."

"Don't tell anybody that I was smoking a cigarette."

She made a scoffing noise. "I wouldn't."

"You told them about Jessie Jane." They walked up the steps, and she put her hand on the doorknob.

"Well, I'm not jealous of the cigarette."

She said it so quickly, so casually, that he didn't process her statement until they were back inside, until Cassidy said something to him about being sure she'd seen a feral hog in the back pasture.

Jealous.

Perry had been jealous of Jessie Jane.

He spent the rest of his night turning that over. But when he went to sleep, he didn't dream. Mostly out of spite.

Chapter 12

I feel as if writing these words is a sin, and yet I know it isn't. He kissed me tonight in the parlor. He had been drinking, and I worry he thought I was his first wife, or that perhaps he didn't think at all. I started to scold him and then his mouth was on mine, and I could not think at all. He came to his senses and part of me wishes he had not.

—Mae Tanner's Diary, February 16th, 1900

Perry had been slightly queasy over her slipup the entire night, and she didn't really feel better as she sat at the kitchen counter in the little cabin the next morning drinking coffee.

Carson hadn't said anything about it, not that they had been alone at all after it happened. Not for more than a few minutes. He had dropped the hope chest off last night, but he had scarcely stayed longer than five minutes. She blamed herself.

He had texted her this morning to say that he was coming by at nine, which was going to be very soon, so she needed to stop ruminating.

She had let last night get weird. She had been way too open in her feelings about Jessie Jane; she didn't know why she cared about her specifically. It didn't make any sense.

And then he had said . . .

That he had never wanted to sleep with Jessie Jane. Not in all the time that he had lived in Rustler Mountain, so of course it wasn't going to change.

That had felt like a stab wound. It had been the worst time ever to make a slipup the way she had. When he had made it so abundantly clear that if he had never wanted a woman, he was never going to.

She knew that. She knew it because . . . obviously.

Just obviously. The fact that he had never touched her, and never even seemed to want to was evidence enough.

All the evidence she needed.

She sang a very long, high note into the echoing silence of the kitchen before she took another sip of her coffee, as if expelling the sound from her body might do something to disrupt the restlessness within her. The embarrassment. Instead, she just was even more embarrassed.

There was a knock on the front door, and she startled. Then she grabbed her sweater off the back of her chair and drank the last of her coffee on the way to the door. She set the mug down on a side table and jerked it open.

There he was. Tall, broad, his blue eyes still clouded with sleep. He was wearing the kind of battered jeans that haunted her dreams. Soft denim that conformed to his muscular thighs, and all the other details that she tried to never look at.

Operative word being *tried*.

"Good morning," he said, sounding gruff.

"Yeah. Great morning," she said, walking out of the house and closing the door behind her. She locked it ostentatiously.

She looked up at him and saw his mouth twitch.

"Sleep well?" she asked.

"Just great," he said.

She got into the passenger seat of the truck and waited for him to join her. She was wondering if she should be the one to say something. He wasn't acting weird, so maybe she didn't need to, but she also wasn't sure if she could just let what she'd said slip by. No. She was going to leave it alone. She wasn't going to say anything.

Because there was no good end to it. She didn't even know how to articulate what she was feeling, so there was no point trying.

"Did you sleep well?" he asked. "I mean, did I put the bed together right?"

"Yeah. I don't feel any lumps under the mattress. So, no errant peas or anything."

"Peas?"

She looked at him, entirely straight-faced. "Because I am a princess, Carson."

"A pirate princess, maybe," he said. "And if I recall, you took offense to that back in the day. Because you didn't understand why you couldn't just be a pirate like I was."

"Well. It seemed sexist," she said. There. They were talking about being kids. Simpler times. Not about whatever last night had been.

"Sorry you feel that way," he said.

"I don't think you are."

She leaned forward and turned his radio on. Then she found the AUX cable and hooked her phone up. "I want to choose the music," she said.

He groaned. "Please no."

"It's a short drive. You'll live. Though I might make Taylor Swift the soundtrack of the renovation."

"I like Taylor Swift," he said.

"Well, then you won't mind my two-hundred-song playlist."

"At least it's not the same song two hundred times, which is definitely what high school Perry would have prepared for me."

"I do love to ruminate on a song. But I know better than to make you suffer for it."

"The character development is truly stunning."

This felt good. It felt easy. It felt like them.

She *tried* not to get lost in *ruminating* about how long it had been since they had felt normal. Maybe there was really no normal. They had been little kids together, and it had been simple. Her heart had nearly burst every time she'd ever looked at Carson Wilder, but she had assumed that he felt the same. She had assumed it was friendship. Why would she think it was anything else?

He was her compass when it came to human connection. Her north star, her baseline. He was everything.

So she had assumed that the feeling in her chest, far too full and nearly painful, was just the feeling you had for your very best friend in all the world. It was only when she started to get breasts, and realized that she was a girl, and he was a boy, and that meant different things when it came to emotions and bodies, that she started to worry that maybe his feelings were different from hers.

When he grew six inches, and she saw him making out with a girl who had her nose pierced in the back of his truck, then she had known for certain.

That not only was he a man, and she well on her way to being a woman, which made them different, but that for him, there were women that he saw differently. She was something else.

But for her, he was the standard. So she had learned to protect herself from those truths over the years. She had done her level best to find a new normal every time something changed.

He'd looked at her once, when they were out at Outlaw Lake and she'd been in a white dress, hoping he'd think she was beautiful. But he'd seemed almost . . . angry, and he hadn't made a move on her, far from it. The way his eyes had skimmed over her had made her skin feel too tight. She'd run away. Swum away, actually.

Then she'd decided that she could find boys to make out with.

To sleep with.

Who didn't look at her as if her being a woman was an inconvenience.

When he'd left, she had to find a new version of normal all over again. And then he had brought back a wife, and the world had turned over yet again.

What was normal?

Them being at Outlaw Lake. That was about it.

She was changing that. He wasn't wrong. What he had said to her last night about her upsetting herself by leaving and then taking it out on him.

No. He wasn't entirely wrong.

She did not play the same song repeatedly all the way down to town, though she did consider it, just to be irritating. Sometimes, there was comfort in acting more like a younger sister, someone who could annoy him and get away with it. Because it felt a little bit more intimate than friendship, and it let her tease him without sounding as if she was flirting.

It didn't feel right this time.

It wasn't honest, anyway.

That was the problem. She was beginning to get more and more frustrated with herself. Because she wasn't honest with him. She had put together a facade that she had continued to refabricate whenever necessary. She presented an image to the world of how she felt about him, but she knew it wasn't true.

She kept her real feelings inside, turning them around like that same song she would play two hundred times because she liked it.

Except she didn't especially like this.

It was a problem with her in general. She got obsessed with just one thing.

Sometimes she wished she could go back in time and undo the moment she had become obsessed with Carson. But then, the thought of doing that made her sad, because he had given her so much joy.

Didn't she get so much from who they were together? Even when she was separated from him, it would be different from if it had never been.

No. She would never have survived her childhood without him. She would have died of loneliness. Of a broken heart.

Because living with her parents had been worse than living alone.

Walking on eggshells was a fact of life with them.

"You're awfully quiet."

"I'm thinking about my parents, actually."

"Oh?"

"I haven't told them yet that I'm leaving." That was true, and she didn't especially want to give him the breakdown of the thought ladder she had climbed to get to the topic of her parents.

"Oh. Well. Will they notice?"

"I mean, they already live over an hour away, but this will be even farther. And selling my grandma's house . . ."

"Do you think your mom is going to be upset about it?"

"Kind of. It feels completely in line with who she is. She didn't help take care of her mother when she was dying, and she never acted like she cared about the house at all, but if I sell it . . ."

"Yeah. That does sound like your mom." He paused for a moment. "I don't know what my mom would sound like in any given situation, because I never see her."

"Aren't we a pair."

"I think it's why we're a pair."

"True."

It was a reminder of exactly what had bonded them. And it wasn't a bad thing.

She always felt like the being-in-love part, the attraction, was shallow in comparison to everything else. Sometimes she got mad at herself for thinking that, because romantic love was important too.

But it was nothing in the face of a lifelong friendship. Surely. What example did either of them have of the true value of love and romance?

Mae Tanner had not moved out to Oregon for love. She had done it out of a sense of self-preservation. She wanted to find the new thing, the best thing, the thing that she needed most.

She had left behind a life of safety, and any number of men who had a romantic interest in her for a man who had written taciturn letters and offered nothing in the way of romance at all.

There were bigger things. Brighter things.

Her mother had dimmed herself loving a man who was awful. She'd had a child with him. Whoever her mom was before, Perry would never know, because she was that child. But at one time, her mom had been a woman who had looked at Perry and decided to name her Periwinkle. And that was possibly the most misguided moment of romantic whimsy ever.

Perry had always had trouble connecting those dots.

But knowing Carson had healed her in a lot of ways. Because he was lovable. There was no argument about that. Even so, his father was mainly uninterested and his mother was absent. But Perry could see there were no flaws in him. His situation made her feel slightly better about herself.

They were, she concluded, integral to one another's development.

When they pulled up to her house, which was now empty, she felt a strange, hollow ache in her chest.

"This is weird," she said as they got out of the truck and made their way up the front porch. She let her hands skim slowly along the banister.

"What is?"

"Just thinking about leaving."

"You could rent the place out. Instead of selling it."

"I could. But purchasing the building in Medford would be dicier. If I had a big lump sum, then I'd be able to be sure I had a few months of rent on hand in case the business took more than it made." She worried her bottom lip. "Maybe I'll think about it. But I would have to manage a tenant all the way over in this town . . ."

"You could find a property manager."

"Granted," she said. "But again, I feel the arrangement might be too unstable. And if I have a savings account . . ."

"What are you really trying to accomplish?" he asked, taking the keys from her hand and unlocking the door, pushing it open.

"I already told you."

"You want more out of life. But you have a successful business here. You have a good life here."

"I'm just ready for something different." It was such a lie. She hated herself for telling it.

"Yeah. Okay. It's just that you seem sad about moving."

"Isn't every big change scary and kind of sad?"

"I don't know."

He seemed genuinely mystified by her question. Instead of continuing the conversation, he walked into the room, and she could see him taking a mental inventory of all the things that were in disrepair.

"What about getting married?" she asked.

His shoulders went rigid. She felt bad for bringing the topic up. Maybe it was inappropriate. Maybe she shouldn't have asked. He had said those things about Alyssa, and then they had dropped the subject, let it evaporate into thin air as if it had never happened. A regrettable detour, just like the dates they had gone on that night in Medford that hadn't amounted to much of anything. They had let the conversation end as well. But here she was. Talking about it again.

"No. It wasn't scary at all. I felt sure and certain. I knew everything was going to work out." He rapped his knuckles against the wall. "Why wouldn't it? I made the decision to do the normal thing. The good thing. I was a goddamn soldier, Perry. And soldiers are good people. They're not outlaws stained by the tainted blood of their ancestors. Nope."

"Carson . . ."

"I . . ." He looked at her, and there was something raw in his eyes. Something tortured. Painful. "I don't know if I can love anybody."

The admission was tortured and pained, ripped from him.

"What are you talking about?"

"It's like . . . my dad. He got married. He had kids. He cheated. He just didn't care about my mother as much as he cared about whatever momentary distraction was sitting in front of them. Just like he didn't give a shit about his kids. He didn't make sure we had food. He didn't tuck us in at night. He didn't care about us. Not really. He tried to. He went through all the motions. He wasn't a criminal. I mean, there were DUIs. But he wasn't going around trying to be a bad person. It was just that . . . there was a limit to how deep his soul went. It was a well with a very finite bottom. I'm afraid that I'm the same."

"Why?"

"I wanted that marriage to be something. I cared about it. So much. When I got Alyssa up here, I realized I didn't know how to talk to her. I realized that we didn't have much to say to each other. She was happy with the house. And so was I. She occupied a space in it that I appreciated. She filled the emptiness in my life, and I enjoyed it. She died and I grieved her."

"Carson," she said softly. "She was your wife. You loved her. You did. You had to have."

She needed that to be true because it had cut her in half when he'd married another woman. To have to unravel every feeling she'd had about his marriage didn't feel fair.

She realized, though, that he had been doing the same thing. Quietly these last two years. Reckoning with his own feelings and how difficult they were.

He had been grappling with this idea that he could love nothing and fix no one. Not even himself.

"I brought her out here, and she was lonely. She told me that. She was lonely, and she said I was holding back and . . . she said that I was emotionally unavailable."

"You're not emotionally unavailable." She responded automatically. She wasn't sure if her words were totally true.

"I was. To her. I know you. I've known you all your life. But I didn't know how to open up to the woman I married. I don't think I know what love even is. I thought it was as simple as looking at a woman and deciding that I could imagine being with her. But I'm not Flynn. Monogamy has never terrified me. It sounded settled. It sounded like I might be fixing something."

"Why didn't you tell me this?" She felt raw and wounded. She felt as if he had stabbed her. She didn't know what to do with his confession. That he carried this much pain was such a hideous thing. "I was just thinking earlier," she said, "that I am so grateful for you. Because if I didn't have a friend like you, Carson, I would have thought that there was something irreparably damaged inside me. I would have thought that was why my parents couldn't love me. Not the way that parents should. But I looked at you, and how wonderful you were, and the way that your parents were. That your mom left, that your dad was so uninterested, and it made me think that maybe I was okay. Because I knew that you were. I am so sorry I didn't do that for you."

"Don't say that, Perry. You did everything for me. You are the most important person in my life. I'm afraid. That I'm my father. I feel guilty that Alyssa died with a shitty husband."

"You were not a shitty husband. Everybody says that marriage is hard, and being newly married is very hard. You guys were just going through a rough patch."

"Yeah. But that was all our marriage ever got to be. When we started out, we wanted the same things. We wanted to move to a small town. We wanted to have kids."

Her heart crumpled just a little bit. She wanted to have kids too.

She understood what he was saying. This idea that you could make yourself a family and protect yourself with it. Make a happy bubble nothing could pop. Protect yourself from all the bad things that had ever happened before.

She understood. He'd tried it and he believed he'd failed. She knew Carson well enough to know that failure of that kind was not acceptable.

She nodded. "Yeah."

"We didn't get to fix it. She died unhappy."

"I think it's probably more nuanced than that. She wasn't unhappy all the time. I'm sure that she hoped to change things with you."

He looked into the distance. "Maybe."

"Listen. I have complicated feelings about Alyssa. All right. But there's one thing I do know: You didn't marry a weak woman. She was strong. And she definitely had her own opinions. She would have left you if she didn't see a way for the two of you to work things out. So she wasn't despairing, and she wasn't without hope or a plan. Whatever she thought was going to happen, she saw a future. Don't give yourself so much credit that you think a woman sat down and died of a brain aneurysm because she couldn't sort out what to do with your two-year-old marriage, Carson."

He looked devastated, and she felt kind of bad. But he needed to hear the truth. "I know you cared about her. I also know that you feel you let her down in some ways. But she didn't exist to be your salvation. That's *your* perspective. She didn't exist to be your success or your failure. She had her own hopes, her own dreams. Maybe she would've stayed with you and worked it out, maybe she would have left. But I doubt she was sitting there waiting to find out if you could love her more."

"Fuck," he said, his voice pained.

"Well. It's true. Give her a little bit more credit and stop seeing her as someone who just existed in the context of you."

This rousing defense of Alyssa wasn't something Perry had seen coming. Not that there was really anything wrong with Alyssa. But Perry had always felt the relationship was wrong. She wasn't sure if she felt validated by Carson's admission or not. And the whole conversation felt strange, because the woman wasn't here to speak for herself. Maybe that was the deepest tragedy in all of this.

Not that Carson had lost his wife.

But that whatever their story, whatever role she played in their marriage, it would always center more around Carson and what the loss meant to him than who Alyssa was as a person.

It wasn't really fair.

But in the wider world, that wasn't true. She had a family who had known her all those years as something other than Carson's wife. And they would grieve for her fully, and wholly.

"All that to say," she said softly, "I don't think it's fair for you to make the memory of her a sad one by making it all about you."

"That is bracing. And true. It's complicated. Because I miss her. I do. I miss being able to dream about what we could be. Because even though it was tough, I could still see what we hoped for. When I asked her to marry me, it all felt possible. A clean house, well-maintained. Me working the land, her setting up a pottery studio. Maybe even opening a souvenir store in town. One she could bring the kids to. I wanted that life. In hindsight, I'm not sure that she fit into it. She wanted a specific kind of husband, and I'm not sure that I actually fit the shape of what she hoped I would be."

Perry thought about that. Long and hard. His words brought up some of the same things she was sorting through with Carson. The way she had always carried a torch for him. And how projecting her desires onto him would've forced him into something she wanted. It was so complicated to attach your hopes and dreams to a specific person.

Though it could never be said that she didn't know him.

She didn't only know him—they were like trees that had grown up shaped around each other. They had bent and twisted around their childhood trauma, but also around their friendship. There were so many good things intertwined with the bad. Branches that had rotten fruit, and branches that grew something delicious. And the good fruit was because of their closeness to each other.

But if she bent his branches in a certain way to please herself, she might break him. So she was left with the arduous task of unwinding herself.

Because what he was talking about was what happened when you tried to force someone into a shape they weren't able to take.

"Anyway. I'd better continue to take inventory."

"Sure."

They walked up the stairs and into one of the far bedrooms. Everything was cleaned out, so she noticed something odd for the first time. The wallpaper was faded and bowed in a spot she hadn't noticed before. She walked over and peeled away the edge, and it gave easily. She frowned. There was a small compartment behind the wallpaper.

In it was a journal.

"What is this?" She stared at it, and then she cracked it open.

She recognized the handwriting. It was Mae Tanner's.

She opened up the first page and saw the date.

This diary picked up a year after the one she had read left off. Perry had read about Mae's arrival in Oregon, and then her description of meetings with the man that she married. But nothing beyond the first few months of their marriage.

"Oh," she said. "This is . . . this is the rest of the story."

"What story?"

"I've told you about Mae Tanner. How she moved out to Oregon as a mail-order bride. She kept a record of her new life in her diary. But this is more. More of her writing. And here is a bundle of letters too," she said, reaching into the compartment again.

"Why was it in there?"

"I don't know. Maybe for safekeeping. But it was kept a little bit too safe."

"Well, you'll want to keep that. Good thing you found it before you sold the place."

"Yes."

She looked around the room, and suddenly everything felt wrong. The idea of leaving this place. When her family history was literally in its walls.

She didn't put a lot of stock in her family's past. Not considering the way her parents were. But this . . .

This link to the past felt important. Important in ways she couldn't articulate. She held the bundle to her chest. "You can . . . continue on."

He nodded. And she took the letters downstairs. She sat on the bottom step and opened the diary up to the center.

When he puts his hands on me, I feel as if I learn new colors, new sonnets . . .

Her eyes widened.

I didn't come here for passion. I had given up the hope of it. Not a single man in Boston ignited desire in me. And when I got here, he looked at me with such cold eyes, I couldn't imagine that he would feel it for me. Not when his heart is so firmly buried in the ground with her. Sometimes it seems the only way we can talk is with our hands. Our mouths.

Perry had not had old-timey erotica on her bingo card.

This stark writing about the sex life of her ancestor was not something she had anticipated. She closed the diary for a moment.

She was breathless.

She was definitely going to read this entry later.

Maybe things had been different between Mae and her husband more than she had ever imagined.

Not that this entry sounded especially happy. Mainly, it sounded as if Mae and her husband shared a strong attraction.

For one moment, Perry wondered what that would be like. To feel an intense attraction for somebody, but not love. Well, she'd been attracted to men she didn't love. But not in the way that Mae was talking about.

For Perry . . . there would have to be deep emotion connected to such intense physical pleasure. The only thing that came close was how she felt for Carson. But he had never touched her. Not in that way.

"Okay. I think I have a fair idea of what I need."

She jumped, and felt guilty about the direction of her thoughts.

"Great," she said.

"I'd better go down to the hardware store."

"I'll go too," she said. "I want to get some new seeds from the nursery next door."

"All right."

That seemed like the best idea. Because she could sit here and ruminate, play that same song over and over again. Or she could get in his truck and try to find her footing again.

Good thing she was used to doing that.

Chapter 13

Is it wrong to write these words down? He claimed his husbandly rights, or perhaps that is the wrong way to say it. I don't have words for what he did to me. For what I did to him. It was not a claiming so much as a mutual dissolution of the walls between us. I wanted what he did, I begged for it. The unknown of the marriage bed once frightened me. But now it's the aftermath of it, of my own heart, that terrifies me.

—Mae Tanner's Diary, February 20th, 1900

Carson was grateful for some time to work at Perry's house alone. He was still raw from their discussion that morning.

Perry had gone back up to his place to plant flowers. He wondered if she had been as rocked by the conversation as he. Probably not. He'd had the strangest feeling talking to Perry earlier that there were things he didn't know about her. It felt impossible. Because they had been in each other's pockets all their lives.

He tended to tell her things pretty quickly. He didn't have any other way to process them.

All the stuff he'd said this morning, it had been underneath the surface for a long time, but he hadn't had the words for it.

He didn't know if he was better off now that he'd given his feelings a shape. But he'd spoken. And now he realized how true it all was. The grief he was grappling with was different from what everybody thought it was.

Yes, it still involved missing a person. Feeling gripped by the tragedy of somebody young losing their life. But his own feeling of failure, of doing the wrong things was a major part of his regret.

His own deep grief that he hadn't been the husband he wished he'd been.

That he hadn't loved Alyssa the way he should.

He hadn't been a hero. But that wasn't even what bothered him most.

It was the deep cold fear that he would never love anyone that way.

That he was born wrong. Born like his father.

Fuck.

He wasn't doing himself any favors. He was supposed to be focusing on restoring Perry's Victorian. Not on anything else.

He pulled his phone out of his pocket and opened up the dating app he'd used to match with Vanessa. He hadn't opened it since that night. He had a message from her. He winced. He felt like a dick. She said she'd had a good time, and that if he was ever in town again, they should catch up. He sent back a brief message, saying when he was in Medford again, he would let her know.

He wouldn't, though. And that felt bad. He didn't like playing these games.

He was surprised to find a few matches pop up locally.

Especially surprised when he saw Marissa Rivera. Who he knew Perry was going to use as a real estate agent when she sold the house.

Dating in Rustler Mountain seemed like a bad idea. Why the hell was he even contemplating it while he was thinking about his own emotional limitations?

Maybe he should keep trying?

Just thinking about getting married again made him feel like throwing up. Because it was a swamp of failure. Of tragedy. It was like war, honestly. No, he and Alyssa hadn't fought like that. That was the problem. It wasn't that it had been an awful marriage. It was just . . . it hadn't been what he had hoped. It certainly hadn't been what he had thought love might be like.

But the problem had to be him.

Because she had been perfect on paper.

He was the one who didn't understand what a functional house was supposed to look like. A functional family.

He swiped on Marissa and waited.

A couple seconds later, he got the notification that it was a match. A message popped up.

A surprise to see you on a dating app.

Yeah, he responded. **I'm surprised too.**

Are you free tonight?

Not tonight. But maybe tomorrow.

Oh. Sure.

We could go out to Barclay's.

That sounds great.

It was different from matching with Vanessa, a woman in a town he didn't live in. A woman he'd never met. He'd gone to high school with Marissa. They might not have been personal friends, but he already knew who she was. That kind of took the pressure off. In some ways. She already knew who he was. She already knew that he had a dead wife. So. That was probably why she was surprised. Or maybe it was because he didn't seem like the kind of person to embrace technology. He wasn't.

He finalized his plans with her and put his phone back in his pocket. Yeah. He was making progress, maybe. Or maybe he was just trying to put distance between himself and his uncomfortable revelations.

He didn't really care which. Tomorrow's date would help him stop thinking about his conversation with Perry earlier. And he wanted that more than anything.

He wanted to fix things. Change them.

He wanted to go back to when they were kids. When it was simple.

When being together was fun and easy and bright.

Was anything fun and easy and bright anymore?

With Perry maybe they could be.

He decided he was going to do whatever he had to do to get them back there. Because she was Perry, and no one else had ever given him what she had.

No one else ever would.

***

Perry was overly warm from planting. Sweat was dripping down her brow, but she was determined to get the rows planted. Carson had said that she could use some of his land, and she was bound and determined to do it. To get a jump on all the growing that she wanted to do, to get stuck into the new life she was going to create.

Because the problem with moving up here was that it was pushing her to spend more time with Carson, and she was losing track of why she was leaving in the first place. The idea of staying, of sinking into the comfort of the familiar, of just finding a way to evolve again with Carson seemed...

Tempting.

You are a weak and spineless ho for that man.

She wished. Because not even.

She stood up and shaded her eyes, looking out over Outlaw Lake. She missed being a kid with him. She missed the time when their friendship had actually been simple. Maybe she had spent the last fifteen years grieving the way things were.

She felt sad that they weren't children, who could laugh and play and be together without the complications of life. Other relationships. Without the awareness that her feelings for him were dangerous. That they were too big.

The oak tree was still there, along with the swing that they had played on when they were kids.

Sometimes it had been a plank to walk. Other times it had been just a swing.

Back then, possibilities were large, and time stretched out so long that anything had the time to be everything.

She had lost that feeling when Carson had married Alyssa.

She couldn't face losing him to another woman, someone like Jessie Jane. *I've lived in the same town with her all my life and I've never been attracted to her...*

He might as well have said that about her.

Perry squared her shoulders and started to walk over to the lake.

"Where you going?"

She turned around, and there he was. His jeans were dirty, covered in dust, likely from his endeavors at her house. His T-shirt was streaked with some kind of residue. He looked tired and gorgeous, and he made her heart hurt.

"I was thinking," she said.

"About what?"

"About how somehow, even though our childhoods weren't easy, they were still simpler than now."

That was honest. At least.

"You look overly warm," he said.

"I'm not," she said. But her face felt hot, and she couldn't work out whether her cheeks were flushed because of Carson's sudden appearance or the summer sun.

She hoped it was the sun.

"I'm good," she said.

"You look hot, Perry."

He had a mischievous glint in his eye, and his words made her feel a sort of discomfiting sensation between her legs.

"Don't you dare."

She extended her arm and held her hand out toward him, as if that might inspire him to keep his distance.

"Don't I dare what?"

"You know full well, Carson."

Because suddenly he had that same light in his eye he had gotten when he was a little boy. When he was up to no good. She knew this version of Carson Wilder all too well.

"I'm not doing anything," he said, holding his hands out.

She could feel it. Bubbling between them. Almost a desperation. To recapture something. A memory she could almost taste. "I'm not a pirate."

"You are definitely a pirate."

"I'm not," she said, lifting the front of her dress up just slightly and beginning to move quickly through the tall grass.

"Well, if you aren't, it doesn't much matter. Because I am."

And that was when she found herself swept right up off the

ground into his strong arms. She was held solidly against the hard-muscled wall of his chest, his strength an entirely different thing than it had been when he was young. He might have grabbed her arm and dragged her along down to the water, but he had never picked her up like this. Never held her.

"Arrrr," he growled in her ear. Goose bumps broke out along her neck, down her arm.

"You are ridiculous," she said.

"No, I'm not," he said.

She expected to find herself dumped straight into the lake. But instead, when they reached the shore, he set her down on the swing.

"You get a trial before I make you walk the plank," he said, pulling the swing back and letting it go. She closed her eyes, just felt for a moment. The breeze hitting her face. She clutched the ropes and opened her eyes right when she reached the top, looking down over the water, glittering and clear.

The swing went back and forth, and she pumped her legs, propelling it forward. Keeping it going. And then she saw Carson strip his shirt off and take a running leap out into the water.

His sharp yell indicated the temperature. Then he popped up from beneath the surface, slinging his head back, and pushing his hair out of his face.

She watched from above, her heart bursting.

Because this was a reminder. Of the time she had been happiest. Of the only person she had ever been happy with.

Her palms felt sweaty, her heart beating just a little bit too hard. And then she thought about letting go. Once the swing was extended out over the water. It had always scared her. She had always been afraid that she would miss. She would end up landing precariously back on shore, or that her jump would be inelegant and she would hurt herself.

She pumped her legs again, reaching her full extension.

He was watching her. And she realized this was how she always wanted him to see her. Like this. The way they had been. Not a war-torn woman who had let him break her heart without his even knowing. Not this version of herself she didn't want to be. This woman who was running away from him because she had let herself be embroiled in an impossible love.

She wanted to be the girl who had loved him. Big-hearted and reckless, not realizing that it could hurt.

She called on that girl. On all of the strength that she had.

And then she let go of the swing, launching herself forward. She screamed. Loud and feral. The last thought she had before she disappeared beneath the water was that she couldn't remember when she had stopped screaming like that.

She couldn't remember when they had stopped playing. When they had stopped being able to find the magic in life.

Maybe around the same time she had realized that the feeling she had for Carson could hurt her. Maybe around the same time she had realized that she couldn't just assume his feelings matched hers.

Maybe around the same time her body had changed shape and become something men thought existed for them to look at, to touch, rather than for her to enjoy in freedom.

Maybe then.

How she missed this.

She swam up to the surface, and she took a great gasp of air when her head broke the water.

"Pirate princess," he said. "We should swim over to the cave and look for buried treasure."

"There is no buried treasure in that cave, my captain," she said. "Only spiders and moss."

"Then let us get the moss and the spiders." He turned and swam away from her, and she followed, paddling beneath the surface, kicking like a frog, because she wasn't the world's best swimmer, and she was out of practice. He swam in long, smooth strokes, and as she swallowed lake water in his wake, she admired the musculature of his shoulders. Because this couldn't be a moment of pure childhood joy, could it?

It was infected by the fact that she was all too adult.

When they finally arrived at the shore of the little island in the lake, she was tired. Much more so than she would like to admit.

Her dress was sticking to her, and she stepped out of the water, shivering just slightly, her chest aching from trying to take in enough air.

"This was just the best idea," she said.

"Yes, it was," he said.

And he was off, scrambling barefoot into the cave. She followed behind.

"I can't see," she said.

He reached out to her and took her hand. And her heart leapt up to her throat.

"Captain," she said.

"Yes, pirate princess?"

"You're unhinged. You're aware of that?"

"Tired," he said. "I'm fucking exhausted. I just wanted to not be for a minute."

"Yeah. I get that."

She had felt that, somehow. They were each other's only refuge. They always had been. This was the only place they could play. The only person they could play with.

"I wonder when the last time we played pirates was? And why we never realized it was the last time."

Maybe it was that moment when he'd looked at her as if he was angry, when she'd swum away from him.

They were too old to be playing games, but they had been anyway.

"It wasn't. Because we're playing now."

She laughed but pulled her hand away from his. Then she reached down and took a jagged rock off the cave floor. "I believe this is a gem," she said.

He smiled at her. "I bet."

She could see just the outline of his face there in the dim light of the cave mouth. She was grateful she couldn't get a great look at his sculpted chest. It had been a minute since she had seen Carson without his shirt. She could piece together an image still, but she wasn't going to, not right now.

She was a pirate princess after all. Not that weak. Much stronger than Perry Bramble.

She wished she were deeply interested in rocks and moss. Sadly, she was more interested in Carson's bare chest. She was answering her own question about when they'd stopped playing pirates and why.

"Okay," she said. "The cave is dark."

"Yeah. Fair."

They turned back out of the cave, and Carson stepped ahead of her, standing on the shoreline. She looked at his bare, broad back, examined the musculature there. He turned his face to the side, and she allowed herself a moment to admire his strong profile.

He started to walk along the edge of the lake, then paused, bending down to pick up a yellow poppy. "Here's some gold," he said.

He turned toward her, and she was momentarily immobilized by the sight of him. The heat in his blue eyes, the definition of the muscles in his chest. His ridged abdomen.

And then he was right there. He held the flower out, but she found she couldn't move her arms. When she didn't respond, he extended the blossom and tucked it gently behind her ear, moving her hair along with it, his thumb brushing her cheekbone.

She looked up at him, her chest so full, she thought it was going to explode.

She couldn't breathe. She couldn't think.

The light in his eyes changed then. And it wasn't like when they were children. Not like when he was a boy. Suddenly, she saw something different there. It was an echo of what she had seen that night out in the truck.

Not completely foreign. But also different. It was more. Deeper. As if whatever had gripped him then was stronger this time.

She was seeing Carson as a man for the first time, she realized. What other women saw when he looked at them. When he was close. When he might kiss them.

That's how he was looking at her. She couldn't breathe. She couldn't move. She couldn't do anything to show him that she wanted it. And that she desperately didn't at the same time. That she wanted to run away. That she wanted to hide. That she wanted to fling herself at him. Right into his arms. If she didn't take this opportunity, when would it ever come up again?

If she took this opportunity, would they still be friends?

He was the only one she could play with.

He was the only one who had ever made her this happy. And this sad. This filled with need.

But he was also the one who never come close to satisfying all the need she carried inside her. He was the problem. He was the solution.

Suddenly, he shifted his hand, his large palm cupping her face. That wasn't ambiguous. It wasn't in her head. That wasn't the touch of a friend. Or a captain to a pirate princess. It was a captain to *his* pirate princess. And that made all the difference in the world.

She wanted to say his name, but her vocal cords wouldn't work. Her tongue couldn't move. Her lips felt conspicuous, and she couldn't force a smile or a word with them either.

She was staring fully into a moment that she had wanted for most of her life.

In which her friend was both familiar and unfamiliar. In which he was both himself and a fantasy version of himself.

She had felt something like this before. This acknowledgment between them. This connection. Suddenly, she knew what it was. It was mutual attraction. It wasn't just her. In those moments when it felt as if they were sharing thoughts, when it felt as if there was something connecting them, it was attraction. Coming from him too.

There weren't enough words in the English language to articulate the way she was feeling now. As if a miracle had happened.

He shifted, moving closer. Her eyes fluttered closed. It was the only way she could think of to tell him yes. The only way she could show him what she was feeling.

So she stood there. With expectation. She stood there, feeling breathless with anticipation.

And then, suddenly, he dropped his hand. He took a step away. And with him went the revelations, the miracle.

She opened her eyes. "Carson?"

"Are you good to swim back?"

She felt confused. She felt completely . . . disoriented.

"I mean, I got here, didn't I?"

"I just want to make sure that you've had enough rest."

He was going to say something any minute now about the kiss. The one that almost happened. For a moment, he had been different, and she had been different, and all the air between them had been different; he couldn't be pretending that it hadn't happened now.

"Come on, pirate princess."

His tone was light, but far too bright. Like a fake veneer slopped over the top of something genuine.

"Carson," she said.

"I'll beat you."

He started to wade into the water, and she just stood there feeling completely stunned. That bastard was running away. He was acting as if nothing had happened. He was . . .

"You're not a pirate captain," she said. "You're a scab." Why not call upon the vocabulary of her youth in this moment? "A yellow-bellied marmot!"

If he heard her, he didn't show it. And anyway, now he was swimming under the water, swimming away.

She growled and gathered up her wet dress, jumping into the water after him, swimming like an outraged, waterlogged cat to try to catch up with him.

What was she doing?

Why was he turning her away?

There had been a moment that almost changed everything. He hadn't allowed it. Why?

She shouldn't push him. She should let it go by. But she was outraged. Because she had realized something. Finally.

The attraction wasn't just her.

At last they reached the shore, and she climbed out. And for one moment, he looked at her, and she saw something in his eyes. Regret. Fear. And then it was gone. As though it had never been there at all.

"Thanks for going on that ridiculous detour with me."

Ridiculous detour? That was what he was calling the moment that had affirmed her entire life? The one that had reminded her of the importance of their friendship, while dismantling the relationship at the same time?

How nice.

"Yeah," she said. "Of course."

Because she was a coward too. She was weak. She wouldn't push. She wanted to bite her own tongue out. She wanted to scream.

But she didn't scream anymore. This last hour had been an anomaly.

Somewhere along the journey to adulthood, she had stopped screaming like a feral animal whenever she felt like it. She had stopped caring for Carson without fear.

She couldn't go back. And apparently, they couldn't go forward. Not into the place that she had hoped. That she had thought, for one, brief, shining moment they might go.

"I'd better go. I have . . . Everything in the house is looking good. I'm going to work on it again tomorrow. But then afterward I'm going out."

She felt as if he had just taken the earth and pulled it out from under her feet like a rug.

"Are you?"

"Yeah. Marissa and I . . ."

"Marissa Rivera? My real estate agent?"

"Yes."

Well. How nice. For all involved in their small town.

But she just smiled. Until she thought her face would break.

Because she wasn't going to show him, not again. She had closed her eyes. She had stood in front of him like that. And what had he been doing? Looking at her with pity?

So she wasn't going to show him now. No. She wasn't.

"Sounds great. I have a date tomorrow too. So I wouldn't have seen you anyway."

"Oh. Great. With who?"

An image of the card with West's number on it burned in her brain. "West Hancock."

She really hoped he was free because if he wasn't, she was walking herself into a ludicrous lie.

"You're kidding."

"No. I'm not."

"After you lectured me on Jessie Jane?"

"I didn't lecture you. Anyway, I don't have a brother that wants to jump West's bones. So I don't have the same conflict you do."

"And *that* was your issue with Jessie Jane? You think that Flynn wants her."

"Yep." She was a liar. She was shocked he didn't call her on it.

"Where are you going?"

Right then, she made a decision. One that was a little bit dark. A little bit mean. And a whole lot reckless. "The Watering Hole."

"*Really?*"

"Yeah. I want to dance."

"Why aren't you going out with Stephen Lee?"

"Stephen is nice," she said, shrugging. "But . . . you know. Stephen is the kind of man you marry. That's not really what I'm in the market for right now. I'm moving, after all. So this is for a good time, not a long time."

That was possibly the meanest thing she'd ever said, and she made a mental apology to Stephen, who would never know she had said that about him, and no internal apologies to Carson, as she turned on her heel and started to walk back toward the cabin.

She hadn't done anything foolish. She hadn't done anything reckless.

And yet she still felt as though something large and chaotic had hit the wall of their friendship.

She would have thought destruction would come with a kiss. Instead, they had cracked the wall with the weight of unspoken words.

It wasn't even fucking worth it.

Chapter 14

I could write sonnets about my nights with him. I never expected this. When I came to Oregon, I thought it was for the freedom the West had to offer. I knew I was trading Boston men I didn't want for a man I didn't know, because a man is a necessary evil in a woman's life. I never thought he would be the centerpiece of my life here. I never thought his hands would consume my every waking thought.

—Mae Tanner's Diary, April 18th, 1900

Carson had ample time to reflect on the damage done down at Outlaw Lake during his time at Perry's house. Which was exactly what he should be doing, instead of imagining the way she had looked in that dress, the sodden fabric clinging to her figure.

He had made a fool out of both of them down by the water.

He couldn't stop picturing it. Over and over.

He had told himself that he was only touching her because he wanted to recapture something they'd had when they were young. When he had picked her up and put her on the swing, his intentions had been innocent enough. But the moment he put his hands on her body, his resolve had been tested. And he had pushed his willpower to the limit. Swum with her across the lake. Gone into the cave.

The whole time, there had been something humming beneath the surface of his skin. An awareness that he had worked so hard to suppress for so long. But it was as if everything had fallen apart on the drag of a cigarette the other night. Or maybe it was when she had told him not to sleep with Jessie Jane. Or maybe it was a thousand other times, and a thousand other places. And it had all built up like grains of sand in an hourglass, nothing on their own, but together amounting to a mountain.

He couldn't quite parse it.

He wasn't sure he needed to. Understanding might not fix anything.

She was going out with West Hancock tonight after all. West, who had a reputation for seducing every woman he passed on the street.

The thought made his stomach go tight.

Perry had *wanted* Carson to kiss her. Her eyes had fluttered closed. He could still remember the way it had felt to touch her face. And he had fucked up. Because there had been a moment when he could have moved away, but instead he had moved closer. There had been a moment when it could have been a glancing touch of his hand on her face rather than his hand cradling her, but he hadn't made that choice. He had made it clear what he was thinking, what he intended to do for one brief moment of insanity.

He had wanted to taste her.

His Perry.

That feeling of possession had swelled inside him.

His. He'd felt it from the moment he had first seen her, when she was nothing but a sprout of a girl standing in the field with large eyes and tangled hair. Bare feet and a sort of hungry look about her.

Mine.

She had been his to hold, his to keep. He'd terrified her that long-ago day he'd wanted her to be his to kiss.

Then down by the lake today he'd torpedoed another kiss.

Because he had known, in an instant, one blinding flash, that if he had kissed her, he would have stripped that soaking dress away from her body, and he would've changed the thing between them irreversibly.

And he couldn't ruin Perry like that. He couldn't ruin *them*.

He had friends. They weren't Perry. He had a sister, and she wasn't Perry. He'd had a wife, but she hadn't been Perry. Only Perry was Perry. She occupied her own space in his life, in his soul. And he didn't know what the hell he would do if he broke her the way he had done so many other things. If he shattered the connection between them.

He had wanted to cut his own tongue out. Telling her that he had a date with Marissa. And now she was supposedly going on a date with West Hancock, who *would* be kissing her, that was sure and certain.

Yeah. He had reflected on all this during the workday, then he had taken a shower in Perry's bathroom, and thought of nothing but her presence in the house. Then he had gotten dressed and ready for his date.

West. Hancock.

He could remember the rumors about him and the entire cheer squad back in high school. There were rumors he'd gotten the preacher's daughter to throw her purity ring into the river and forsake her vows to God for him.

West. Hancock.

He hated that guy, he really did.

He hadn't before now. It was a spontaneously occurring hatred that was very deep and very real all the same.

A question was burning in the back of his mind. He wasn't entirely sure he wanted the answer to it. Why had she been standing there waiting to kiss him if she had a date?

Why did you almost kiss her, asshole?

He didn't want to answer that question. So instead, he sent Marissa a message that he was headed toward the restaurant and began to move in that direction.

Away from all of the bad decisions he had made in the last twenty-four hours. Before he could mess something else up. He was headed right toward something . . .

It was living. That was what he was trying to do. The date felt pointless, but he wasn't going to focus on that. He was just trying to be normal. He was trying not to be sad. Someone his family didn't worry about. Someone Perry wasn't concerned about leaving.

She doesn't seem all that concerned, does she?

With gritted teeth he got into his truck.

He had a date.

Lucky him.

Chapter 15

When he kisses me, I wonder who he sees. If it's her, I might die.

—Mae Tanner's Diary, June 21st, 1900

Perry could admit that her decision-making during the day had been erratic. She had gone to Medford in the morning, had gone to the mall, and had bought an extremely short dress. The bonus feature of the extremely short dress was that it was also very tight. And left absolutely no detail of her body to the imagination. It wasn't her usual thing, but it was entirely possible she was dressing for revenge.

She had spent so much time in her head, so much time analyzing everything, that she decided to turn her brain off. She didn't want to rehash that almost kiss. To rake it over and over. What she wanted to do was live. Feel. Something for somebody else.

Or maybe just for herself.

After that, she went back to Rustler Mountain. She texted West and asked if he wanted to meet her at the Watering Hole that night.

She could have done it earlier. But she sent a picture of herself in the fitting room in the dress, and he responded with a fire emoji and a yes.

So she'd gone and basically announced to the man that she was DTF. Great.

Adrenaline fueled her through getting dressed and ready. It got her all the way down to the Watering Hole itself. Then she started to question herself a little bit. She parked her car against the curb right around the same time West pulled his motorcycle up to the front.

He was wearing a white T-shirt and black jeans. He was hot—really, there was no denying it. He definitely fell into the outlaw category of Rustler Mountain lore.

Well. Apparently, she could easily make that her thing.

Though West didn't seem to have any interest in reforming. Unlike Carson. Who cared so much and felt he was accomplishing so little.

"Perry the florist," he said, appraising her. He clearly liked the dress. "I didn't expect all this."

"Really? You know the company I keep. I like an outlaw." Apparently, she did know how to flirt. How nice for her.

"True. Though I'm a little surprised your Wilder isn't with you like he was the other night."

"Where Carson is or isn't—that isn't my problem or yours tonight."

"Great. Let's go get that drink."

He put his hand low on her back, definitely grazing her ass, not that she was complaining, because this was what she wanted. To be reckless. To do something without thinking. To do something that wasn't about Carson or the future. Because she was bruised and battered and tied up in knots, because she felt every action had so much consequence. And she just wanted . . .

The truth was she didn't want West. But she wanted to feel something, and she thought he might be the easiest road to that feeling. Maybe it wasn't fair to him, but she didn't take him for the kind of man who would care.

He opened the door to the Watering Hole and held it for her. She walked in ahead of him and was overwhelmed by the noise and the smell of booze inside the place.

"Wasn't your dad like a banker or something?"

"My dad is a prick," she said, smiling. "But he was a mortgage broker. I suppose he still is. And we went to church every Sunday."

"Interesting," he said, sidling up to the bar. "Gus," he said to the bartender, "I'll have a beer. You know what I like. And the lady will have . . ."

"Beer," she said.

"So are you rebelling against your dad?" he asked, leaning against the bar and looking at her.

She smiled. "Something like that."

"Fine by me."

"I imagine daddy issues often work in your favor."

"I certainly don't mind it if you want to call me daddy."

This was really an elite opportunity for her to take a step off the straight and narrow. She might not be a virgin, but she usually wasn't one for casual sex. But this casual sex could potentially serve a purpose. To give herself a clean slate. To wipe yesterday afternoon out of her mind.

Carson had made his position clear. There really was no point pushing it any further.

In fact it was stupid.

She wished she had someone she could talk to who wasn't Carson. She'd suddenly realized that there was a deficit in her life that she should have tried to fill a long time ago. If you fell in love with a guy who was your best friend, you should do your level best to find someone else you could confide in, so you weren't out at a bar tempting fate with a stranger.

Not that he was a stranger danger level of stranger. He was a known entity. West had been enough years ahead of her in school that she didn't know him well, but she knew he had a reputation for only mild mischief about town.

"Carson is fixing our wagon, right?" he asked, an abrupt change of pace that had nothing to do with what she could call him.

"Yes," she said. "Jessie Jane brought it up to the ranch a couple of days ago. I live there."

"Interesting."

"What?"

"All of the above, really. That any Wilder would consent to fix our wagon, that you live on the ranch. You know. All of that. It's interesting."

"Right. Well. I don't know that it's that interesting."

"They hate us. All because of some ancient family feud that I can't even be bothered to think about. History doesn't solve a damn thing."

"Well. History doesn't. I think it's kind of up to us to solve the messes that history made. Don't you?"

She realized that she was headed down the wrong path. She shook her head. "You know what? Never mind. Let's dance."

They were seated in a window at dinner, directly across from the Watering Hole. And he hadn't been able to help himself—he had glanced out the window at some point to see if he could spot Perry, and once he had started, he hadn't been able to stop. It wasn't really fair, because Marissa was making perfectly pleasant conversation, and he should absolutely be giving her his full attention. But once Perry's little car pulled up against the curb, his concentration had been shot.

Right at the same time, a motorcycle had rumbled up. And when West had gotten off the bike and Perry had gotten out of her car in the shortest damned dress he'd ever seen her in, he suddenly understood.

Perry had fired shots. Perry was deliberately creating drama.

Because there was no way that she was out on a date with West Hancock at random. No way she was wearing that dress for nothing.

She was trying to make him mad.

She didn't plan on your watching her out a window, asshole.

Maybe not. But she was poking at him, and he was getting fired up. It was working, dammit.

He tried to keep his focus on Marissa. She was beautiful. Absolutely beautiful. And dinner was great. She was interesting, and he should be listening to her. But in his mind, Perry's name was echoing on loop.

"Do you want to head over to the Watering Hole?" He waited to ask the question until she had taken her last bite.

She looked surprised. And then there was a slight shift in her expression that suggested she knew she shouldn't have been surprised.

After all, he was a Wilder, so of course he would want to go to a disreputable bar.

"Sure."

Which made him suspect his being disreputable was part of why she was going out with him. Though, to be fair, he was not as disreputable as his younger brother, and Austin was completely reformed. He hadn't given much thought to his reputation in a very long time. He'd had bigger issues. He supposed he was going to end up thinking about it again and often if he was actually going to date.

"Great. I'll get the check."

He flagged the waitress and gave her his debit card. He hadn't thought this through, he realized, as they headed across the street toward the bar. Because they were going to be walking into the same space that Perry and West were in, and he didn't exactly have a plan.

"What do you like to drink?" he asked as he opened the bar door for her.

"I don't know. You can choose."

"Okay," he said.

"Carson," Gus said from behind the bar, giving him a broad smile. "Good to see you."

"Good to see you too, Gus."

"Usual?"

"Yes. And something for the lady. Bartender's choice."

He looked at Marissa, and he could see that he had made a mistake somehow. By letting the bartender choose. Well, hell, he didn't have any thoughts about what this woman he didn't know might want to drink. His lack of interest was probably what she sensed. Was probably what bothered her.

He looked across the room and saw Perry on the dance floor with West. She had her arms wrapped around Hancock's neck, and he felt a knot tighten in his stomach.

She had been standing right in front of him yesterday. He had touched her face. And now she had her arms around another man's neck?

You're jealous.

Jealous.

The word echoed inside him, and he wasn't quite sure why.

He didn't like it. He didn't know what the hell to do with it. It wasn't . . . it wasn't them. It wasn't him. He had never been jealous over a woman in his life, let alone his best friend.

That was a pointless exercise if ever there was one.

You're the patron saint of pointless exercises, Carson Wilder.

He shoved that thought to the side. It was truer than he would like to admit. Trying to be a hero. Trying to be a husband. He did love a pointless fucking exercise.

Dating with no real goal. Trying to get excited about having sex?

In truth, he hadn't missed it.

His mind skipped back to Perry yesterday, and he felt his whole body try to reject the answering arousal. Arousal. Over his friend. His best friend. But that guy was touching her. Touching her like she was someone whose clothes he wanted to take off. That felt like a violation. Carson knew that Perry wasn't a virgin. So men had taken her clothes off. They had touched her; they had kissed her.

His vision went a little bit blurry.

"Do you want to sit down?" Marissa touched his arm.

"Sure," he said. He realized he could only manage to spare her the slightest glance. He felt like an asshole. He really had engineered this whole thing in a pretty foolish manner.

But he had acted without thinking. He had been compelled by . . . the Perry of it all.

He recalled that night when she had come to visit him, eaten pizza in his kitchen, but not the crust, and told him that they were codependent. And now when he pictured that scene in his mind, he imagined her holding a grenade. Pulling the pin out and leaving the explosive in the center of the table. What she had done had tripped all these internal mechanisms that had been left undetonated for years. They were disrupted now. Ready to explode.

What are you going to do?

He didn't have an answer. Yesterday, he hadn't done a thing.

Except he had. He had. He had touched her face. She had closed her eyes.

It had been something. It hadn't been nothing. He saw a table with four chairs and began to walk toward it just as Perry and West separated and started to move off the dance floor. "Oh, look," said Carson, feigning surprise. "It's my friend Perry."

"Oh," said Marissa, smiling. "She contacted me about selling her house."

"I know," he said. "I'm renovating it."

"I could come and look at it," said Marissa, as she took a seat. "I can tell you which things to focus on."

"That would be great," he said. "Do you mind if I ask them to join us?" He smiled, trying to be the sort of charming that he had never been.

"No," said Marissa, looking a little bit confused, but not upset.

"Great."

He took two steps toward the dance floor, and Perry caught his gaze. Her eyes widened, and then a little crease appeared between her eyebrows. "Hey, what are the chances of meeting you here?" Except, he had been told that she was going to be here. And even though Perry didn't know that he had seen her outside, she knew that he knew that she was coming here on her date. He wasn't subtle. He didn't care.

"Carson . . ."

"Would you like to sit with us?"

Perry smiled, but it wasn't really a smile. It looked more as if she was baring her teeth.

But she was playing with him.

He was sure of it.

So he was going to play right back.

"Of course," Perry said.

West stuck his hand out, and Carson looked at it. "Haven't seen you in a minute, Carson," he said.

"No," Carson said, extending his hand.

It took him a moment to realize that neither man had said it was good to see each other. Well. A mutual feeling, then. Not anything that needed to be corrected.

They sat at the table. He made introductions between West and Marissa.

"We haven't eaten," Perry said. "Do you want French fries?"

"We ate," said Marissa.

"Oh. So you just decided to come here after?" Perry asked the question pleasantly, but she slid Carson a sideways glance.

"That's what happened," said Carson.

"Neat," said Perry. He had a feeling she did not find it neat at all. But he hadn't actually asked her opinion. West was bad news. And Carson knew it. The guy had a rap sheet longer than his brothers'. And yeah, technically Austin had never been convicted of anything, and it was all petty stuff. It was pretty much the same with West. Petty crimes committed before they had become adults. Still. *Still.* Not good enough for Perry.

He was here with the real estate agent, for God's sake. Perry should be here with a real estate agent—it would be more in line with her goals.

Except apparently she hadn't wanted to find a man that she could have a baby with tonight. She just wanted to . . .

He held back the onslaught of mental images that came with that thought.

"So Perry," said Marissa. "What's prompting you to move?"

That kicked off a conversation between the two women, and he and West just sat there. Listening.

"Oh, I love this song," said Perry when the band started playing a new country hit.

"Let's get out there," said West, extending his hand, and Carson nearly bit his tongue off.

"Carson," Marissa said quietly. "What exactly is going on?"

"Nothing," said Carson. "I mean, we're here at a bar."

"You're not with me, though. Are you?"

She said it softly, and without malice, but it felt as if she had taken a very small knife and flicked it right under his skin, flaying it delicately from the bone. Cutting right down to the marrow.

"I don't know what you mean by that."

"You wanted to come over here because Perry was here."

He thought about lying. But what was the point? He wasn't going to marry Marissa. She wasn't going to want to go on a date with him again. He had messed up. He didn't want to sleep with her. He didn't want . . .

He wanted *Perry*.

Gut. *Punch*.

He couldn't breathe.

God. He didn't want that to be true. Because what the fuck was he supposed to do with it?

He had tried to hold all this back for so long. The flood of it. He'd wanted to be her hero.

Right now, with his body strung as taut as a wire, he felt better equipped to be her outlaw fantasy.

Because if she was here with West, she had one, didn't she?

Well, he was right here.

"I don't like that she's out with him," he said.

"Right. Because?"

"He's not a good guy," he growled.

She nodded. "A lot of people say that about the Wilders."

"I know," he said.

"I know that you and Perry are friends," Marissa said slowly. "Everybody does. But . . . you seem jealous."

"I'm not jealous," he said, his gut going tight. "I . . . I'm fucking jealous."

She let out a sigh. "You're a nice guy. I didn't swipe on you thinking you would have no baggage. But I was kind of thinking that . . . it would be a different kind."

Caron ground his teeth together. "You figured your competition would be dead?"

She blanched. "Ouch. But yes."

"I don't know what's going on," he said.

"And that's fair. Because life is weird. But I don't want to be in the middle of . . . all that. I like Perry."

"Yeah. Me too. That's the problem." On every level. He liked Perry. He more than liked her. She was a cornerstone of his existence. The way he felt tonight was shallow in comparison to every other feeling he had for her. This was . . . nothing. But it was eating him alive, and he didn't know what to do about it.

"Thank you for dinner," she said. "I'll pay for my drink on the way out."

"You don't have to do that," he said.

"Okay. I'll take you up on that." She patted the table. "Thanks again. Dating advice," she said as she stood up. "Don't involve your dates in the drama you're having with the woman you actually want."

Guilt lanced him. "I didn't know," he said. Which sounded so stupid. He was thirty-four years old. Why didn't he know?

Her expression softened. "That's okay." She sighed. "Actually, I can see that you didn't. I kind of hope it works out for you. But . . . get it together, Carson. So that it can."

She turned and left, and Carson just sat there, while Perry danced with West and he felt like the biggest chump on the planet. He got up to go to the bathroom, and on his way back a couple of things happened.

Perry and West left the dance floor, and West backed Perry up against a wall, just as Carson circled into their vicinity. Then West lowered his head and pressed his mouth to Perry's. And Carson didn't even make a decision. He didn't even think about it. He just grabbed West by the shoulder and shoved him away from Perry.

"What the fuck?" He was the one who asked. Him. The guy who was not on the date with Perry.

The guy who didn't have the right to ask.

"Carson!" Perry said, sounding as if she was scolding a child.

"Back off," Carson said to West, putting his body between the other man and Perry.

"I didn't force her to do anything," said West.

"He didn't," said Perry. "I wanted to kiss him. Stop acting like my protective older brother." She moved away, as if that finished it. As if he had interceded because he thought that West was forcing himself on her, which had never occurred to him at all.

He growled. "I don't care. He needs to stay away from you."

West squared up to him. "Are we about to have a bar fight? Because now that I think about it, that might have been the last time I saw you, Wilder. Didn't I put you through the window in this very bar back when you were here with a fake ID?"

"See how well it works now that I'm not sixteen," Carson said.

"Oh, knock it off," she said. "Both of you. And you." She rounded on Carson and grabbed him by the shirt. "You're coming out back with me."

She dragged him through the hallway, and out the exit. Into the alleyway behind the bar. "What the fuck, Carson?" she asked. "What the fuck are you doing? I am here on a date. You knew that I was going to be here. Why did you drag your date over here and insert yourself into my business? And then why did you . . . interrupt me?"

"He's not good enough for you. I looked out the window and I saw you here with him, and it doesn't make sense, Perry. I just didn't fully . . . grasp it until I saw you with him. If I had, I would have told you that he was bad news and you needed to stay away from him."

"Are you kidding me? Carson Wilder, your whole family has a reputation for being nothing more than a bunch of outlaws, and you are using all that town-history stuff against somebody else? What is the matter with you?"

"This is the matter with me," he said. "It's not right, Perry. You deserve better than him. You said you wanted to get married. You said you wanted to have babies. You're not going to do that with him. And you know it."

"I didn't know that you were a prude, Carson. There's a little thing called recreational sex, and I'm allowed to do it. Just because you haven't figured out what to do with yourself since you lost Alyssa doesn't mean that I have to wait. I am not in a convent just because you've taken a vow of chastity. This is exactly what I was talking about. We are not linked in this way."

"That's a lie. We are."

"We never happened."

"He's just . . . he's wrong for you. You deserve better."

And then Perry exploded. As if she was a volcano in which pressure had been building and building, and then it simply couldn't contain itself anymore. "Shut up!" she shouted. "You shut up. This is such bullshit. You could have given me better any time over the last twenty-five years and you didn't. You gave better to other women. You *married* another woman. Don't get mad because you've suddenly decided you want me now that I've put myself out of reach."

"You've been out of reach before," he said, having no idea why he was trying to defend his position, and really having no idea what his position even was anymore.

"No. I was never out of reach. *You* were, Carson. You're the one who left town. You joined the Army, you . . ."

"That was different," he said.

"Obviously," she said. "Obviously you feel like it's different with me right now or you wouldn't be here posturing like a gorilla."

She moved closer to him, her eyes bright. And he remembered the moment that West had put his hands on her. Pushed her up against the wall.

Put his mouth on her.

He took a step toward her. "*Posturing*," he said. "That's what you think I'm doing? Posturing? I've been your best friend since we were children, and you think that I'm *posturing*?"

"What else would you call it, Carson? Because you're not going to do a fucking thing. You're going to beat your chest and act outraged. Then you won't do anything. Because you're a coward."

She moved toward him, and she shoved him in the shoulder, just as he had done to West.

He gripped her wrist. And he pushed her back up against the

wall. Beneath his thumb he could feel her pulse beating quickly. He couldn't catch his breath. He couldn't catch his thoughts.

It was Perry who moved. Perry who started to move toward him. And he growled. "Don't."

She froze. Anger poured through him. Confusion. Desire. He wanted her. And in that moment, everything became crystal clear. The horse had bolted. Yesterday his self-control had been both belated and pointless. Because it was too late. He had been desperately trying to identify the moment everything changed. Maybe it was when she had pulled the pin out of the grenade. Maybe it had been when the grenade was made in the first place. He didn't have a good answer. But it was clear to him now that there was no going back. There was no saving their friendship. There was no saving them.

He had given words to what he was feeling. Attraction. Desire. He had let her beauty become specific. He had allowed himself to imagine what it would be like to touch it. And then he had touched it. Yesterday. Today, he had made it clear he couldn't abide someone else doing it. Yeah. It was too late. He had no control over it anymore. But he had control of when. And he would not . . . he wouldn't let it be like this. Not his Perry.

"Our first kiss is not going be when I'm mad at you," he said, his voice low.

Perry moved away from him, her eyes bright, her breath coming out in short, choppy bursts.

He thought his own heart might beat straight through the walls of his chest.

"Our first kiss?" she asked.

"Yeah. Because I am going to kiss you, Perry. But not just once. Once I do . . . there won't be any stopping it. There will be the first, then the second. Then we'll lose count. We might fuck each other up. We *already* fucked this up. So I'm not going to let it start out mad."

In case it ends that way.

He didn't say that. Instead, he turned away from her and walked back into the bar. He walked up to the counter, and he ignored West when the guy came up behind him, gnawing at him like an annoying terrier.

"Mine and Marissa's. I'll get West and Perry's too."

"Do you really think I'm going to let this go unanswered?" West asked.

Carson kept his back to West as he paid the tab.

"I'm talking to you," West said.

Carson turned sharply, fire and murder in his blood.

"I'll kill you," Carson said. "And you think I'm kidding. You think I'm kidding, because this isn't the Old West, but let me tell you something. You wouldn't be the first man that I've killed. I learned that if you do it for the United States government, you're a hero. I wonder what they would call me if I took *you* out."

Then he walked right out of the bar. And onto the street. He couldn't quite get a handle on everything that had just happened.

"Carson!"

It was Perry. He just kept walking. Down the street toward his truck.

"Carson!"

He didn't stop. And then something hit him square between the shoulder blades. "Ow!" He turned around. And saw Perry's shoe on the sidewalk.

"Are you out of your mind?" He picked her little ballet flat up off the ground. "What is the matter with you?" he asked.

"*You're* the matter with me," she said. "You ruined my date. You hit my date. Then you said all that about kissing, and you walked away without doing anything."

"I'm trying to get my head on straight."

"Why bother? It hasn't been for years."

"Oh, and you're doing so great."

"I'm not!" she shouted. "What about anything that I have said or done in the last few weeks indicates to you that I'm doing great? I'm leaving this town. My house. Everything because I am not doing great. And this is why . . . this is why you infuriate me. Because I'm leaving, because . . . and that is the only reason that you're talking about kissing me. Because at no other point . . ."

"It's not *why*," he said. "Can we not scream at each other in the street?"

"Why not? You know everybody already thinks we're fucking, Carson."

"But we're not," he said, her words scalding him.

"No. We're not. I'm aware. And you have never shown the slightest bit of interest. You've never . . ."

Right then, he remembered. That she had been jealous of Jessie Jane. She had said so.

She'd also said . . . she had complicated feelings about Alyssa.

"Were you really jealous of Jessie Jane?"

"Wow. You just hit a man that kissed me."

"I did! Because *I'm* jealous!" he shouted.

Those words echoed down the whole block. In his whole chest. Fine.

There was no point putting a lid on any of this now.

"Why?" She put her hands on her hips. "You told me yourself, you're not attracted to Jessie Jane, and you never have been, because you've known her your whole life. I'm not any different. You left this town, and you found a wife. You found the one you wanted, and you never even considered me."

She started to walk away from him, toward her car. With only one shoe.

He couldn't let her do that.

He went after her and took her arm. "Talk to me," he said.

"I don't want to. I don't want to talk about this. I have spent so many years *not* talking to you about this."

"What? I tell you everything. I can't even . . . I did hit your date. I followed you into the bar, because I can't keep this inside me. It's been driving me crazy the past few days . . ."

"Aren't you lucky? Aren't you lucky to have the spontaneous occurrence of wanting something that you can't have for *days*."

"Perry..."

She exploded then, her arms thrown wide, her blond hair wild around her. "I've wanted you forever, you dumb fucking idiot."

He couldn't find any words to respond to that, so when she turned away, he didn't stop her. He just stood there like a fool.

He felt she had torn strips off him. He had been left in shreds.

And then she got into her car. With one shoe on her foot, and one in his hand.

But this wasn't over. Not tonight.

He'd be damned.

He had a strong feeling that, whatever happened, he *would* be damned.

Chapter 16

He is my husband, and I have him. He is in my bed every night. Why do I still feel that something is missing between us? If he asked, I would tell him I loved him. But I fear the answer he would give if I asked him the same.

—Mae Tanner's Diary, June 30th, 1900

Perry probably shouldn't be driving. She was crying. She was shaking. What had happened out in the alley had been . . . exhilarating. Terrifying. It was like a dream, but not in a fun way. It felt bizarre and distorted. Because she had always imagined that if she and Carson ever crossed the line in their friendship, it would be sweet. But this had been so angry. And he had been so raw. The things he had said to her . . .

She'd been so turned on, and so angry. And then he had walked away from her without saying anything.

Did he think he got control of everything because he had woken up sometime today and decided he wanted her?

She pulled up to the cabin and wiped her eyes. Cursed as she walked across the gravel.

She wasn't foolish enough to think that he wasn't going to follow her. He was. But she had wanted to have a small implosion first. Because what was she supposed to say?

I love you, and it's ruining my life?

She couldn't do that. Carson cared about her. A lot. She didn't question that. She could not bear the thought that he would try to give her something he didn't actually want to give.

She walked into the little cabin, the one that he had shared with his wife when he'd first brought her back to Rustler Mountain.

She had been the best woman in his wedding. She had stood at the altar beside him while he waited for another woman. That was a sick sort of self-torture. She would never forget that memory.

This was awful. This was actually her worst nightmare. Because they were in a horrible in-between place—they could no longer just be friends, or pretend that the subject had never come up. They'd crossed that precarious line you walked when you were friends with somebody you could potentially be attracted to. Now they had to figure out how to navigate this perilous new territory.

Because she also knew that it wasn't going to be true love forever.

He'd already chosen someone else.

She was never going to be able to get over that. She hadn't fully realized it until that moment. She'd been right in front of him, and he hadn't chosen her. So she did love him, in a fashion. But she could never live with him knowing that he had wanted a life with someone different. That she was the consolation prize.

For a moment, she had thought tonight might change something. But all his talk about love really meant was that he had given whatever love he had to a different woman. Even if he thought it wasn't a deep enough well of love. Even if he thought it was limited in some fashion, it didn't especially matter. It was all he had to give. And he hadn't given it to her.

She heard his tires on the gravel.

She didn't even feel angry. Not anymore.

Just sad. Sorry for herself. For the woman she was and the girl she'd been.

He didn't knock. He just opened her front door as if he had the right. And the air changed. The feeling inside her shifted. It was as though reality fell away. They were back in the alley, but they were also here. They were standing by the edge of Outlaw Lake. He moved toward her, purpose on his face. "Are you still mad at me?"

She wasn't an idiot. She knew the right answer to that question.

He'd given it to her in the alley.

"No," she said, lying through her teeth.

He nodded and moved nearer to her. He cupped her cheek, never looking away from her, never breaking eye contact. He moved his thumb along her cheekbone. And she closed her eyes. Then opened them, because she couldn't bear to miss a moment of this.

This moment that was either self-indulgence or self-immolation, she couldn't be sure which. Either way, it was too late to turn back. She had said she wanted him. She had screamed it to him in the street. She had thrown her shoe at him.

At this point, turning away would be like going swimming, and then refusing to stand outside because it had started to rain. They were already wet.

He lowered his head and let out a breath. She took it in. His mouth hadn't even touched hers, but she had shared air with him. It was a deep, shattering intimacy that made her heart beat so hard it hurt. That made her ache between her legs.

She tilted her chin, just as he moved to claim her mouth.

She couldn't even remember the kiss she'd gotten from a different man only a half hour ago. Carson obliterated it. He obliterated everything.

Her good intentions. Her years of restraint.

She was kissing Carson Wilder, and he was kissing her.

Just yesterday she'd experienced the life-altering revelation that he was attracted to her. And this was yet another world-ending moment. Another complete and total shift of her reality.

His mouth was firm and hot, it was home, and it was something else entirely. Because he was Carson, but he was a stranger. She had never kissed him before. She had never watched him kiss a woman, not like this. Not with sexual intent.

She gave thanks for that. Because this felt like a unique experience.

He cupped her face with hands that were large and rough. She felt so safe. And imperiled all at once. He angled his head, parting her lips, sliding his tongue against hers, and she let out a sigh. It turned into a moan as he sifted his fingers through her hair, then moved them down her back, down to cup her ass.

She wrapped her arms around his neck, arched against him.

They needed to talk. But they'd spent twenty-five years talking. Avoiding this moment. And somehow, they had been brought here anyway.

Somehow, this was where they had ended up.

"I was never supposed to do this," he said against her mouth, and it prompted questions in her that she would have to ask later. Because she couldn't ask them now. All she could do was whimper as he kissed her like he never wanted to do anything else. As he kissed her like he had never wanted anyone else.

He made her ache. But she was smart enough to know that it was just this moment. It was just this.

It wasn't just sex, because that was impossible. Because she was Perry, and he was Carson.

"My pirate princess," he whispered in her ear, and she thought she was going to come then and there.

"*Oh,*" she said, an inarticulate noise of need.

"I want you," he said, his eyes so intense. They were blazing with hunger.

She had never seen him look at anybody like that.

"Why?"

She wanted to punch herself in the face. She didn't need to introduce talking. Not to this. They had done all their talking. They didn't need any more.

"I don't know when it started," he said. "And I realize that is a really stupid thing to say."

She couldn't speak. The words wouldn't come.

"I just know that I do. It's like breathing. I didn't decide to do it. I didn't think about it. Suddenly, I'm just aware of it. And now I can't do a damn thing but focus on it."

It was actually the best thing he could've said. His need wasn't sudden. It wasn't because she was leaving. It wasn't even just because she had kissed somebody else. It wasn't a lie.

"I want you too," she whispered.

He cupped her face again and lowered his head, kissing her deeper, longer. It was the best kiss of her life.

She had always known. She had always known that his mouth would fit against hers perfectly. It wasn't weird that it was happening now. It seemed absurd that it never had before.

It was more intimate than any kiss she had ever received. Because of course she had kissed men in the past, some that she knew, and ones she didn't know so well. But she didn't know anybody like Carson. He held a piece of her soul, always.

He was the very first and always. Maybe not the first to touch her, but the one who had made her understand why you might want to be touched. Why pressing your mouth against another person's wasn't gross.

No. Not at all. It was everything.

They stood there in the living room, kissing. Her arms around his neck, his roaming over her body.

And then she tugged the front of his shirt. Just a little. Just slightly in the direction of her bedroom. And she found herself being picked up. Like he was the pirate captain to his pirate princess, and he was going to make her walk the plank.

Except she wouldn't tumble into the water this time. It would be into bed. With him. With Carson.

She started to shiver.

"Are you okay?" he asked against her mouth as he set her down, her one bare foot cold against the floor.

"Yes," she said.

"Nervous?"

She laughed. "No."

He growled and brought her close again, kissing her. She kicked her remaining shoe off. He took off his. Suddenly, that tight little dress she had put on earlier felt like a burden. She had known that dress had one purpose. To be taken off by a man. She simply hadn't imagined that it would be this man.

Not tonight, anyway. She had imagined him taking her dress off a hundred times. Until she had stopped letting herself do that. He was the foundational text of her sexual fantasies. There was no getting away from that. She didn't even want to. She wanted to savor every moment. Every touch. She wanted to watch him watch her. She wanted to have the full experience of him desiring her.

Because it had been a revelation yesterday when she had realized that he wanted her too. She wanted to hang on to that. She wanted to fully experience it.

The way his hands moved down her body, the way he unzipped her dress. "It's a beautiful dress," he said as he kissed her neck and pulled the garment away from her body, discarding it on the floor. She gave thanks for the black lace bra and underwear she wore, which were sexier than her everyday wear. But she had been on a date.

"Damn, Perry," he said, pressing his forehead against hers, his breathing jagged.

"Are you nervous?" she asked.

He huffed a breath. "*Yes.* I haven't been with anybody in . . ."

"Me either. I lied. In the car. It's been at least as long as it's been for you."

Because she had lied also in the alleyway. She *had* put herself in a convent. Because she had been sorting through the disastrous implications of Carson not being married anymore and all of her great and terrible feelings for him.

"But it's not really that," he said. "It's you. It's *you*. The first time I saw you . . . you were mine, Perry. You were mine."

She didn't know what he meant by that. But her heart reacted to it. Her whole body did. She felt as if she was going to go up in flames. She wanted to get closer to him. His clothes were in the way. She just wanted to be closer.

She started to tug at his shirt.

She was undressing Carson.

Her hands were shaking violently. She moved them over his bare torso. Over all his muscles. She had permission to touch him now. This object of her never-ending fantasies. She pressed a kiss to the hollow of his throat, then down on his chest. He grunted. She felt greedy now. Desperate. He was a mirage that might vanish at any moment. Was this real? Was she just hallucinating?

She'd finally driven herself mad. But he was firm and solid beneath her fingertips. Hot. His chest hair rough beneath the touch of her hand, his heart raging there.

She scraped her fingertips down his abdomen, the hard ridges of his abs. "You are . . . you are gorgeous," she said.

She held his face in her hands and stared at him. She knew that she was being intense and weird, but it was Carson, and she couldn't help herself. For years, this was her darkest secret, the one she kept locked away in the deepest part of her soul. The wall that held it back had sprung a leak, and water had been dripping from the crack for weeks, maybe years. But now it had burst open. And it was all just pouring out. There was nothing she could do to stop it. Not anymore.

She didn't even want to.

She kissed him. Desperate. And he unhooked her bra, kissing her neck, moving down, growling as he took one nipple into his mouth and sucked it in deep. She watched him. The profile of her best friend's face as he tasted her. Her head fell back; her internal muscles pulsed with desire. She was wet, slick for him. If he touched her now, he would know how much she wanted him. It would be obvious.

She wouldn't be embarrassed. How could she be?

Because this madness had taken over both of them, and maybe for the first time since they were children, they each wanted the same thing with the same amount of ferocity as the other.

Just like playing pirates.

She was seized with a longing for the recklessness they'd had then. With the desire for that wildness to be theirs. To be his pirate princess. She had never felt closer to that fantasy than she did now.

"Beautiful," he whispered, kissing her along her jaw, sifting his fingers through her hair. Then he laid her down on the bed. He kissed right between the valley of her breasts, down her stomach.

The whiskers on his chin rubbed the sensitive skin on her stomach. He paused at the waistband of her panties. He lowered his head for a moment, resting his forehead right on her stomach as if he was saying a prayer. Then he took her underwear down, slowly. His breathing jagged, tortured, as he revealed that most intimate place.

She had the thought that maybe she should be embarrassed. But she just wasn't. Because she wanted this so much. She wanted him to see. Her. All of her. She was desperate for this. She had been for a really long time.

He pushed her thighs apart, his breathing becoming labored. And then it became clear just why he had bowed his head to pray.

He moved between her legs and tasted her, his mouth soft at first, then firmer, more demanding.

She gripped his shoulders, gasping. He moved his hand beneath her ass, lifted her up from the bed and started to eat her with intent. Never. Never in all her life had she . . .

Yes, men had tried. But she had never been all that into it. This was . . . this was something else. It was personal. It was him. It was her. It was, perhaps, the most direct way they could have ever defiled their friendship. And she was absolutely here for it.

She was clinging to him, hard. So hard that she realized she was digging her nails into the back of his head, and it was probably too much. She released her hold on him, and everything unraveled inside her. She shattered. Gasping, shivering, crying out with her release. And then she realized what she really wanted. To do the exact same for him.

She moved away from him, sliding up to the top of the bed. He went up on his knees, and she moved to him, wrapping her arm around his neck, pressing her naked body to his. His jeans were rough against her hipbones. She started to undo his belt, the closure on his pants.

She was still shaking. Dammit. She didn't know if she was going to be able to stop. She was about to see Carson, all of him. She already knew she would think he was beautiful.

But when she reached her hand down into his underwear,

wrapped her fingers around him, she gasped. Because he was a large man, and he was large everywhere, it turned out.

She let out a shuddering breath. She began to stroke him slowly, pushing the fabric of his jeans and underwear down and freeing him.

Then she lowered her head and took him into her mouth.

"Fuck," he said, his head falling back as she tasted him.

As she indulged herself in the way that he just had. And it was even better, quite honestly. Because she was tasting him. Touching him. Because she was finally, finally touching him like this.

She lost herself, completely.

Until his grip tightened in her hair. "Have mercy on me," he said. "I've only got so much self-control."

"I don't need your self-control," she said, looking up at him.

"Perry . . ."

She moved up against him, kissing him. He wrapped his arm around her waist and brought her down on the bed. He kicked the rest of his clothes off, moved his hand between her thighs and started stroking her.

"I'm ready," she said, her voice shaky, thin. He pushed two fingers inside her, sliding his thumb over the sensitive bundle of nerves there. She groaned, arching her hips against him.

"Maybe I want to tease you a little bit more. Maybe I want to draw it out. Because when I take you for the first time . . . It's the first time."

And there would be more. That was the rest of it. It wasn't just tonight. It made her want to weep. But she also wondered how he had just gotten so sure.

It would be wonderful. She knew that. Maybe he did too.

He stroked her inside, and she gasped, her orgasm shocking her, jolting her halfway off the mattress. He claimed her mouth, withdrew his fingers from her, and positioned himself between her thighs. Then he thrust home, his size a shock, but in the very best way.

She raked her nails down his arms as he began to move. Wrapped her legs around his lean hips as he thrust deep. Impossibly so.

"Carson," she whispered.

"Princess," he said, kissing her neck.

And she was undone.

He was inside her. Carson Wilder. The boy of her fantasies, the man of her dreams. Hers. Hers.

You're mine.

And they were each other's.

She lost herself in the pagan rhythm that he established. She met his each and every thrust. She drew blood and cried out his name. She didn't want it to end, but when it did, it was a blaze of riotous glory, pleasure like she had never known. Her body tightened around his, and she unraveled while pleasure took her words, her thoughts, and left her only with him. He cried out his own release, pouring himself into her.

Afterward, there was no sound except for their labored breathing.

He lay down beside her on the bed, staring at her.

And she felt herself losing touch with consciousness. Three orgasms. She was wrung out.

Except she had a feeling it wasn't really the orgasms. It was him. Having sex with her best friend for the first time.

He stroked her face, and she decided to close her eyes just for a moment.

When she opened them again, she realized that she had fallen asleep. Carson was sitting on the foot of her bed, his broad back to her. He was wearing his jeans. His head was lowered, and his posture was tense.

He was still there, though.

She wasn't confused, not even for a moment. Because even in her dream she hadn't forgotten that she'd just had sex with Carson.

She sat up, clutching the sheets to her breasts, which was a silly and belated display of modesty. He wasn't even looking at her, and he had already seen everything. She touched his back.

"I didn't use a condom," he said.

"Oh."

A pang of something that should have been horror tightened her stomach.

"If you need to get . . . I don't know, a pill or . . ."

"Do you want me to?"

He turned to look at her. "Not especially."

The odds of her being pregnant, at thirty-two, after a single sexual encounter, were low. But not zero, she knew. He was telling her he wouldn't judge her if she wanted to make those odds lower. She tried to take a breath.

A baby. Carson's baby. Actually, she wanted that a lot. But . . . it would trap them both in a really specific kind of heaven and hell. It would make a lot of decisions for them.

"I don't want to either."

He nodded. "I'll be more careful next time."

She nodded. "Yeah. You want there to be a next time?"

His face was drawn and haggard. "I don't think there's any choice."

"You sound delighted by that," she said.

"I don't know what it means for us."

It was right there between them. The obvious thing. They could just decide to be together. He had said that he didn't even want her to take the morning-after pill. She knew that she didn't want to. If they had a baby together . . . she wouldn't leave. She would stay. She would push aside all her hurt about Alyssa. About not being chosen first. She would let the pregnancy force them together.

They could just decide to do that.

To forget everything that had come before. To be all in now.

Except he'd said he didn't want to get married again. And he'd said he didn't think he could love.

And she knew that she loved him in ways that might kill her.

She thought about her mother. The way she had been entirely addicted to what her father made her feel.

Carson wasn't her dad.

But she did know what it meant when a woman loved a man

more than he loved her. She knew what it looked like. She knew all the bad and unhealthy decisions that could stem from that. She wouldn't allow that to happen. Not to them. She cared too much about him.

"The horse has bolted," he said, his voice rough. "And I'm afraid that things are different now."

She nodded. "Yes."

"You're still leaving Rustler Mountain."

"I am," she said, a hitch in her breath. It was her decision. She could decide to stay. She could decide not to put a down payment on that place in Medford. She could decide to just stay with him.

"Remember what you said?" she began, pushing herself up and letting the sheet fall away. "About how you kept trying to figure out the future. So that you could make it something good and easy. And how maybe you just needed to try to live. Maybe we just have to try to live through this. And see what happens."

"That sounds really dangerous," he said.

He would get no argument from her.

"Except it's you. And it's me. And the one thing I do know, Carson, is that I can't imagine life without you."

"You're going to make one, though."

"Not any more than you did. You went into the Army, and you married somebody else."

His face went blank. "I did."

"But we're still us."

"Yeah."

"And the way we've been us has taken a lot of different shapes, hasn't it?"

"Yes."

"So this is a different shape that we're in right now."

He nodded slowly and moved toward her, cupping her face. "I can't imagine going back. Because now I know what you look like underneath your clothes."

As romantic proclamations went, it wasn't the most florid.

But it was sincere.

"You should move your things into my house."

Her heart stopped. His house, where he had lived with Alyssa. Yes, they had shared this place for a while, but not this bed. This cabin hadn't been their home.

"No," she said. "We're not doing that. I'm not playing house with you."

Because that's what it would be. Playing. This wasn't really what he wanted. It wasn't what he was choosing. He could've chosen her at any point. He hadn't.

"I don't want anyone to know," she said.

She didn't want their friendship to be changed everywhere. Suddenly, now that she had the intimacy she had always wanted, she almost wished their relationship could go back to being what it was. Because that had been something she knew how to live with. It had been something comfortable.

"Right." He chuckled. "I mean, you're my best friend, Perry. You would be the only person I would tell."

She understood the weirdness of that. "Me too."

"I want to kiss you," he said.

"You don't have to ask."

"I just wanted to be sure. I didn't know if there were going to be times when you needed me to go back to just being your friend."

She frowned, pain lancing her chest. She put her hand on his face. Then she leaned forward and kissed him. Slowly. Gently. "I was your friend the whole time I was doing that."

He nodded.

"When we're alone, we can be however we want."

For now.

She refused to think about forever, the future, or the date of her next period. She refused to think past the end of her mattress. And when he kissed her again, and it quickly intensified, she decided she wasn't going to think again for the rest of the night.

Chapter 17

She was part of his life. I accept that. She gave him his children, whom I love now as my own. She made this man who he is, in his stubbornness, his grief, and his hard-won smile. But it is difficult to accept her when I have never loved anyone but him, and I fear someone in the grave holds more of him than I ever will.

—Mae Tanner's Diary, August 18th, 1900

Carson didn't sleep. And when he finally decided to get out of bed, it was early, the sky outside gray.

He looked at Perry, sleeping. They had slept together all night. She'd kept her hand on his shoulder, and he had lain there, looking at her. Trying to come to terms with what had happened. Trying to sort through it all.

It had been the most explosive sexual encounter of his entire life, and he knew that had nothing to do with the amount of time it had been since he'd been with somebody. It wasn't about pent-up desire. It was about Perry.

The small miracle of seeing her beneath her clothes. Of tasting her. Touching her. He had walled off his longing for so many years. His own decision, in many ways.

Because he had decided no. He had decided that it couldn't happen. And now it was. She had told him not to overthink it. Not to plan. But that was a difficult thing to do. Because she was Perry. What he wanted desperately was to . . . It wasn't even about doing the right thing by her. It was about not breaking her. All those old family traumas felt so close to the surface now.

He went into the kitchen and started hunting around for the coffee.

And then he saw the journal that she had taken out of the wall the other day.

Old family heirlooms. This town was full of them.

Austin had managed to make sense of his whole life by excavating the past. He had healed so many wounds because of something other people had felt two hundred years ago. Carson wasn't sure he understood that. But then he thought about the house in town. It had been built to house a family. And the man who had built it had lost the woman he loved. Then he had sent away for a mail-order bride. What a strange experience it must've been for her. To be something that had been ordered. Not the woman he had chosen to love.

That thought gripped him, and he had a hard time letting go of it.

He also thought about the Wilder house, down the street from Perry's Victorian. Austin Wilder had built that house for his wife. Had built a facade of respectability, all while remaining a true Wilder. An outlaw. He had died for his sins. Whatever work his brother Austin had done to try to shed a little bit more light on their ancestor, the man had still been a criminal. He might not have been a murderer, but whether his life had ended shot dead in the street or in a jail cell, it probably didn't make much difference.

He had built that house with his own hands, dreaming about making a perfect life for a woman he had fallen in love with, but because of who he was, that dream had never been realized. Because of his own sins, he hadn't been able to make that home matter.

Yeah. He couldn't find the kind of joy in the past that his brother did.

Not even close.

What he liked about history was the reminder that life went on. That people change, but also stayed the same. That time rolled like thunder, and you weren't all that important in the grand scheme of things. That he liked. Whether it made any kind of sense or not.

He took his hand off the diary and started to make a pot of coffee.

A few minutes later, he heard the sound of footsteps on the wood floor.

"Good morning," he said, his voice rough.

Perry stopped in the doorway, wearing nothing more than his T-shirt, and lust gripped him hard.

They'd used a condom the second time they'd had sex. But not the first. He wasn't sure if he actually hoped they were safe. Part of him could easily imagine a whole new life. Perry with his baby.

It was enough to make him feel that the wind had been knocked out of him.

Are you just doing the same thing you did with Alyssa? Looking for a wife-shaped person to give you stability?

He immediately rejected that notion. Because Perry wasn't just the shape of anything. She was significant.

She mattered.

She was Perry.

"How did you sleep?" he asked.

"Good. I haven't had anybody make me coffee in the morning in a long time."

"I'm a full-service experience."

She laughed. This was a strange sort of intimacy that they hadn't experienced before. Him wearing only jeans, her wearing the other half of his clothes. He could still taste her. He was getting hard again. That was new. Not being able to control himself when he looked at her.

He had locked his need down so tight.

But he didn't have to keep it locked down now. So he crossed the room, bent his head and kissed her. He had only meant it to be a quick greeting. But it heated up quick. She wrapped her arms around his neck, arching against him.

"Perry," he whispered, nuzzling her neck, kissing her there.

"I have to open my store," she said.

"Don't you have to take a shower first?" he asked.

She looked at him and blinked. "We could take a shower together."

"Yes, we could."

Lust gripped him hard.

There were no rules between them now. Or at least, there were new ones. He could get in the shower with her and watch the water sluice over her skin. He could lick it off her.

He was suddenly so turned on he couldn't see straight. He picked her up off the floor, holding her like a sack over his shoulder as he marched toward the bathroom.

She screeched. "Put me down!"

He slapped her ass. "No," he said.

She yelped and wiggled against him. Oh, he *liked* that. So did she. They might have to play around a little bit.

Play.

Perry was the only person he had ever played with. Whether it was pirates or . . . he had a feeling they were going to find some other games they could play.

When he set her down and turned the water on, he was at the end of his rope. He pulled her against him and kissed her until their lips felt bruised while the water heated up.

"I am very excited to help you get ready," he said.

They stripped naked and got into the small space. The warm water poured over their skin. He kissed her deep and long.

And then he got the soap, and slicked up his hands, moving them over her beautiful body.

He pushed her against the wall and rubbed himself against her. He had forgotten a condom. He was an idiot. And he knew he couldn't take a chance with her again. But he hooked her leg over his hip and rubbed against the place where she was most sensitive. Until she cried out. Until he lost it completely. Until they both came, the sounds of pleasure echoing off the shower walls.

She slid down his body. He rinsed her off. And then he took her to her room and helped her get dressed, which was actually kind of fun, though not as much fun as taking her clothes off.

"The coffee is probably done," he said.

"I bet," she laughed.

This was actually great. Because it was Perry. And he liked her so much. And the sex was absolutely fantastic. "I'm going to buy a bunch of condoms today," he said.

She let out a short bark of a laugh. "Okay, Carson."

"Well. I'm mad that we couldn't finish that the way I wanted to."

"I wouldn't have minded," she said, her cheeks turning pink.

"Don't play dangerous games, Perry." Because he wouldn't really have minded either. He gritted his teeth. "I'm going to protect you."

She nodded. "Thank you."

It was a strange, fragmented thank-you. But sincere. As if he really was the one protecting her, but he couldn't quite parse that.

"Want me to drive you down, sweetheart?"

He had never called her that before. It had just fallen out of his mouth. And she looked a little bit uncomfortable. "I'm sorry," he said. "I don't have to do that."

She shook her head. "You can do whatever you want."

"I'm going to hold you to that later."

"Okay."

"Let me drive you. I'll pick you up when the store closes."

She nodded. "Okay."

He got dressed, and the two of them left together. She had said that she wasn't going to play house with him. And he was very aware that that was what this morning felt like. Except it didn't feel like anything he'd ever experienced before.

He didn't know how he was supposed to get anything done today, with the memory of her body beneath his hands. The memory of her flavor on his tongue.

"I can still taste you," he said, when they were halfway down the driveway.

Perry squeaked. "Why would you say that?"

"Because I like the way you taste?"

"You're dirty," she said.

"Yeah. You don't know that about me, do you?"

She blinked, and then turned her head to look at him. "No. I don't."

"It's one of the few things you don't know about me, actually. And I don't know about you. Are *you* dirty, Perry?"

She straightened, her hands in her lap. "I would define myself as being not entirely prudish, but not . . . I wouldn't want to advertise myself as a freak."

"Interesting."

"Which is not to put limits on you. Or this."

"Noted."

"What do you like?" she asked, her voice suddenly getting husky.

"You," he said without hesitation. "Everything you've done. Everything we can do."

"Yes, but I meant before, with other women."

"Before doesn't matter. Because you're you. And I've never . . . I realized when I was carrying you to the shower, I've never had fun really with anyone but you. Even this is fun. In a way that it never has been. Yeah, it always feels good. But not like this."

He always told her what he was thinking, so it seemed normal to tell her this too.

"Yeah."

"What's it like for you?"

She looked at him. "My favorite flavor of ice cream."

He didn't know what to say to that. He didn't know what it meant. And he didn't know if he really wanted to dig into it. Because it just sounded nice.

He wanted to be that for her. Her favorite something.

"That's why I took my time licking you," she said.

He felt as if he'd been punched in the gut. "That really was cruel," he said.

"Think about it today while you work on the house." She said it cheerily, right as they pulled up to the florist shop.

"You're mean," he said.

She hopped out of the passenger side of the truck and waved at him. "Goodbye, Carson."

Then she unlocked the front door of the florist shop and disappeared inside.

And he had nothing left to do but head on in to work on her house. Where he had no doubt that thoughts of her would crowd every moment.

When he got halfway through the day, he realized that he had something to look forward to. Something he was very much looking forward to. And that was a miracle all on its own. A miracle that he had thanks to Perry.

So maybe it was a good thing he had lost his mind last night at the bar.

It had gotten him something he hadn't even known he wanted quite so badly.

Now he had to figure out just what to do with it, with her, to keep them from falling apart.

Chapter 18

I tried to talk to him tonight, about feelings and hearts and hopes. He said he has trouble speaking of such things. I'm afraid of what he might say if he tried.

—Mae Tanner's Diary, August 28th, 1900

Perry was having difficulty focusing on anything. In the space of one night her entire life had changed. Her assumptions about everything. She and Carson had done things to each other that she had never done with anyone. Things that she had never imagined she would do with *him*, because it was a dream and a fantasy that she had buried well and often.

Images of what had happened never stopped playing over and over in her mind. A constant reminder of how hot last night had been.

You slept with your best friend. It was the best sex you've ever had.

You can't wait to do it again.

You get to do it again.

Yes. All true.

Yet she had never felt so much as if she were standing on the edge of a perilous cliff, in danger of going over at the slightest breeze.

She was bustling about, creating a bouquet out of some blossoms left over from a special order, something to have for spontaneous purchases, when her shop door opened, and Marissa Rivera walked in.

Perry stood, frozen for a moment. She had never even come close to being the other woman. And while she knew that one date with Carson did not make Marissa his girlfriend, she did feel weird about the way everything had happened last night. In fact, she hadn't even really had time to hear how things had gone down between Carson and Marissa, because they had been too busy with their screaming fight in the street, and then all the sex.

"Hi, Perry," said Marissa. "I just wanted to let you know that I heard the Medford building is going on the market early."

The announcement was so different from what Perry had been thinking about that it took her a second to catch up with reality.

"Oh?"

"Yes. So . . . I don't know where you're at right now, but it would be best if we could secure some kind of financing and get an offer in. I know you don't have the house up for sale yet . . ."

"Yeah. No. It's . . . you're right. I need to do something. If I want that building."

"I'm sorry about the timeline. I grumbled at the seller's agent, but he just said that things change, and they need to off-load the building quicker than they thought."

"Maybe I should put the house up for rent."

"That's not a bad idea."

Perry nodded. "I . . . Carson is . . . he's working on the house and . . ."

"I know," said Marissa. "We don't have to be awkward about him."

"I would love to say that I'm not awkward about him, but it is a little bit awkward right now." It was also supposed to be a secret. She was the one who had told Carson it needed to stay a secret, and now she was the one who had let the cat out of the bag.

"I told him last night that it was obvious he was jealous of your date."

Perry blinked. "Did you?"

"Yes. He was frothing at the mouth. I thought you guys were just friends. I didn't know I was getting in the middle of something. I'm sorry."

"Oh, you don't owe *me* an apology," said Perry. "Carson owes us both an apology." When she said that, she realized it was true.

Because he was the one who had dragged Marissa into the middle of things when . . .

Okay, she'd done the same thing to West. But West wasn't here. For her part, she hadn't done anything to Marissa.

"Because you know, he's certainly never been interested in me before," Perry explained. "So all of that last night was . . . it was unexpected."

"Well. I'm glad there wasn't something I was supposed to know that I missed."

Perry shook her head. "No. I was never upset with you. A little upset at myself. *Definitely* upset at him."

"I guess my next question is, are you actually still going to move?"

That question paralyzed Perry for a second. "Yes," she said. "I don't . . ." She sighed. "I've known Carson since I was seven. He had twenty-five years to do something about us. He didn't. He's not promising anything. You know, his wife died a year and half ago . . ."

"Yeah," Marissa said. "You don't have to tell me. It's complicated. I get it. I'm really asking in a professional capacity. Unless you need to talk about it in a personal capacity."

"You really are a girl's girl, Marissa, and I appreciate it. But I don't know how to talk about it."

Marissa nodded. "I'm sorry. That's heavy."

"Maybe it doesn't have to be. Maybe I'm making it more difficult than it needs to be."

"I doubt it. What is love if not consensual torture?"

Perry couldn't argue with that.

Because so far, being romantic with Carson felt mildly torturous in ways both good and bad.

Her phone lit up, and she saw Carson's name.

"Speaking of . . ."

"Let me know about the offer. Or if you need any help with anything. I can talk to Randall down at Mountain Mortgage about getting something going."

"Yeah. Okay. I'll . . . I'll be in touch."

But she was already opening her phone even as Marissa was leaving, and she felt guilty, because she should've devoted her whole attention to the other woman. Marissa had been so much nicer than she needed to be. But Perry was desperate to read Carson's text.

Dinner with Austin tonight? Millie invited us.

Sure.

It was such a normal thing. Routine for them. She hadn't been baking or anything, though. She hadn't gotten used to working farther away from where she was living. She hadn't gotten used to the new kitchen.

Whatever. She was making excuses about not baking when the truth was, she was just distracted by Carson.

Dinner was going to be the two of them at his brother's house pretending they hadn't had sex.

She wondered how that would play out.

How is your day going?

She smiled at his text. **Fine.**

I've been thinking about you.

Don't, she responded.

Why not?

It was too much like their letters, in which she'd poured her heart out, and had started to believe their shared confidences meant something. Now there was sex between the words they were trading, and if she wasn't careful, she was going to start hoping for love again.

She didn't say that.

She also didn't say: *I think about you all the time.*

Because that was the road to insanity.

For the rest of the afternoon, she was simply counting minutes until he came to get her, and she was left pondering exactly how she had ended up in this situation. How trying to put distance between herself and Carson had resulted in her being more wrapped around him and obsessing to a degree she hadn't done since she was a teenage girl.

When he walked in the door right at five o'clock, her heart nearly burst out of her chest.

She wasn't sure what she was supposed to do. They had decided to keep their romance to themselves. But it seemed wrong not to go and kiss him.

He answered the question of what to do when he walked straight through the store, behind the counter, and cupped her cheek with his hand, breaking the barriers of their friendship in one easy move, before moving in to kiss her on the mouth. "I've been wanting to do that all day."

"You realize the entire town is out there."

"Yeah," he said, making eye contact with her.

"Carson," she said, feeling pained.

"Sorry. I don't know how not to touch you. Which I know is wild, considering . . ."

"You didn't touch me for twenty-five years?"

"You didn't touch me either."

That shut her up. Because as often as she'd felt she had been wronged, he was right. She had never said anything. She had never touched him.

For a very long time, she had sat in a lot of quiet fury about his not choosing her. She had let life make her scared.

She had learned to push everything down.

Now it was all rising back up, and maybe that was a good thing.

Their relationship had never been fragile. Maybe that was the truth she needed to cling to. They had survived his going to war, they had survived his marrying another woman, and her telling him they were codependent.

They had survived his attempts at not being on this earth.

She had no idea where this was headed. But they had never been fragile.

"Should we stop and get something for dinner?"

"Maybe."

"Let's do it, so things don't seem weird."

"What do you mean?"

"Normally, I bring bread or something."

He frowned. "Yeah. I guess so."

"You haven't noticed that? And that I've been not making bread since . . . well, since all of this started."

"Yeah. When you came to my house and told me that you were leaving town."

"I'm doing a great job of leaving," she said. She tapped the countertop. "Marissa came by. She told me that the florist shop in Medford is going up for sale earlier than expected."

"Oh," he said. "So . . . what are you going to do?"

"I don't know," she said. "I really don't. I'm not . . . I'm not sure what the right thing to do is. Because I really did want to have more money in my bank account before taking on a mortgage."

"You can list the house as is. But I'm definitely going to need a couple more weeks to finish what I've started."

"Maybe I'll rent it out. I'm starting to question my decision to sell. Finding the extra journal in the wall reminded me how much that house is part of my family. Part of me."

"Yeah," he said.

"I have a complicated relationship with my family. You know that. But not with my grandmother. And I know she didn't want the house to be a burden. But it isn't. It's never been anything but a gift. I just wonder if I'm missing something. I . . ."

She bit her tongue. "Carson . . . I told you that I've wanted you for a long time."

He nodded slowly.

"That was why I wanted to leave."

He looked stunned. "You said . . ."

"I get it. I know what I said. But I don't really have anything to protect now. Because . . . you know. Because I basically flung myself at you and . . ."

"I flung myself at you too. You're not alone in this, Perry."

"But all those things I yelled at you last night in the street. I've been wanting you. And spending so much time with you just felt pointless. It felt like a roadblock. To the rest of my life. Because how was I ever going to meet a man and marry him, and have kids with him, when I was in this relationship with you? When you were away it was easier. When you were married it was . . . *easy* isn't the word."

"I'm sorry," he said. "I'm . . . I'm so sorry."

She shook her head, and she made what she knew was a terrible face. "Please don't apologize to me. This is a huge reason why I never wanted to have this conversation. I cannot bear for you to feel sorry for me."

"I don't. I feel . . . regret. I don't pity you, Perry. But I decided when you started looking pretty to me, when you started to become a woman, I decided that I could never take advantage of you. You know . . . you know how I see myself. My family. I made a decision because I wanted to protect you. But instead, I hurt you. This is my whole damned life, isn't it? I never wanted to hurt you, ever. I wanted to spare you, and I fucked things up anyway. I hate that. I'm sorry, because . . ."

"You don't have to protect me from what you feel," she said, still trying to sort through the implications of what he was saying.

"I think sometimes I don't even realize what I'm holding back because I haven't processed all of it. If I don't say it out loud to you, I think a lot of my thoughts go without being understood. But you're right. When I was a horny teenage boy and I was with you all the time, I *did* want you. And I decided to make you into something other than a woman to desire. My saint. My angel. My Perry. So that I wouldn't. I stopped it. And any time it ever threatened to pop up, I would end it. Because it seemed right. I just wanted to protect you. I still do."

She realized that this was his version of pushing down feelings that were too big to comprehend. He was a man, so the realization had taken a physical shape first. She had loved him before she had felt attraction like that. He had known when she had started to get breasts that he wanted to touch them. The urge was very male.

But it was honest. And she could understand it.

She also realized that life had hurt him, badly, and taught him early not to care, just as it had her. Which meant they had curtailed their romantic feelings at a very young age out of a sense of self-preservation, and why wouldn't they?

"We're really kind of a mess," she said.

He nodded. "Yeah."

"I don't need to make a decision about the building right now."

And right then, she felt the same ambivalence as she did about being pregnant. Maybe if the Medford building ended up being unavailable, and all of her plans fell through, she could just say, oh well. Maybe everything would be fine. Maybe she could throw her hands up and say that fate had intervened.

After all, there had been a lot of things that had happened to Carson and her that they hadn't chosen. Maybe some good things could fall into place the same way.

He nodded. "Okay."

"You can finish the house, and then if the building's still available, I'll make some decisions. If not, maybe I'll have to go back to the drawing board, but . . . I can't commit to anything right now."

"Good. All right."

She was buying them both time. To sit with these revelations. To sit with this new stage of their relationship. She closed up the florist shop and got into his truck. They went to the grocery store and walked down the short aisles with a small cart, grabbing dinner rolls and a pie. Then they headed back up toward the ranch.

She wondered if they looked as changed as she felt. Because when she looked at him, she just saw his naked body now. She had a feeling when he looked at her, he saw the same. So she wondered what everybody else was going to see.

"Well, here we go," she said.

He laughed and grabbed the bag with the pie and the bread.

When they walked into the house, everyone was already there: Millie and Austin, Cassidy, Flynn, and Dalton.

"Hey, traitor," said Flynn.

Perry was deeply confused by Flynn's greeting until she realized that he was talking to Carson, and that it was a reference to his restoring the wagon for Jessie Jane. It felt as if that controversy had originated a whole different lifetime ago. She now couldn't believe it had set her off. But it had.

"Hi yourself," said Carson.

"Leave him alone," said Cassidy, fussing around Carson.

"Why are you being nice to me?" Carson asked his sister, batting her hand away when she went to touch his cowboy hat.

"Because," she said, "somebody should."

Perry frowned. She realized that Cassidy wasn't looking at her. Interesting.

"I'm going to bring the pie and bread into the kitchen," she said, taking them back from Carson.

"Cassidy," said Perry, "you want to come with me?"

She had noticed Cassidy was being a little standoffish with her. She hadn't been chatty when she'd served her dessert the other night. But Cassidy was a Wilder and that meant she was sometimes twitchy, so Perry didn't take it personally. Especially since she was dealing with her own stuff—namely, banging Cassidy's brother.

Cassidy met her gaze and she worried momentarily that Cassidy could read her mind.

Of course she couldn't.

She was not going to let Carson's little sister be mad at her. She had known Cassidy since she was a kid. If Cassidy had a beef with her, then Perry was going to hear about it.

"Sure," said Cassidy, accompanying her into the kitchen.

"What's going on?" Perry asked.

"Nothing," said Cassidy.

"That's not true. You're being nice to Carson, and I think it's because you're mad at me."

"I don't understand why you're leaving," Cassidy said. "And the longer I think about it, the more it doesn't make any sense."

Perry hadn't considered that her move would hurt Cassidy as well as Carson. Oh, Cassidy wasn't saying that, and likely, she wasn't going to. That wasn't the point, though. She was defending Carson's feelings, but Perry could see there was something else.

"I haven't decided if I am leaving, actually. Just because some things came up with the building, and I might not actually be able to go."

"Oh," said Cassidy. "But you want to."

"Yes. But it has nothing to do with you, or your family, or how I feel about anybody."

"I didn't say that it did," said Cassidy, stubbornly.

"You didn't. But I know how you feel. Because I also have terrible parents that basically don't care what I do. And I understand what it's like when somebody takes off, and it feels like a direct reaction to you."

Carson's joining the military had felt that way. Carson's marrying someone else had felt that way. Because while she had loved him wildly, she had also been immature. So in her mind, everything he did related to her.

She hadn't fully realized that until this moment. Until looking at the expression in Cassidy's eyes had reminded her of the pain she had experienced.

"I know that Austin has Millie now. But for most of my life you were basically the only woman around."

Perry had never considered that, and it felt like a stab wound that she hadn't. She had been so wrapped up in her own stuff.

"You're the closest thing I have to a sister," Perry said. "And you're a good one."

"Oh." Cassidy's eyes filled with tears and Perry moved over to her, pulling her close. She really hadn't considered everyone she would be leaving behind. She had been so eager to sever that bond. To create her new life.

"There are so many things I don't want to leave behind."

"I don't understand, then," Cassidy said, looking bleak.

"Sometimes you have to change your surroundings in order to change yourself. That's the best way I can describe it." She released her hold on Cassidy.

"But what about Carson?"

"I need Carson to take care of himself for a little bit," she said.

"I thought he was your best friend."

"He is. And more besides. But . . . things happen."

She had probably revealed too much. And Cassidy clearly didn't know what to make of her admission. Perry didn't clarify.

Soon, it was time for all of them to sit down to dinner, and the seriousness of the moment evaporated. Dalton and Flynn performed what was essentially a comedy routine, the quick rhythm of their barbs bouncing back and forth across the table while Cassidy injected dry commentary to bring them back down to earth.

Millie smiled, serene, and Perry often wondered what Millie thought, being dropped into the center of this clan. The siblings were so rowdy, and very much not the kind of family you'd expect a librarian to choose to marry into.

But then, Austin had always been something of an enigma. A little bit dangerous, a little bit studious.

It was odd that she had never quite realized until today how deep some of Carson's emotions were buried. How much he thought about things. Except when he didn't want to think about them and cut them off at the source. Probably because he felt things as deeply as his brother did.

But Carson built things, rather than reading. Austin took information in, digested it for years. He had written a book. Carson made things. Maybe that was what he was trying to say about his marriage. He had been trying to build something.

She shook off her introspection and just enjoyed the conversation.

She got up to go to the bathroom, and on her way back, she ran into Carson. He wrapped his arm around her waist, pulled her against the wall, and kissed her.

Until she was breathless.

"What are you doing?" she asked, laughing because she couldn't help herself.

"I was thinking, what if I hadn't stopped myself from wanting this? Think of all the trouble we would've gotten into."

That was terrifying.

"God. We would've had a baby when I was sixteen."

He laughed, low and throaty. "Probably."

"We would've been a disaster," she pointed out.

"We definitely would've been sneaking around this house." He kissed her again.

"Carson," she said as he slid his hand down to her ass and nuzzled her neck. "I want you. I want you so bad."

Then he moved away from her and walked ahead of her back toward the kitchen. She blinked, going after him.

He was being feral, and she couldn't say she disliked it. It was the pirate in him. And perhaps the pirate in her responded. That was how the rest of the evening went. She slid her hand beneath the table and grazed his arousal. He caught her alone in the living room for a second and wrapped his arm around her, squeezing her breasts. When everyone came in, he moved away as if nothing had happened. Flynn and Dalton set a card table up in the center of the living room and decided to play poker.

"One second," said Carson. "I have to grab change out of my truck."

"Oh," said Perry. "Me too."

As soon as they were outside, Perry found herself pressed against the side of the house, with Carson kissing her deep and fierce.

"I think I need to fuck you against a wall," he whispered in her ear.

"Yes," she whispered. "Please."

"I'd do it against this one right now if we had even a couple more minutes."

"I bet I could make you finish very, very quickly," she said.

"Don't tempt me," he whispered against her mouth.

"Oh God!" They turned and saw Cassidy standing on the porch, her mouth dropped open. "Why is this my life?"

He and Perry moved away from each other. Perry straightened her dress, even though it wasn't really askew.

"Cassidy," said Carson. "Don't say anything."

She clamped her mouth shut and turned on her heel, going back into the house.

Carson rested his forehead against Perry's. "Okay. That was very careless. I'm sorry."

"It's fine," she said. "In the sense that I wasn't being any more careful than you."

"Fair," he said. "I'll talk to her."

"It's fine. I'm not ashamed of this."

"I never thought that you were," he said. "I never thought that was why you wanted to keep it between us."

She nodded. "Good. It's just . . . we don't have any answers yet . . . and we don't want to be rushed into giving them to anyone, or to ourselves."

"Exactly," he said.

She sighed. "I suppose we should go back."

"I really do have to get money out of my truck."

He did, and they went back inside, where the poker game was being dealt; there were two empty seats for them. Cassidy was sitting at the table with scarlet cheeks, but she hadn't said anything. They could tell, because no one else was reacting.

When they finished the game and it was time to finally go back to her place, she could breathe again. Because then he kissed her. And they went to bed.

She had demanded that they not play house. But they were doing this again. Carson had made good on his word to buy condoms.

Right now, everything felt pretty amazing.

Perry was going to cling to amazing for as long as they could have it.

The next day, Carson decided to work on the ranch a bit before heading over to Perry's place, and he wasn't terribly surprised when his sister rode up to him out in the north pasture.

"Well," she said. "Since I am now the keeper of the world's most insane secret, maybe you could actually give me some details."

"Why do you want details?"

"Because," she said. "You are . . . I don't know. You've never been the same since Alyssa died. Perry is your best friend, but you were making out with her hot and heavy. That is totally in opposition to what you were telling Flynn about dating again. And sex and all of that. And much as I don't want to know about that part of your life, I can't figure out what the hell is going on."

"Well. Join the club."

"Oh," said Cassidy. "You're really too old to not have a handle on your life."

Carson couldn't help it. He threw his head back and laughed. "Oh, bad news, kid. Uncertainty is the name of the game. That's just how it is. I don't know what the hell I'm doing. Maybe you will when you're thirty-four. I kind of doubt it."

"Don't tell me that. I'm going to be in a great place when I'm thirty-four."

"Tell me all about it, Cass."

"I'm going to have my own ranch. I'm going to have bees, and I'm going to meet a nice guy who's not from here. Maybe he'll even take me different places."

"Yeah. Let's circle back on that in ten years and see how it went."

"That's not nice."

"You're going to be okay in ten years," he said, feeling guilty now. "But you might not have done all the things you thought. That's all."

She frowned. "I know that . . ."

"No. You don't really know. About me, or anything. Me either, to tell you the truth. Not all the time. I'm not grieving Alyssa in the way that you think. I'm just messed up."

"Oh."

"You look disappointed."

"I don't know what you mean by 'messed up.'"

"I'm just still dealing with our childhood. Mine was different from yours, I grant. But we had the same dad."

"I just thought that your problem was . . ."

"My wife dying. I get it. I kind of wish it were. Because then maybe I would have given her something better. But it's not. My problem is me. And the fact that no matter how hard I try, I can't seem to get to the bottom of the bullshit of having Dad as my dad. Or of having Mom leave."

"I thought I would be over that by your age."

"Sorry."

"I've been really upset about Perry leaving. Last night when I talked to her, I realized it's because whenever someone does something like that, it feels like abandonment. And that's not normal. But it's . . . I'm having a really hard time not making everything about my mom leaving me forever on Christmas, you know?"

"Oh yeah. I absolutely know. The problem with life is that it keeps going. And because it keeps going, it keeps flinging new shit at you."

"That's not encouraging," she said.

"Well, it's something to look out for. Because the thing is, it's just layer upon layer. Until you can't figure out how you ended up where you are. Until you end up really far away from what you used to want. And then you have to figure out how to get back to it."

"Is Perry what you want?"

The words were stark, simple. The question he had been avoiding asking for a very long time.

"I can't imagine life without her," he said.

"Because it's always seemed to me that she was really special to you. But I just accepted that you didn't have a physical relationship with her. I'm not going to lie." Cassidy wrinkled her nose. "That was a little bit like walking in on my siblings kissing each other."

He laughed. "Well. There you go. Another layer of trauma for you, Cass. Sorry about that. Perry isn't my sister. Never has been."

Cassidy looked profoundly bummed out. "Yeah. Well. I get that."

"We just didn't want to tell anybody about this because we don't know what's happening. Because she might still leave. Because . . . I'm unpacking some things."

"You could just marry her. You know, Flynn said it back at the bar, and now that I know you like making out with her, it doesn't make sense to me why you don't. You could give her a baby. You could just be happy."

The words were so tantalizing. So sweet.

"I wish I could be sure of that. But it isn't about me. It's about her." Because he already knew what happened when he wanted something to work out badly enough that he didn't actually think it through.

And he wasn't sure he had learned that lesson yet.

"Why can't this damned family just be happy?" Cassidy said, shaking her head.

"God help you when you end up in love, Cassidy."

She shook her head. "I'm not going to make a drama out of it. I'll find someone who fits in with my life and makes . . . sense." Her cheeks went pink. "It will be easy."

"You're tempting fate."

"Good thing I don't believe in fate."

"You don't?" he asked.

She shook her head. "No. It's nobody's fate to be left on Christmas by their mother."

Great point, honestly. "Yeah. Well. That makes sense."

"The good news is," said Cassidy, "if nothing is up to fate, you get to decide."

His younger sister decided to ride off then, her brown hair tangling in the wind as she did.

She was young. Her perspective on the situation reflected that. There was anger underneath her words, and a certainty that she could control the outcomes of things he knew you couldn't always control. Carson did believe in fate. Because he'd tried to take control of his life, and it hadn't worked.

But there was also some truth in what she said. There were things a man got to decide. He just had to figure out what those things were.

Chapter 19

The town feels empty without you. I don't know how to explain it. Sometimes I think if I go wait by Outlaw Lake, you'll appear and tell me you're my pirate captain and we have to go on an adventure. I can't wait until you come home so that it feels like home again.

—A letter from Perry Bramble to Carson Wilder

After work the next day, Perry went straight to her old place, where Carson was working diligently. She brought a picnic blanket, and a picnic basket that she'd picked up at the grocery store. She just felt like . . . doing something. Being with him. Giving him something nice. This was the only thing she could think of.

"Hey," he said, getting up from the floor where he had his nail gun out.

"Hey."

He walked over and wrapped his arm around her neck, pulling her in for a quick, rough kiss. How had they ever not done that by way of greeting? How was she ever going to forget that they'd once had this?

She was very conscious of the cliff's edge again.

We're not fragile.

"I talked to Cassidy this morning."

"Oh?" she asked.

"Yeah. Apparently, she felt like she walked in on her siblings kissing."

Perry guffawed. She couldn't help it. "You know, of all the things that you've ever been to me, a brother isn't one of them."

"No. Absolutely not."

She thought it was funny that he was so certain of that too. That he had never thought of her as a sister.

"I'm so hungry. Thank you for this."

"Yeah," she said. "I wanted to . . . give you something. You know, as a thank-you for fixing my house. And also get you some protein to keep your strength up for later."

He lifted his brows. "Later?"

"Yeah. I think you know."

He chuckled. "Yeah, I do."

She sat on the blanket that she'd brought and started to get the food out. A rotisserie chicken, coleslaw, and potato salad. She got out the paper plates and plastic utensils, and the two of them dug in. There was something about this moment that reminded her of when they were kids. Of when Austin had brought them simple meals from the grocery store. When Perry had been hiding from her family. And Carson's house had been empty of all responsible adults.

"I was always really grateful to have you," he said, as if he had read her mind.

"Me too. You were safe to me in a way that nothing else was. Plus, we could be noisy at your house. Because even though your dad was a piece of work, he didn't care about noise."

"No. He didn't. Damn." He looked down. "I'm so sorry that your house was such a disaster. I feel like I know about it, but I don't know about it. Because we grew up together, so we didn't really talk about all that."

"I know. You were the first person that I ever told about my dad hitting my mom. No one else would have believed it. Everybody liked him so much. And when things declined between them, they just moved away. To a different community, where people could get to know them all over again. You know, the versions of them they wanted people to know. I'm sure my dad is an elder at the church. And he doesn't see anything wrong with how he is. Because he's just the head of the household, and everybody should do what he wants. He's an asshole and a hypocrite, but he doesn't see it."

"I've never regretted punching him in the face."

She laughed. "You were my hero for that, honestly." She was quiet for a moment. "Sometimes it wasn't even his hitting her or me that felt the worst. It was the calm before the explosion because you knew it would . . . just come out of nowhere. The house was just a terrible, awful place to be. I knew he might lose it at any moment, and I always felt like I had to be quiet. I always felt like I had to watch my step. I never felt like I was allowed to be in my own house. Not as myself. I could be a cute, quiet little girl. A good reflection of him. Of the kind of father he wanted the world to believe he was. Neither of my parents have ever cared about who I was, or what I wanted. I never really felt like I knew who I was until you. You taught me how to be wild. In a way that I was never allowed to be. You gave me a childhood, Carson."

He looked dumbfounded by that. "I never figured I had the power to give anybody much of anything. My brothers and I didn't have a terrible childhood, I guess. The ranch was what we had. Our dad was who we knew. Later, it kind of hit me that it was messed up that our mom left. Later, that felt painful. At the time I just kind of accepted it. She wasn't there. I thought maybe she had no choice. But you know, you figure out how the world works later . . ." He was silent for a moment. "One time a teacher told me that our mom left because she was a nice woman, who couldn't stand to deal with rowdy kids like us."

"No," she said, outrage blooming in her chest. "Who said that?"

"Mrs. Converse. You know, she was a sour old lemon."

"Yes, she was. That is the cruelest thing that anyone could ever say to a child."

"I had just put a garter snake in her desk."

"It doesn't matter. She was the adult. You were a child. And obviously acting out because of the way your home life was."

"Not just my home life. The whole town. We were bad seeds from birth. And there were very few people around here who believed any different."

"My dad thought you were bad news. I was forbidden to see you. And that was why I did. I didn't know that it was wrong. I didn't know that it was wrong for men to hit their wives. I didn't know that dads were supposed to be kind to their children. To look at them. Because in public we were the family that you saw on TV. So I thought everybody had secrets like ours. I thought it was how men were. It wasn't until later that I knew it was wrong. But even when I didn't know . . . I didn't want to obey him. I didn't care about what he wanted. That was why I went to visit you. To see for myself. He said that you were bad. That we were respectable. But I could never see anything respectable about us. When I met you, somehow it was like I had a different way to look at the world. Like I had a decoder ring. Because if you were bad, and we were good, but you were the single kindest person I had ever met, then I knew my dad was a liar. I knew he was wrong." She pulled her knees up to her chest. "That was important."

Carson looked down at his hands. "I didn't know. That I did that for you."

"You did so much for me. That's only one of the things." She took a breath. "You made my life happier. You gave me a childhood. You taught me how to play. I would've just been a perfect little doll sitting on a shelf all the time if it wasn't for you."

"You did the same thing for me," he said. "I was wild, and I was a pretty bad kid. But you brought some fun to it. You made me less self-destructive."

Hope. That was the theme of it all. They had given each other hope for a life that was different from the one they knew.

That, she realized, had been an integral, important part of their friendship. They had lost it somewhere along the way. They had stopped believing that anything was possible. She was very aware of there being a before and an after. Of there being a time when she could believe that anything might happen, and a time when she had stopped believing. Obviously, it had been true for him too.

Maybe the turning point was when you stopped believing you could love each other.

She pushed that thought away. It was a deep, sad thought, and she didn't know what to do with it.

"I was mad at you when you took Elizabeth Grant to prom," she said.

He looked at her. "Were you?"

Yeah. That was one of the things that had gotten between them. When they were little, it hadn't mattered that he was a boy and she was a girl. It had started to matter. It had started to make her feel sad. And she had started to wish that she hadn't met him as a child, so that he could see her in a different way.

"Perry, I thought . . . once, down at the lake, I wanted to kiss you."

His words were like a bomb going off in her chest. She tried to catch her breath and found that she couldn't. She tried to breathe but it got caught.

"You looked scared of me," he said. "And you were . . . your dad was such a bastard. I didn't want to be another man who scared you. I didn't want to be a man to you, if that made me scary. I wanted to be your hero. I never wanted you to run from me."

She was gasping for air, for sanity. "I was running from *me*."

"You remember that?"

"Yes. Clearly. I . . . I wore the dress because it was see-through. I wanted you to notice me that way . . . I didn't know you wanted to kiss me. I thought you were mad. Like you saw my body through that dress and hated that I was a woman. Or . . . I don't really know what I thought. I was a virgin, and I was confused. I knew I wanted you, and I knew that I wanted you to see me, but I didn't know what it meant. Now that we've been together, I get why it felt dangerous. We're not like anything else."

He shook his head. "No, we aren't."

"I was running from something that was too . . . too big. And I could have asked you, but I was afraid."

He leaned in and touched her chin. "Why?" He looked torn up in a way that devastated her.

"It wasn't you. It wasn't your fault. In the absence of decent parents, teachers mean a lot. Mrs. Converse hurt you. It was . . . it was the principal, Jack Condzella, who made me afraid. He'd always been so nice to me, but when I tried to tell him about my dad hurting my mom, hurting me, he said I had to be careful saying things like that because it could ruin my father." Her throat went dry. "He wouldn't listen to me. But it was more than that. It was never that he didn't believe me; it was that my dad was more important than I was."

"When was that, Perry?"

She blinked. "I was maybe eleven."

"Why didn't you tell me?"

"I was humiliated. And I didn't know what to say. He didn't care. I never wanted to talk about it. I never wanted to repeat it."

Carson was breathing hard, fury and murder in his eyes. "School personnel are mandatory reporters."

She nodded. "I know. I know they are, but he didn't protect me. He just made me feel like . . . what I was afraid of was true. I didn't matter. What I said didn't matter and I let it affect me for a long time. I let that make me scared. That was the time when I started questioning myself, how loud I shouted when we played."

He shook his head and pressed his forehead to hers. "That was wrong, what happened to you. I wish I could have protected you from it."

"It wasn't your job to protect me from everything." The truth was, Carson's attempt to protect her had caused its own kind of pain.

Despite his good intentions.

But it was just life; she was beginning to accept that. There were so many beautiful, wonderful things, and also so much tragedy. So many opportunities to hold on to pain forever, or . . . let it go so you could experience something new.

"You really went swimming in that white dress so I could see your underwear through the fabric, Periwinkle?" he asked, his tone vaguely scolding, rough and sexy.

"I did. But I was playing with something more dangerous than I was ready to handle."

The truth was, the fire between them would have burned them both up back then. Maybe it would have been worth it. Maybe.

"I wanted to dance with you," she whispered. "I dreamed of it."

He kissed her forehead, and she closed her eyes. "I can dance with you now."

She wasn't sure if that was enough to erase her regret. But she wanted to dance with him anyway.

He took his phone out of his pocket and flicked through it for a moment. Then he pushed PLAY on a song that she liked. He knew she liked it, because he knew her. Then he extended his hand and pulled them both up to a standing position. He pulled her close, his fingers laced with hers as he began to sway her in time to the music. This didn't feel like friendship with sex. This felt like something else. It felt like something deep.

It felt like letters sent from overseas and the hope of building a future. It felt like a stolen, breathless moment at Outlaw Lake, and the decision to stay instead of run.

It made her heart swell, and her chest ache.

It made her long for things she didn't want to put into words. But he held her close. And then he twirled her, and she was dizzy when she came back to him, when she rested her head against his chest. They danced like that until the song ended.

Over their lives, over the years, she'd felt there were shifts happening inside them. But it had never actually happened. Until now. Until this.

Perry hadn't understood the true bravery behind Mae Tanner's decision to pack her life up. She'd thought of leaving home herself, but it wasn't the leaving that took courage. What took real bravery was deciding to be the author of her own story.

It was unwinding herself from the expectations of other people and doing the brave thing for herself even when no one else could make sense of it.

It had been brave because Mae had stepped away from all the things that could have protected her.

Perry was so very, very good at protecting herself.

She'd seen moving away as a radical act, but had it just been running?

Carson gripped her wrists, his eyes blazing into hers, the shift between them hot, sudden.

She could see it now, the intensity he'd felt back then that poor teenage virgin Perry had thought was anger. All this stunning male intensity that she'd been so certain was rage at her woman's body. It was, in a fashion. But not the way she'd thought.

"Come home with me," he said.

"Carson . . ." Her stomach went tight. "I can't."

"Why not?"

"I can't sleep in a bed that you shared with her."

She felt like her skin had been pulled tight over her entire body.

She wasn't trying to hurt him, she wasn't trying to rub stinging nettles into a wound neither of them could magically heal, but she needed to say something.

They were going to have to talk about it. She was going to have to give him some honesty. "I wanted you back then, Carson. *And* I was your friend. I don't want you to feel like I was lying the whole time. I think that's what's the hardest about this. It feels dishonest. Like I wasn't really your friend. Or like I was lying in wait, only there because I wanted you in a physical way. But that wasn't it. That wasn't what I was doing. Not ever. Sometimes I could be happy with what we had. Sometimes I thought things were changing, and then they didn't, and I learned to accept being just friends all over again. You went away, you left me. And it was like I was broken in half. I only felt right when you came back."

He nodded. "Me too. I missed you so much while I was gone. You don't even know. The military was hell, Perry."

"You never talk about it."

"Because we quit talking."

She realized how true that was. They saw each other, and they took solace in each other. They were there for each other. But they knew so many things about each other's lives that they didn't often dig deep as they had been recently.

They could exist beside each other in quiet comfort, and there was something nice about that. But it didn't leave room for him to share what the military had done to him. She hadn't wanted to know. He had revealed bits and pieces of his marriage in the last couple of weeks. She had never asked before then. It wasn't by accident.

"When you came back engaged, I thought I was going to die." She didn't like to think about that time. She didn't like to revisit it at all. Not in her own mind, much less bring it back to his.

"I hated her," she said. "I really hated her, Carson. At first. But then it turned out that she was a really nice woman. And I thought you loved her. I thought she made you happy. That meant I couldn't hate her. How could I? She gave you something no one else did. But a little over a week ago, you told me that wasn't true. And I've had to figure out what I think about that, about everything, since then." She shook her head. "I know it sounds selfish, I know it sounds bad to say that your tragedy hurt me too. But it did." She took a deep breath. "You're supposed to marry your best friend, right? So if you got married to somebody else, then I couldn't be your best friend anymore."

He grabbed hold of her arms; he held her close. He held her hard. "Perry," he said, "you were always my best friend."

"But I just knew then that nothing was ever going to happen between us. Don't you understand that? Because I think part of me always did think that we would . . . you know everybody in town kind of thought that too."

"I just didn't want to break you."

"You did." Tears fell down her cheeks. "You did. You broke me because you didn't choose me." The words were plaintive and small. "And maybe I don't have any pride. Maybe that's my problem. Because I don't even think I should be with you now. Because you didn't choose me. You chose her. And she's gone. How am I supposed to contend with that? I'm still angry, but it's tragic. I'm afraid I'm a petulant, greedy woman."

"Perry," he said. "I wanted to save you from this, from me."

"Carson, you were all I wanted. I can never . . . I can never be special enough. Oh, I hate it. I hate saying it. It sounds so small, and so ridiculous. But no one has ever put me first. My dad didn't choose to be a decent person. My mom didn't choose to make me her priority. The principal didn't think I was as important as my dad. You didn't choose me. To be your girl. The same issue keeps repeating itself, and I am thirty-two years old, so I know how immature I sound."

"I'm really sorry," he said. "I just didn't want to hurt you. I mean that. Perry, I did choose you. To be the most important person in my life. The most important. That's what you have been to me always. She wasn't . . ."

He turned away. She knew that this conversation was impossible. It felt unfair. "There was never any point in my life when I saw an example of a good marriage, one that mattered. When I met you, you were more important to me than anything else. I wanted to protect our friendship."

"But I don't understand why you got married at all."

"Because . . . it was selfish. I thought it would fix me."

"Why couldn't you have been selfish with me?"

"I don't . . . Perry," he said. "It was different with us—it always was. Alyssa was an army brat and she was from a family that . . . functioned so I knew she could help me build a life."

"I'm not good enough because my family is broken?"

"No, but I convinced myself I needed someone who at least knew what normal felt like. Who understood how I was and the cost of the military. Someone I didn't have to explain it all to. I just wanted to feel fixed. All I had to do was be that hero she wanted. And I thought I could make a stable life with her. But I still wanted to keep you. In a box over there."

Her heart was beating so fast, she thought it might burst through her chest altogether. "The women in your life don't exist just for you."

"I know. I know that. I am living with the consequences of that mistake. In the regret I feel for what that marriage did to you and to her. What it did to me. I just wanted to change the way I felt. And I thought I could do that using external forces. I was an idiot."

"I wish I could understand," she said.

"Why didn't you tell me?" he asked.

She could see that his eyes were tortured.

"Why didn't I tell you what?"

"You wanted me? Why didn't you kiss me, Perry? When we were teenagers, why didn't you?"

"Because I was scared. I was scared you would reject me. I was scared that I would ruin our friendship. I was more afraid of life without you than I was of not kissing you."

She was seized by the conviction that she had to love Carson and everything he had done, all the decisions he had made in his life. There were some hard things.

But he was hers now. And he was here.

Every gruesome step had somehow brought them here, and yes, maybe they should have done this years ago. But maybe declaring their feelings then wouldn't have protected them. She had to stop fantasizing about it. She had to stop wishing. She had to love the man as he was right here. Because that was love. And anything else was . . .

Protecting herself. That was what she had been doing. Using Carson as a shield. To protect her from any other man. Any other relationship or love. To protect her from the dysfunction in her household. To protect her even from the love that she felt for him. Because as long as she kept him out of reach, it could happen. The possibility existed. There was safety there.

She had been angry at him.

It was wretched and unfair. She was being dishonest. With herself most of all.

She had blamed him for the fact that he had never looked her way. But he was right. Why had she never told him how she felt? She had always been a pirate right along with him, fearless. But she had hidden all of her spark, all of her desires; she had accepted ice cream she didn't even want to avoid the pain of being denied the ice cream she might not be able to have.

God. What a horrendous thing to realize. She had loved her own safety more than she had loved Carson.

This anger she felt over not being picked was valid. But the way she'd let it define her every feeling for him in the years since wasn't.

She'd held a piece of herself back ever since the principal she'd trusted had made it clear to her what mattered was her father, not her.

That moment with Carson, when he'd looked at her in fury by the lake—fury she now knew was tortured, teenage desire—that had been an excuse.

She was safe as long as she wanted Carson, the man she could never have. As long as she loved him, she could never love any of the other men she slept with. There was no chance a relationship could ever overtake her. Could make her lose control.

She'd built a little house to hide all her little traumas, so she could walk around out in the world and pretend to be normal. Oh, she dated and she was just fine. Her only problem was that her best friend had her heart, but never her body. Everything else was just great.

It was a lie.

And she'd used that lie to make sure she never had to see what life would actually be like if she had Carson.

He was right.

Even in her letters, she hadn't said everything. Just in case. She was always leaving space for herself to wiggle away, just as she'd done at the lake all those years ago.

And she'd had the nerve to call *him* a coward.

She suddenly felt caged by her cowardice. She didn't want to be this version of herself. She wanted to be the pirate child who'd run barefoot with him through the weeds and screamed as she'd jumped off the swing. She wanted to be wild and free and all the things that life had taught them had too high a cost.

They'd been like Adam and Eve in Genesis. That day by the lake they'd realized they were naked—even if not literally. That he was a man and she was a woman. That they had to make decisions to protect what they were, to protect themselves.

At least that was why she had run from him.

Over the years they'd doubled down on their caution every time they'd drifted.

She wanted her wild back.

He moved to her then, his eyes intense. "Don't be scared of me."

"I'm not," she said. "I'm not. Not now. I won't be. Not ever again."

"My pirate princess," he whispered, his mouth crashing over hers.

They kissed and she gripped his shirt, dragging him down to the floor of the old house, this place he was restoring for her to sell to someone else.

This place that had housed her family, her ancestor who had come west for freedom and found passion along with it.

"I'm not a pirate princess," she said, rising up onto her knees and shifting herself so that she was straddling him as he sat back. "I'm a pirate queen. Your pirate queen. And you're mine."

He growled, moving his hand up to the back of her hair, gripping it, tugging. There was a feral light in his eyes, and she loved it. Something wild that she had never seen before. It had certainly never been directed at her. Even though their recent encounters had been passionate, this was different. It was all their history, and everything new, crashing in on each other. All their new promises, their new revelations, and all the old tarnished but beautiful things.

There was nothing and no one between them. She was done with protecting herself. She was laying it to rest. Nothing else mattered. Nothing but this. Nothing but him. Nothing but everything they could be.

She pulled his shirt up over his head and threw it onto the floor. She raked her nails down his chest, reveling in the feel of his muscles beneath her fingertips. She took her own shirt off, her bra. She pressed her body to his. She wanted him close. With nothing between them. She was the only one who had him like this. And that was the honest truth.

No one had ever known him the way she did.

He wanted to be her hero. He was already her hero. He was more than that. He was the little boy he had been in the man he had become. He was all of the painful things, all of the things that he tried to forget. All the things he'd tried to accomplish. He was everything he had ever done, and every goal he felt he'd fallen short of. To her, he was perfect. And that was all that had ever mattered. Because he had been there when she needed him.

And yes, there had been times when it had felt as if she had lost him, but part of that was her own inability to tell him what she needed. So she was going to show him now.

She kissed him. Deep and long. She ground herself against him, reveled in the feel of his heart between her legs.

"Carson," she breathed against his mouth.

"Perry."

These were their vows. They would save more formal words for their friends. His family. They would make a legal commitment to each other, and it would matter. But this, this was what was real. These were the things that really needed to be said and done between them.

He pressed his palm to the center of her back, moved over her, pressing her against the floor. He unbuttoned her pants, stripped them off, left her naked. And then he was naked too.

"Carson," she said. "I need you. Inside me. You have no idea how long I've wanted this. How long I wanted you."

"I want you too," he said. "I didn't let myself want this. I couldn't let myself want you, Perry. You're too perfect. You're too beautiful. You were everything, and I knew that I could never be enough for you."

He pressed a kiss to her collarbone, to her shoulder. Maybe he was making it up. Maybe he was trying to make it all okay now. But she didn't care. She couldn't care. Because every word he said healed something inside her.

"I'm going to be enough. I swear it," he vowed.

She nodded. She took that vow. She held it close. She let it expand inside her. Along with all the love that she felt for him.

"I used to fantasize about you," she whispered. "You were what made me realize why a kiss might be wonderful. You were the man who made me understand desire."

His elbows buckled just slightly. "I don't deserve that."

"Yes, you do. Carson Wilder, you have always been my hero."

He claimed her mouth in a deep, ferocious kiss. Consumed her. Until the flames consumed them both.

He put his hand between her thighs and began to stroke her. Carson, touching her like this. She would never get over it. No matter how many times it happened. Because she had wanted this so much in secret, and now it was out in the open. Now they were telling each other the truth.

And it was so glorious. Almost too much. He stroked her until the rest of their life flashed before her eyes. Until she was clinging to him, crying out his name.

And when he entered her, inch by inch, she put her hands on his shoulders, she met his gaze. She didn't let herself close anything off. Any feeling.

She let it be like it was the first time. For both of them. Like there had never been anyone else. Because they were Carson and Perry. And no one else was them. No one else ever would be. How could she be second, when no one else could ever be her? It was a deep, profound feeling. To allow herself to be special.

Her own fear, her own feeling of being inadequate, had hurt her. It hadn't protected her. She had kept herself in prison.

She had to let herself out. Carson couldn't do that for her. He had already said beautiful things to her. He had already made it clear that he felt a lot for her.

But he couldn't make the insecurity go away. She had to make that go away on her own. She had to stop resenting what had come before and accept everything about the man who was inside her now. The man she loved.

She gave thanks. For this moment. For who he was. She wasn't going to give thanks for all of the terrible things. The feeling of abandonment. The abuse. The things he had seen in war. The loss.

No. She wasn't going to give thanks for those. But she could give thanks for the people they were on the other side. The people they were in spite of everything. And maybe a little bit because of it. She gave thanks for how strong he was. How wonderful. How glorious.

"I love you," she whispered. And then again as he thrust deep. "I love you."

They had said that to each other before. But this time, it wasn't out of habit. Not out of routine. She hoped he understood. Because she didn't have more words. She didn't have anything more articulate at all.

They were committing themselves to each other. They were committing to a future together. So she clung to him. And she said it again. "I love you, Carson."

And when the release washed over them both, she said it like an incantation. Because she had held back for all this time. Because she hadn't really known what it meant.

She did now. It meant being brave. It meant accepting the timeline of their journey.

It meant accepting him. Everything that he was. Everything that he had been.

She loved him.

She was Perry. He was Carson.

The pirate-ship captain and his pirate queen.

And everything that they were or ever had been was something they shared. But the best part was now they were going to share everything they were ever going to be.

Perry held that truth close, because it was all the hope she had ever been looking for.

Chapter 20

I think about you all the time. We were under gunfire today—shrapnel was flying everywhere and all I could see was your face.

—A letter from Carson Wilder to Perry Bramble

He and Perry spent the night at his place, in the room he'd shared with Alyssa. Carson didn't sleep well. He sat on the edge of the bed and stared at the window until the light turned gray.

She'd said that she loved him.

He thought he might be dying of something.

Without putting much thought into it, he put his clothes on and drove over to Austin's. The life of a rancher began early, and he knew his brother would be out working already.

He wasn't disappointed.

"Howdy," Carson said as he walked into the barn.

"Hi. Why do you look like you're about to tell me you're doing more work for the enemy?"

He frowned. Oh, right. The wagon. Everybody was so upset about that damned wagon. It didn't matter to him. The Hancock family didn't matter to him. Well, he still wanted to punch West in the face a little bit. But other than that, they didn't matter.

"I need to have a talk with you about something. Something big."

"Okay. What?" Austin looked worried.

"About Perry. I don't know what . . . to do."

Austin turned his face sideways and looked at him out of the corner of his eye. "What?"

"I kissed her." He cleared his throat. "And then I slept with her. Several times."

"Lord almighty."

"Yeah. I . . . was never going to do that."

"It's about damned time, you dumb asshole," Austin said.

"What?"

"You're obsessed with her. Your life starts and stops because of her. When you married Alyssa, I figured I was wrong about that. I know you grieved Alyssa but you can't keep yourself away from Perry. She's your person."

She was his person. He knew that. He was on the verge of losing her too. On the verge of her moving and starting a different life and having babies with someone else, and it made him want to die.

"I want her," he said, and then he gave voice to what had been burning up inside him all night. "And I can't think of a good reason not to marry her."

Austin nodded, slowly. "Are you in love with her?"

Everything in him rejected the possibility, just as he hadn't been able to process her declaration of love last night.

"I don't need words with her. She's been there my whole life."

Austin squared off with him, his arms crossed over his broad chest. "Does she need the words?"

"Marrying someone else fractured my relationship with her, and Alyssa's death didn't fix it. Perry was unhappy that I married someone else and now she's wanting to leave and make a family with someone else. I have to keep her with me. I'm going to have to sort the logistics of it out after the fact."

"Carson, that is not a thing you sort out after the fact."

"She's my best friend. If I don't do something, she's going to leave. She's going to move away."

"And that's a bad thing?"

"Yes. Because I don't know what I would do without her."

"You like sleeping with her?"

"What kind of question is that?"

Austin shrugged. "It's a valid one."

"Yes. I do." That was underselling it. It was the best sex he'd ever had in his life. She blew his mind constantly. Not only was it hot, but they also laughed. They sometimes made each other shake. He had made her cry. It was everything. Just like they were. He couldn't even begin to explain it to his brother, and he wasn't going to try. That was private. It was for them.

"So, the sex is good, you can't bear the thought of not being with her . . . but you're not sure if you love her?"

"I don't even know what that means. Everyone in our family had such toxic romantic relationships."

"I'm doing okay."

"Yes. You're doing great. But . . . I've been married before. I thought I was in love before."

"Just because you have feelings for Perry now doesn't mean you weren't in love with your wife."

"You know, I wish that was what I was struggling with. I wasn't in love with my wife. And I feel awful about that. I just . . . I'm sorting through that. I don't know what to do with it. And I don't know how to feel okay about it. I'm also terrified that I'm walking into a bad situation."

Austin frowned. "You didn't love Alyssa? How the hell do you figure that?"

"I just wanted to marry someone I thought could be good for me, and I did. It was selfish as shit. I know that. It's why I've been so . . . it's why I couldn't seem to get back up again. Because all I've ever wanted is to be better than our dad, and somehow I walked myself right into being him. I used Alyssa." He shook his head, something breaking inside him. "I didn't mean to."

"Of course you didn't. You know there's a big fucking difference between what our dad did—having a wife and kids and continuing to do what he wanted—and being a man who wants to do the right thing, the good thing, and makes a mistake."

"I guess, but Alyssa knew, Austin."

"If she hadn't died, it would have been a divorce, not a tragedy."

Perry had tried to tell him that. She'd tried to tell him that

Alyssa's life didn't come down to her relationship with him, but he'd had a hard time accepting that.

This morning, though, he realized it was true.

She'd had a life, a family. There was a reason he'd let her parents bury her back in the place she called home, with her family. It was where her life would have ended if it had only ended at a different time.

He would have been just a bump in the road.

Maybe that's what she would have been for him too.

He nodded slowly. "I never wanted to be divorced either. I guess it's hard to come to terms with how much you've screwed up . . . everything. But now I just want Perry with me."

Austin sighed. "First of all, no situation with you and Perry could ever be terrible. You know her better than you know anybody else in the world."

"Yeah."

"She makes you happy."

He thought of all the years. All the games. All the kisses. All the Perry. "Yes."

"You don't have to be scared of being happy."

His brother's words felt radical. Maybe they shouldn't. They did, though.

"Perry's special. She always has been. I never wanted to protect anything in my whole life—I just wanted to protect myself. And then Perry showed up on the ranch, and I wanted to hang on to her and never let her go. I also thought she should probably run away. But I didn't want her to."

"I know what we went through as kids was tough but . . ."

"What you are you talking about?" Carson asked.

"Mom leaving."

"She did what she had to do. I'm not happy about it. But I—"

"You can't tell me that's not what you see. Whenever somebody leaves."

He gritted his teeth. "I've always figured I needed to be different from Dad. Because women left Dad."

"That's true."

"I want to be the opposite. I want to be Perry's hero."

Suddenly, he felt different. Different than he had since Alyssa's death. He had given up. On everything. And he had decided that he was just going to try to live in the moment. But that wasn't enough for Perry.

He wanted to give her everything. He wanted to be Perry's hero.

"Carson . . ."

"This is going to be . . . it's maybe what should've happened all along. We fit. It makes sense. I'm going to tell her that."

"I'd caution you that she might want more romance than this," Austin said.

Austin didn't know Perry; Carson did. Because of that special connection. One that Carson didn't know how to put into words. But soon he would have a word for it. Perry was Perry. His best friend. The person he'd always known. The one who had always been there. And soon she would be his wife. He'd had a wife before. But the word would mean something different when it was Perry.

"You don't know her like I do," Carson said. "She wants safety and security, and I can give her that."

Austin gave him a long look. "If you say so."

"If she'll have me, I guess I have a wedding to plan. Are you up for being best man?"

Austin smiled. "I've never been the *best* man. But I'll always be your best man."

Chapter 21

My heart almost exploded when I read that you were shot at. I need you to come home to me, or I'll never be home anywhere. What would I do without my hero?

—*A letter from Perry Bramble to Carson Wilder*

Perry wished that she had someone to talk to about what had happened. About what was changing. She only had Carson. And that was sort of her eternal problem. So when Carson walked into the florist shop right after she closed, she felt relieved, and of course a little scared, because her friend was the one she was having a whole situation about.

Her friend was the one she'd said *I love you* to, and he hadn't said anything back.

Still, she just wanted to be with him.

He opened up the door, and there was a tension on his face that she couldn't quite read. There was definitely something on his mind.

"Hi," she said.

"Hi," he said as he went to her, his mouth crashing down on hers, the kiss so deep and hard, it made her lose her breath.

"Very hi," she said, her heart fluttering.

Maybe there was nothing to worry about. Or at the very least, no real problem to solve.

"Let's go for a walk, Perry."

"A walk?"

"Yes. I want . . . I need to talk to you."

Her heart did freeze then, right in her chest, and she wasn't sure she wanted to walk on the street where anyone could see them, not when she didn't know what he was going to say.

But she took his hand and let him lead her out of the florist shop, down the street toward the house that she was still planning to sell.

There was a large hedge in front, with flowers on it, and he stopped and picked one, turning and tucking it behind her ear. Just as he had done down by Outlaw Lake, when he had almost kissed her, but didn't. This time, he wrapped his arms around her and pulled her in for a kiss. It was long, leisurely.

"Oh," she breathed when they parted.

"I keep giving you flowers that are probably just weeds to you," he said.

"No," she said. "I grow flowers. I make bouquets for people. You know, no one ever gives them to me. Except for you." He looked stunned by that. "That's what makes flowers beautiful, you know. That somebody thought to give them to you."

"I'm going to keep giving you flowers," he said, his voice rough. And that felt the closest thing to a promise that anyone had ever made her.

Her heart was pounding hard. She felt dizzy. This was so sweet and beautiful. And almost everything. Almost.

"I need to talk to you about something important," he said.

"What's that?" He looked so grave, and that wasn't him. Not usually. But last night, what had passed between them had been something beyond friendship, beyond passion. She had given words to it, but he hadn't.

Last night, things had shifted irrevocably. At least inside her. She was ready. She was ready to move forward. There was so much garbage in her past. She hadn't chosen to grow up the way she had, she hadn't chosen a great many things, but she had chosen to live holding pain to her chest. She had chosen to hide parts of herself, and she just didn't want to do that anymore.

"I want to marry you," he said suddenly.

She felt as if the wind had been knocked out of her. "You what?"

"I mean it." He looked so sincere. Bright-eyed with his intensity. Her best friend. Telling her that he wanted to marry her. He was standing there next to that flower bush, looking like the whole world, and she didn't know what the hell she was supposed to do with that.

"I thought you didn't want to get married again."

"This is different. This isn't just two people deciding to get married. Perry, we share so much. So many years. So many changes. So much of who we are. I have never wanted to protect or care for anyone as much as I want to care for you. I made some decisions about how to go about that and they were wrong. Because this probably should've happened years ago. It should've been us. Let me give you this huge ring. Let me give you a good life."

"Oh . . ."

"Please. Be my wife. And my Perry. The way you have been. And I'm going to be the man you need me to be. I promise. I'm going to be someone you can be proud of."

"Carson. You have always been mine. You've always been a man that I could be proud of. You."

He cut her off, kissing her. Hard and deep. And then they parted, and with shaking hands he put the ring on her finger. She clung to him. "I . . ."

Something held her back. Something made it hard for her to speak. She should tell him again that she loved him. Because she did. He spoke with casual ease; he always had. But not her, because it was so bound up in other feelings.

"But I . . . I'm leaving Rustler Mountain."

"Don't leave."

"What?"

"Or let me go with you. I don't care."

"But that's not . . . don't . . . you don't want to get married again," she repeated. "You said it yourself. You said that you didn't want to get married again," she said, recalling the words he'd said to her at the beginning of all this.

"I know. But I changed my mind. Because this is how I can take care of you, and I want to do it. No holding each other back, no codependency. We can have a wedding. A big wedding in a church. Or we could get married down by the lake where we met. I don't care. I don't care where the fuck we get married, as long as we do."

"Why?"

"Because I need you," he said.

His voice was so guttural, so sincere. She didn't doubt it for a single moment. He drew her close, cupped her face with his hands. "I will give you whatever you want. I will give you whatever fucking thing you want, Perry. Anything."

"Love me," she said.

Because it was as simple as that. As simple and as impossible as that. It was the one thing she had never asked for. It was the one thing that she knew she needed to push for. Yes. Loving him meant loving him in spite of the decisions that he had made in the past. Loving him with an acceptance of those things. But that didn't mean she had to accept less than she deserved. It didn't mean that she had to accept less than what she truly wanted, which was for Carson to love her as wildly and madly and deeply as she loved him. She wasn't hiding anymore. Now that she had made that decision, she couldn't.

There was no way. She couldn't possibly hold herself back. She couldn't possibly keep herself from saying what she wanted now. What she needed.

"Perry I . . ."

"Carson, I told you. I said it to you last night, and you didn't say anything back to me. I love you."

"I do love you," he said.

"I know. You tell me that. But not the way I want you to mean it. Carson, I love you. I think I . . . I think I always have. It wasn't until I was sure that I could love you without hanging on to the things I was upset about that I felt I could say it. But I finally did. You married Alyssa, and I'm okay with that. You had feelings for her first. But . . ."

"Perry . . . I can't do that. I already told you that. I'm not built for that kind of love. I'm not built for anything of the kind."

"No. That's not true."

"It is. And if they were just words, Perry, I would give them to you. If all they were was words, I would just say them. Because I have said them. To her, to you. I said them. But the thing I cannot do, the thing I will not do, is lie. I won't say *yes* imagining that I'm going to sort all of it out later. I just won't. I won't say that I'll marry you and promise you things I don't know I can give. But I know that I want us to be forever. I need you with me. Whatever that looks like, whatever we call it. And I'll spend my lifetime sorting all of that out. I swear it. But I'm not going to lie to you."

She felt . . . devastated. This was not what she had hoped for. Not ever. And this was why she had never said anything before. The truth was, she hadn't been strong enough back then to weather this. Oh, poor young Perry, this would've killed her.

Thirty-two-year-old Perry wasn't a fan, but when she had made the decision to love Carson with all of herself, she had also sworn she would walk away if she had to.

It wasn't her. She wasn't the problem. Before, she had believed she might be. Maybe she wasn't good enough. Important enough. But standing there, looking at Carson, one of the most wonderful men she had ever known, telling her that he couldn't love, she realized that the world was just a broken place.

It was broken, and that was why her father behaved the way he did. It was broken, and that was why her mother fought for a love that only hurt her. It was broken, and that was why her principal had made it clear that her father was more important than Perry. That what he did for work, who he was in the community, mattered more than the safety of a little girl.

The world was broken. And that was why Carson didn't know what the feelings inside him meant, and worse, didn't want to have them because they scared him.

He wanted to be an invulnerable mountain, and she was asking him to do the one thing that frightened him.

"I don't need you to be a hero," she said.

"I have to be," he said.

"No. I never needed that from you. You are enough for me all on your own."

"You don't know what you're saying. I . . . I'm not good enough."

"I do. I was your best friend while you were running around kicking up trouble in town. I was your best friend while you were getting in bar fights. I know that you're human. I love you all the same. I don't need you to do this thing that you're trying to do, where you act like a locked box. I don't need it. *You* need it."

It occurred to her then, how true that was. He was the one who needed to be invulnerable. And it kept on hurting him. But he didn't see it. Because it felt like protection. She could relate to that. Keeping her feelings for him to herself had felt like protection too.

She had to wonder if she had created this situation. What if she had told him how she felt when they were younger? What if she had made him feel safer about love all the way back then? What if he hadn't felt the need to go into the military? To scar himself with all the things he'd seen. What if he hadn't felt the need to marry somebody else? What if her love had simply been enough? She would never know. She could never go back and fix it. She could never, ever. She could only move forward.

And she had to stop trying to protect herself. No matter how hard it was.

"I've always loved you," she said. "I loved you while you were away, I loved you the whole time you were married to somebody else. I loved you."

"I don't deserve this," he said. "How can you have loved me all that time? I was a bad husband to Alyssa, Perry. And I don't want to be a bad husband to you. I'll . . . We'll be us. But I don't know how to be anything other than me."

"You're holding something back."

"I have to," he said.

"Not with me. Why don't you trust me?"

"It's not you, Perry. I don't trust the world. I can't. How can I?

Because I went overseas to try to fix things. And all I saw was what a mess it all is. Because I got married, and I brought that woman back here. That good woman, who needed me to be something I couldn't be. Who was going to leave me, because I wasn't right for her in the end. She died my unhappy wife. Because I wasn't enough. And that is how unfair the world is. But we are already a couple—why does it have to be something more? I just . . ."

"You know why it has to be more, or you wouldn't ask me to marry you. You just keep on having sex with me and calling me your best friend. You know why it has to be more. You're just turning away from . . . I don't even know. Like you said, if it's only words, why do they terrify you so much? If it's only words, then why can't you just say them?"

"Because. Because there was a point where Alyssa wanted me to say certain things, and I tried. And that was why she stayed with me and was miserable. And I . . . I want you to marry me, but I also . . . I just thought you knew me well enough to know what I could offer you. So now I'm standing here feeling like a jackass because you—"

"No. Don't put this on me. You know me. Why would you think that I would marry you without even the slightest bit of assurance that you love me? That you could love me."

"I do. As my best friend in the entire world. As the woman that I—"

"It's not even the words, Carson. Not really. It's that I don't want you to keep part of yourself locked away. Because you know what, I think you do love me. But the problem is that you swerve every time we get close."

The minute she said that, she realized it was true. "Because what were the letters? Those letters you wrote me from war—they were so different from everything else that you ever said to me. What did they mean? What did they mean if they weren't leading to your saying that you love me?"

"Perry I could never . . . I knew that I could never—"

"You could never, but here you are. So what is it you're running from? Why do you keep getting so close and then throwing a bomb in the middle of it? I don't understand. I don't understand. And I need you to figure that out. Before I can marry you. Before I can tell you that I'm not going to move away. I love you so much, and that was why I had to leave. That's the honest truth. I'm sorry I didn't tell you that. I'm sorry I didn't look you dead in the face that night at your kitchen table and say I can't share my pizza crust with you anymore because I love you and it's killing me. Because every time I breathe your air, it is making me die inside. Because I want us to be more. Because I want us to be everything. I was too scared to say that. Because I was so scared that I felt it. It is terrifying. This whole thing is terrifying."

"Then why? Why are we doing any of it? This has been good. This has been really good, and I don't understand why you want to fuck it up, Perry. Why?"

"Because I didn't wake up yesterday and realize this about us. I've known it. I have had over twenty years of pushing it down. Of trying to be different. Of trying to feel different. You just showed up at the party, what . . . a couple of weeks ago? When I decided to do something that you didn't approve of. Something that made you feel like you were losing your hold on me. Because you're okay not loving me as long as I'm within reach. That's what worries you: Can you get to me when you need me? And that isn't fair to me. I changed the game, and so you realized you had to do something. But the problem is that I know you." She felt as if she was dying, as if her chest was going to explode.

She wiped at her cheeks, and she was devastated to realize that tears weren't falling. It felt as though they should be. It felt as though she should be dissolving from the inside.

"I know you well enough to know that what you really want is that twelve-step program toward getting your life settled. And you like to collect the markers so you can see if you're doing all the right things, stacking them up in all the right ways. You see proposals and marriage licenses and military service as the ways to put your life right. I don't want to be one of your markers. I would marry you in a field. With no papers. With nothing but vows. In many ways, I did that years ago. With all the love in my heart. But until you can feel that, until you can really, truly let your guard down, with me, with anyone, we can't have it. Everybody thought you were grieving your wife so intensely that you couldn't be reached, but you just wanted us to think that because you didn't want to have to explain yourself. Because you didn't want to have to talk about how fucked up your feelings are."

"They're a mess," he said, nearly exploding there on the public street, where anyone could see them. Where anyone could hear them. "If I cut my chest open and showed you what my feelings look like, you would run a mile. Because everything just feels messed up. Everything I try to do. Everything I try to care about. And I never wanted to involve you. Not ever. But here we are. So I can offer you marriage. I can keep you with me. I could be the father of your children."

"Be the love of my life," she said. "I don't know what you're holding back. I don't have a crystal ball. I don't have magic insight into your soul. I just know that you're holding something back. You have to figure out what. You have to. For us. Because I'll walk away."

"You're going to punish me because I can't heal on command?"

That hurt. It was like a sword, driven straight through her midsection. "That isn't fair. I've been here for twenty-five years. And I have tried. I have tried so many ways with you. And you have tried so many ways without me. Running off to the military. Coming home with another woman. It's always you trying to fix all of this without including me. And right now, this is the first time that you have actually tried to figure out how we can fit together. Not just me being put on ice. Not me being on hold for you. This is the first time that you have ever tried to make you and me work. So I'm sorry that you're not getting your way immediately. I'm sorry that it didn't come together right away. You have no idea. But I have been trying for years."

She sighed, took a breath. And that breath, painful and still, reminded her of why she couldn't say yes right now. What she believed was that she and Carson Wilder were meant to be together. Yes, she had run from it. But he had run all the harder. And now she had to stand her ground, because she could not let them continue to repeat these mistakes. Because they would. They would be together, but they would find themselves unhealthy. They would find themselves broken. They would find themselves unable to be what they needed each other to be. And she didn't want that. She wanted to marry the love of her life, knowing that she was the love of his. She wanted all the dark corners of him. All the things that he had spent all these years protecting her from. She believed that taking this stand would push him. But it was breaking her.

"My greatest sin was not being brave enough when I was eleven. To tell you that I loved you. Not being brave enough when I was sixteen to kiss you when you scowled at me like that in my see-through dress. Actually, I did tell you how I really felt in a letter, but it was returned as undeliverable. My greatest sin was not showing you that letter when you came home. It was not telling you before you got married that I didn't want you to. It was not risking my heart so that we could have it all. But I'm risking it now. It's all or it's nothing."

"Perry..."

She turned and started to walk away, and he grabbed hold of her arm. "I think I might die without you."

"Don't do that. Figure out how to live with me."

She inhaled, deep, jagged. And then she did the hardest thing she'd ever done in her life: She walked away from Carson Wilder and his proposal.

Because she deserved the world. She was going to wait until he gave it to her. Because the simple truth was, he deserved the world too. And someone had to be strong enough to make him claim it.

She went back to the cabin, and she packed a bag. She opened up her little wooden Carson box and took everything out of it, all the things she'd saved all those years.

She held them, turned them over.

Will u go to the woods w/me after school? Y or N circle.

Her heart crumpled. She sobbed as she dug through her underwear. She wasn't going to bring everything, she just needed to get some space tonight. She knew he would come after her.

She was weak. She would go with him.

She needed to be strong.

And in the bottom of the drawer she was digging in, she found the letter.

To Carson Wilder, returned as undeliverable.

The letter that had missed him.

She held it and stroked the closed envelope. She'd said it all now. And it had amounted to nothing. She carried the letter into the kitchen and stopped when she saw Mae's second diary sitting there on the counter. She hadn't read it because she'd been so caught up in her life with Carson that she just . . . hadn't.

She tucked it under her arm and set the unopened envelope down on the counter. She touched the other envelopes there, the letters.

She heard an engine and startled, half hoping it was Carson, half dreading, because who else came up here?

She looked out the window and saw Cassidy's truck.

Cassidy pulled up to the front and Perry held her breath. Then Cassidy came to the door and Perry realized she couldn't ignore her. Not now.

She opened it right before Cassidy knocked. "Oh," Cassidy said. "Hi."

"Hi. I just . . . I wanted to say I'm sorry for being mean to you. About leaving. And that I was weird about you kissing my brother."

She sighed. "Come on in."

Cassidy did, and Perry went to the counter, shuffling her envelope addressed to Carson down to the bottom of the other envelopes because she didn't need Cass spotting it and commenting.

"He's in love with you. I mean, Flynn thinks so. So does Dalton."

Perry nodded slowly. "I kind of think so too. But he doesn't want to deal with it."

Cassidy frowned. "Oh. What the hell?"

"Emotional damage, I think," said Perry.

"Well, that's . . . that's stupid. Did he break your heart?"

Cassidy looked so outraged on her behalf, it genuinely warmed her.

"He did, actually. But you know what? I love him. I always have. And that isn't going to change because of this. Same as it won't change how I feel about you and your family."

"It changes how I feel about him," Cassidy said. "I'm going to put a snake in his boot."

"You don't need to do that. But . . . I'm going to lay low for a couple of days. I'm trying to trust that he'll come around because . . . if any couple is meant to be, I think we might be."

"I don't know that I believe in all that," Cassidy said. "But I know that what you have is special, and if I ever fall in love, I want to have that kind of thing. A friendship that becomes more. It seems like the right way to do it, the real way. I want Carson to choose to get his head out of his ass and choose you."

"Me too, Cass. Me too." She sighed. "He asked me to marry him, but he couldn't say he loved me. And I refuse to settle for less. For both our sakes."

Cassidy looked at her, and her smile shocked Perry. "You really are a badass, Perry Bramble. It takes a lot to force a man to stew in his own juices."

Perry held that close.

Mae Tanner had gone west for a new life. She'd done the hard thing.

Perry was doing the hard thing too.

She was going to hold out for what spoke to her soul. Hold out for it all.

When you knew the whole Wild West was out there, how could you ever settle for less?

Chapter 22

I'll come home to you, I promise. Now you know it's true, and so do I. I would never break a promise to you, pirate princess.

—*A letter from Carson Wilder to Perry Bramble*

Carson didn't know what had happened. He felt like he had been gutted. Like he had been left to bleed out on the streets of Rustler Mountain. He couldn't make sense of it.

It was . . .

He didn't know how to give Perry what she was asking for. He . . .

You do. But you're scared of what it will cost you.

He knew that he had to keep a piece of himself protected or when he lost the people he cared for, he'd fall apart. He would never again be a helpless child who had been too much for his own mother to handle.

He knew he had to be a hero, or he ruined everything he touched. His childhood, his marriage . . .

He knew . . .

There were reasons. There were reasons that he had done all of these things. And he . . . he couldn't think of a damn one right then.

He found himself driving to Austin's house. Because if anybody would understand, it was his brother. Because his brother was the one who had experienced the same loss that he had when they were children.

He knew what it was like to live in absolute despair when you lost the one parent you thought maybe loved you.

Austin had somehow healed and fallen in love and got married, and Carson didn't know how to do that. He had gone through the motions once. Now he was doing it again, and he didn't know what set those motions apart from feeling. Except that he didn't have Perry . . .

He couldn't breathe. He felt like he was bleeding.

He showed up at the front of the house clutching his chest.

"Have you been shot?" Austin asked as he jerked the door open.

"I fucking feel like I have," he said.

His hands were shaking. Jesus.

He hadn't even shaken like this when he'd had to walk out of the hospital without Alyssa. Which made him feel guilty all over again because of how he'd failed her. He'd tried. And Perry had had the nerve to look him right in the eye when he made a marriage proposal to her and tell him that he still wasn't enough.

The problem was *her*. The problem was her and her inability to recognize that what they had was good enough. That what they had mattered. That was the problem. She was the problem.

"*She's* the problem," he said.

"Perry?"

"Damn right. I proposed to her. She turned me down."

"Why?"

"Because I'm not in love with her."

"We had that whole conversation, and your takeaway was to propose and tell her you don't love her?"

"No. That I'm not *in love*. I don't even know what that is. I don't even know . . ."

"You're unhinged. Sit down."

"What does that mean? I have been her best friend all her life."

"Which means you should have known that offering to marry her without offering her your heart was going to blow up in your face."

He growled. "Offering her something I can't actually give her will blow up in *my* face?"

"Look at yourself. You think you don't love her?"

"I'm afraid I can't feel love. Not the way that other people do. And I won't lie to her."

Austin stared him down, as only an older brother could. "Are you afraid you can't feel love, or afraid that you will?"

He frowned. "I don't understand what you mean by that."

"You're afraid of how strong it is, and you're trying to protect yourself."

"I wanted to protect *her* from *this*."

"From you? From you sitting here bleeding out over her rejecting you? This isn't about you not feeling enough, asshole. I think you're protecting yourself. And I get it. I did not want to fall in love with Millie. I had a whole lot of excuses about how the town saw me. How everyone saw our family. But they were just that—excuses. Our childhood was really tough. It doesn't exactly set you up for success. And on top of that, you know so much about how vulnerable Perry was as a kid. I'm not surprised at all that your inclination is to protect her."

Carson pressed his palm to his chest, to the devastated wound he felt there. "I'm worried something is dead. Inside me."

"That you worry about it tells me everything I need to know." Austin huffed a laugh. "Our dad never worried about how he treated us. Our mom left us without a backward glance. You're neither one of them." He paused for a moment. "And you're in love with her."

"If that were true, wouldn't she know it? She wouldn't have turned me down, because she would have sensed that I was in love with her."

"No, you dumb fuck. That's not the issue. The issue is that you're going to have to explain to her why it never happened before. Why you married somebody else, and how the way you feel for *her* is different."

"I . . ." He started trying to take a full breath and found that he could. "I don't have any idea what to say to that. I really don't."

"I think you do. It's not so much what's happening now. It's that you have to repair the things that came before. Because I'm just going to tell you, as your older brother, I think she's always been the one. I thought for a long time maybe you just didn't feel romantic about her. But I think anyone who knows you recognizes that Perry is your soulmate, whatever form that takes. So yeah, I thought for a while there that maybe for the two of you that meant friendship. But when you told me that you'd slept with her . . . Listen, it's none of my business, but I'm confused. Did the physical attraction for her pop up after or . . ."

"I didn't want to feel it. I didn't want to have it because . . . she would . . . wreck me. And I knew that. I fucking knew it, Austin. I knew beyond a shadow of a doubt that loving that woman would destroy me.

"I didn't want to ever lose Perry. I look at how Dad was, with women, with everything. I tried . . ."

"You tried to think your way into things that aren't logical. You tried to think your way into winning at life, but that's the problem. It's messy, and it's full of feelings. Think about it. When you go to restore an old building, or a hope chest, or a wagon, you don't know what you're getting into until you actually get down to the substance of it, right?"

He gritted his teeth. "Maybe."

"No maybe. It's true. Because I've heard you talk about it. So if you were to go over to the old Wilder building right now, you could take a cursory look around the place and make a plan, but until you actually started gutting it, you wouldn't really know how much work there was to do."

"True enough," he said.

"That's life, little brother. You can know things, and you can know what you want. But you can never outsmart the part of living that is feeling. Not ever. 'Cause that's just how it works. By trying to stay a step ahead of those feelings, you're fixing the wrong things. Sometimes you have to open up the walls and . . . take a chance."

"That's a bad metaphor, because you don't even know what you're looking for inside the walls."

"No, I don't. But you do. So you know what I'm trying to say."

"I . . ."

The truth was, he knew exactly what his brother was trying to say. And he also knew that it lined up with exactly what he had been feeling. That in his bid to fix things, he had broken them. That in his desire to be a good man, what he had really been trying to do was be a safe man. Because he had seen something in Perry from the moment he had locked eyes on her—he had seen . . . fate. That thing he tried so hard not to believe in. Soulmates . . . he had never wanted to believe that was true. Because it would mean there was just one person out there for you, and if you messed it up, you could never be happy.

And if he couldn't be enough for Perry, and he lost her, then he would be nothing.

He had deliberately chosen the easier things. Without realizing it. He had chosen the military because it had been easier than staying in Rustler Mountain and trying to build his restoration business, trying to show that he was good through the work of his hands. He had decided to do it by being a soldier. By wearing a uniform that everyone esteemed.

And he had . . .

Perry wasn't wrong about the letters. The letters.

She had said that she'd sent him one that hadn't been opened.

It made him feel like such an ass. He hadn't opened it because he had started dating Alyssa. They had gotten engaged so fast because it felt imperative, because part of him had known . . .

All this time, he had been putting obstacles in front of asking Perry Bramble to be his wife, and he had been running out of excuses. Running out of reasons.

Maybe that was the real reason he went into the military. To run away. So that he didn't have to face the truth about loving her. About wanting her.

Maybe that was the substance of it.

He felt all the color drain from his face. All the blood drain from his body.

"You've been lying to yourself for a long time, I think," said Austin.

"What should I do?"

"I think that's the thing: You have to start being honest. Brutally honest. With yourself, with Perry. You have to. Anything less is doing her a disservice. Anything less is what got you here in the first place. If you weren't trying to protect yourself, what would you have done?"

"I have to think about it."

"Then think about it. But you've already had twenty-five years. So don't keep thinking too long." Carson felt . . . undone. Austin reached out and put his hand on his shoulder. "You made some mistakes. Join the club. Maybe you weren't always a hero. The question is, what are you going to do with that? There are things that you can't make amends for, and I get that. But you have to live. You have to let go."

"But . . . if I don't . . . I don't have to change anything."

"Life is change, little brother. I'm sorry to say."

Carson thought that was bullshit.

Chapter 23

You write beautifully. I am honored to get to know this part of your soul.

—*A letter from Mae Tanner to her husband, Jedidiah Tanner, passed in their own home*

Perry lay on the floor of her old bedroom, wrapped in a sleeping bag, Mae's diary tucked up against her chest.

It was so much more than old-timey porn.

Mae wrote stunning entries about how she could connect with Jedidiah's body, but how his heart seemed closed off. She begged him for more every night with her kiss.

They were married already, bound together, and she was living in the shadow of another woman. Perry's heart ached for her.

Perry was angry she'd left the letters on the counter, because she knew they were important. Because Mae started to reference them in her diary.

He shares his heart best in writing.

Perry could relate.

She could also relate to the push and pull, the way Mae's husband would give and then take back.

The diary ended abruptly, with no resolution, and Perry screamed into the empty void of the house.

How could it end like that? With her not knowing?

How could Perry find the map to her own happy ending, if she couldn't even find it in the lives of her ancestors?

She lowered her head to her pillow and cried for a lonely woman who had slept in this house pining for a man she feared could never love her back.

As she did the same thing a hundred and twenty-five years later.

Chapter 24

You're a fool, and I hope you know it. But I will answer you: Love is what we have already been doing. Every day.

—*A letter from Mae Tanner to her husband, Jedidiah Tanner, passed in their own home*

Carson turned and walked out of his brother's house, then drove over to the cabin, because Perry was his person. He needed her. No matter what. But when he got there, she wasn't inside. It was late in the evening, and she wasn't there. No purse, no driver's license. He went into her bathroom and saw that her makeup case wasn't sitting on the vanity as it had been the nights when he'd stayed here. Some of her things were still here, but some were definitely packed up. Like she was halfway gone.

On shaking legs, he went into the kitchen.

And he saw them. The stack of letters he'd found in the wall of her house. He picked up one of the letters that had the name Mae written on the front.

> Dear Mae,
> I'm not a man of words. Even in writing I struggle with them. But it's better to do it this way than it is to do it face-to-face. I was a failure of a husband to my wife. She was a good mother to my children, and I grieve what I could not give her. I find myself afraid that I won't be able to give you what you need either. You have filled this place with so much warmth. And you have warmed my bed better than anyone. My body aches for

you. But it's my heart . . . That's what I don't know how to handle.
　Your husband,
　Jedediah

An eerie echo from the past. Carson had worked on the Victorian. The house that this couple had lived in a hundred and twenty-five years ago. They were people, just as he was. And they had worried about the same things he and Perry did. He had always found comfort in the past because of the way it spoke to how life simply kept going on. But this . . . this echo of his own pain was . . . it was terrifying.

Had men been so frightened of their own hearts through all of history?

He opened up the next letter.

Dear Mae,
　I don't deserve the gift you gave me. Your body. The sweet words. I couldn't give them back to you—they froze inside me. This is not what I want to be. And yet it's thirty years of habits that I don't know how to break. They don't teach men how to give words to feelings. They teach us how to build a house, how to hunt for food. But not this. And I feel like we could all die of starvation because of it. In our souls. Does that make sense?

Yes. It did make sense. He had doubled down on being tough. He had doubled down on being a hero. Because it was better than being a victim. Because it was better than wishing you were dead because you didn't have your mother.

　They don't teach you how to sit with pain. With your own mistakes. And yet here I am baptized in mine. I might love you, Mae. I'm not rightly sure I know what it means, except the first time that I saw you, I felt you were mine.

Mine.

The first time you touched me, I thought I was going to go up in flames. When you gave me your body, I knew that I wanted to honor it, cherish it like nothing ever before. Maybe that's love. Will you give me this lifetime to figure that out? Perhaps you can tell me what it is.

Love,
Jedediah

Except Perry wasn't giving him a lifetime to figure it out.
Perry has already given you a lifetime.
The words stung. And he picked up the next letter, the last letter.

Dearest Mae,
I'm writing you this letter twenty years after the last one. We've learned to talk since then. I lived a life before you, but I can barely recall it. Because my heart began to beat the moment we met. You taught me to love you, and that was a gift. I could tell you these words now. I don't need to write them anymore. But I like the permanence of putting pen to paper and leaving the mark of my heart behind.

I love you, and I don't question it. Not in the slightest. I love you, and I know what that means. Through children, small and now grown. Through life, both happy and sad. All those vows that they have you say before the preacher, I understand them now. But I made those vows to another woman, and never really understood. Not in truth. I understood the struggle of marriage. I understood the duty of it, but I did not understand the honor. Now I understand the joy. Of sharing the good and the bad. Of sharing all that we are. Now I understand that there is no darkness so vast it can swallow up the light of our love.

I do not know why I feared it so. Yes, love is a fearsome thing. With the power to knock my feet out from under me. But without it, I didn't truly understand what it meant to have my feet beneath me.

It is only by accepting the danger of it, the terror of it, that

I have truly learned to live. If the Lord allows me to love you for twenty more years, I will consider it the greatest gift of my life.
  Love, your husband,
  Jedediah

He stared at that letter. Marveled at its perspective. The things this man had learned in the years between one letter and the next.

There was a lifetime contained between those two letters.

Events that Carson himself could only guess at without knowing the whole story. And he realized he didn't need to.

He realized he was looking for guarantees in places where he couldn't find them. And when he couldn't have those guarantees, he had been looking for safety. He had been running from the one certain thing, because he knew the power of it. He was never going to get a guarantee. He was simply going to have to accept that this thing between himself and Perry had always been there. It had the power to devastate, the power to destroy. And also the power to let him live a happier life than he had ever before imagined.

There was one last letter there in the stack. But it was not to Mae Tanner.

It was to Carson Wilder. Returned to sender nearly four years ago.

Dear Carson,
  When you sent me that letter about how close you came to dying, I thought I was going to die.
  I need you with me. I need you to live. I love you. I love you. You are the most important thing to me. You have been from the day we met. My hero in every way. I'm lost without you here. It doesn't matter how many other men I try to date. How many I try to care about. I'm afraid you're the standard. I'm not sure where that leaves me. Except that I miss you. And when you come home, I don't want things to change. I want us to keep talking like this. I want us to see where this takes us.
  Love,
  Perry

He felt as if his heart was going to explode. And through the lens of that letter, he saw himself clearly.

He saw what he'd been missing. In his lack of bravery, his unwillingness to risk himself, his heart, he had missed Perry.

Their whole relationship was this unopened letter. She had tried. He had run.

He had to find Perry. He could call her. But he had an inkling of where she might be. And he was going to follow it.

Chapter 25

You write even more beautifully than you make love, and that is truly a feat. Was it brave of me to come west? Or was this always the path to you, a glowing thread that led me from the safety of Boston to the wilds of Oregon, to you? It is fate, I suppose, of a kind. But it could never have happened without the first step I made toward you. Nor could it have happened if you hadn't then run toward me.

—A letter from Mae Tanner to her husband, Jedidiah Tanner, on their second anniversary, left on his pillow

Perry was curled in a ball, exhausted from weeping and feeling pathetic. She had said everything. She had taken the chance. And now he was going to have to figure it out. She couldn't do it for him. She couldn't.

There was a hard, heavy knock on the door downstairs, and she nearly jumped out of her skin.

She felt relief wash over her. Because there was only one person it could be.

Her trust in him, in them, had been rewarded.

She scrambled out of her sleeping bag and clattered down the stairs. Then she jerked the door open and saw him standing there. His eyes were glittering, the emotion in their depths raw. "I have messed up so many times."

"Carson . . ."

"I can't even begin, Perry. I don't know where to start."

"The beginning."

"I was such a wild kid. I thought my mom loved me, no matter what. Those were the two true things about me before I met you. And then my mom left. I realized that there was something wrong with me. With how I was. I felt hollowed out, so lonely, so . . . useless. And I never wanted to feel that way again."

He took a deep breath. "Then I met you. And this feeling burst inside me, this certainty. That you were mine. I wanted it to mean a thousand other things, a thousand other things than what it did. What it has always meant. I spent a lifetime running from the certainty of us. From the . . . our fate. And you're right. Every time you got close, I turned away. When I could see through your dress that time down by the lake . . . I was so glad that you ran, because if you hadn't, I might've lost my head. I doused myself in the cold water for a different reason that day. Damn. And then . . . when you started writing to me . . . you were a window into a life that I wanted, one I didn't think I could have. Not safely. Not with you. So I met somebody else, and I decided to marry her. She needed me, and I needed . . . something that didn't terrify me."

He took a breath. "Because I thought marrying someone else would make you . . . manageable." The word broke, his voice broke. "I didn't want you to be bigger than everything—bigger than the sky, bigger than my heart. I didn't want it. Because that level of emotion terrifies me. I can feel it. I wanted it to drown in that lake along with me, but failing that, I hoped that I had left it behind. And then there was you."

He shook his head. "There was you. And I strong-armed fate every which way I could. I dragged other people into it. I hurt them. I hurt you. Do you know . . . ?" He looked up, and she knew there were tears in his eyes. "The last fight that Alyssa and I had, she said the biggest problem was she knew that I could give more, because I gave to you. She said it was clear that I cared about you more than I did her." He took a breath, as if he was surfacing from the lake even then. "I was so angry. So . . . so fucking angry, because I vowed that I was never going to be a cheater. I wasn't going to be like my dad. Not ever. I promised that. I swore it. But I was unfaithful in my heart. I never imagined kissing you or having sex with you. But there was a part of my heart that always belonged to you. I tried so hard to protect myself because I was so afraid if I loved you, I'd disappoint you eventually and I'd lose you. It was the one thing I didn't think I could live with."

He shook his head. "It would've been us, Perry. In the end. My marriage was going to end, sooner or later. Because you are the one for me. You are the love of my life, and I ran from that so far, so fast, and so hard that I put us through all this hell. And I'm sorry. I'm sorry that it took me this long, that I took so many detours."

She hadn't been sure what she'd expected, but it wasn't that. It wasn't hearing that part of him had felt the certainty from the beginning. And she'd had no idea of the devastation he'd felt as a small boy.

"Carson," she whispered. "It was never your job to save everyone. You were doing your best.

"When we were little," she said, "I knew that I loved you with all my heart, and I didn't know that friends and lovers were two different things. When I became aware of that, I got scared. And I understood you might not feel the same way. That was when I started hiding my feelings. It was when I started trying to date other men. I always thought of it like ice cream."

"What now?"

"You have a favorite flavor of ice cream?"

"Sure."

"And you're *my* favorite flavor. But I couldn't have you. So I settled for the flavors I could get easily. But they were never you. I didn't marry any of them, but it . . . it's the same kind of thing. It was wanting to protect myself, wanting to protect what we had. But . . . I always wanted this. I always wanted your love."

"You always had it. I'm just such an idiot. Such a coward. I've made some peace with the mistakes I made with Alyssa. But it's tough. One thing I'm certain of, though, is the depth of my feeling for you. It scares the hell out of me." He took a deep breath. "I read your letter. The one I didn't get. I think part of me knew it was coming. And that's why . . . Perry, all I was doing was trying to put obstacles in the way of being with you. Because being with you terrified me. If I had you and I lost you, I don't know what I would've done. I still don't know. But I also read . . . I read the letters between Mae and her husband. I know he built this house for another woman initially, but in the end it was for Mae. It was for their life. He loved her, above everything else."

"He did?"

"Yes."

"I just always thought she . . . I thought that whatever their feelings were, their marriage was practical. An arrangement."

"No. He said that their love had the power to knock his feet out from beneath him. But without her love he didn't know what it was to have his feet planted. That made more sense to me than anything ever has. Without you I don't know who I am. I'm not sure that I really know yet. Because I only let myself have part of you. Part of us. Now I wanted it all. And I can't promise you that I'm going to be different overnight. But I'm always going to open up when I should. Hell, I might close down. But I'm going to choose you. I'm going to choose to work on it, every day of my life from here on out."

"Carson," she breathed. "I love you. And I'm so glad that . . . that we made it here. Because it was a hell of a journey."

"I was emotionally unavailable because my heart belongs to you. But that terrified the hell out of me, and so I did everything I could to find a way to keep you without risking anything. I'm done with that. I want you. Always and forever you, Perry."

Perry flung herself into his arms, and he held her close. "You are the love of my life. You make me feel that feeling. So big and terrible that I ran from it back then. But I'm not running anymore."

He kissed her lips. "My pirate princess."

"Where will we live?"

"I'll move to Medford for you."

"I don't think that's necessary."

"But I would. I'd give up the ranch. We could go to Applebee's every Friday."

"Let's stay here." She looked around the house, and she realized . . .

He had fixed it up, just for them. They were going to have their happy ending here, just like Jedidiah and Mae.

"All right," he said. "Let's make our home here. And you can grow as many flowers as you want up by Outlaw Lake. We'll make it our second home."

"I like that."

"And I love you."

Perry Bramble loved Carson Wilder with all of her heart. And that heart was no longer shattered.

It was whole, and so was she.

Epilogue

They did get married by the lake, Perry in a white dress that was reminiscent of the one she'd worn all those years ago with a mind to tempt him—and she did tempt him.

In ways that took his breath away. He understood, then, exactly what Jedediah Tanner had meant when he said that while he had made wedding vows once before; he didn't really understand what they meant until the second time. Carson was the same. Because this time, his heart belonged fully to the woman he was promising himself to. This time, he understood the risk, the reward.

This time, he wasn't rushing into something to run from what he really wanted. What he really needed. This was the first time, really. When he looked at Perry, he saw a hope for the future he had never even realized he could want.

When he looked at Perry, he understood love without fear. Because that was what they had both decided on. They had spent twenty-five years building up trust in each other, and it had taken all that time to transform that into the courage to love each other without walls.

But now that they did . . .

It made everything else small in comparison. Because it was no longer a hopeless world, not to him.

He didn't need to be a hero. He only needed to be Perry Bramble's husband.

When they kissed, and their friends and family clapped and cheered, he held her close. "I really did marry my best friend," he whispered. "And I knew it."

"What did you know?" she whispered.

"You were mine all along."

Please read on for a sample of the next
Rustler Mountain novel by Maisey Yates,
Lonesome Ridge.

Chapter 1

I never was a lady, but now I think I've gone too far.

—Belle Martin's Diary, July 1865

Jessie Jane Hancock was the proud owner of a whole collection of toxic traits.

Generally, she found them to be a good time at the very least. But currently, her desperate need to climb impossible mountains was eating at her. Making her life downright miserable, in fact.

So miserable that she got distracted and did something she rarely ever did: Jessie Jane missed a trick. Which was how she found herself tumbling off her horse face-first into the arena dirt.

"Whoa, there."

She popped up and looked across the arena at her older brother West, who was not on his way to help her up but sitting there on the back of his horse, his arms crossed across his broad chest as he stared at her.

"Thanks for the help," she groused as she stood up, before hauling herself onto the back of her horse.

West only looked at her, the maddening fool. "If you fall off the horse, you have to get back on again. No one can do it for you."

"Well, aren't you a big old Magic Eight Ball."

"I've been called a lot of things, Jess, but rarely that."

"*Rarely* isn't *never*, West."

She was supposed to be rehearsing the new routine for this summer's opening of Butch Hancock's Wild West Show. Instead, she was stewing. About the upcoming mayoral election. The thing was, everyone hated the current mayor.

Well. That wasn't true, because Danielle LeFevre *had* been elected. But she was a mean girl. She had been a mean girl in high school, and she was mean now. She had very notoriously stolen the town librarian's fiancé—and Jessie Jane definitely believed that the man in question needed to be held equally accountable. But the man in question was basically a turnip with testicles. So she held him less responsible because he was an idiot.

Danielle wasn't an idiot. For all that she was an awful human being.

Rustler Mountain was a small town nestled in the southern Oregon mountains only eight miles from the California border. It had a rich gold rush and Wild West history and was steeped in myth and legend. The Hancock family had made money off that myth and legend for years.

Because with their family reputation, there was nothing else to do but lean into it.

In Rustler Mountain, things were black and white. It was as simple as good guys and bad guys. Some of the town was descended from lawmen. While others . . . well, they were outlaws.

The Wilder family being the most notorious of the outlaws: Back in the late 1800s, Austin Wilder had been shot dead in the main street of Rustler Mountain by Sheriff Lee Talbot. Of course, a hundred and fifty years later a Talbot and a Wilder had married, and suddenly the narrative of the town had been disrupted.

It was as if a mountain that had stood unchanging for centuries had suddenly ruptured and reordered the landscape around it.

Those clearly defined lines weren't so clearly defined anymore.

There had been big pushes to correct some of the misinformation that had stood as history for well over a century, and as that narrative had changed, so had some of the ways the town worked.

She couldn't lie—it was a little bit annoying to have more of the nice townies in her favorite dive bar on the weekends. But it was also nice to have some more locals showing up to the Hancocks' Wild West Show.

Their show, which featured reenactments and trick riding, along with rodeo events, was extremely popular with the inhabitants of adjacent communities, but was often overlooked by their own. But again, that had to do with the reputation of the Hancock family.

A reputation that rarely bothered her. Except now . . .

"I can hear you thinking."

"I doubt it. I think deep thoughts operate on a frequency you can't actually hear."

West snorted. "If only. But unfortunately, I know you too well."

"That viper is running *unopposed*."

"The viper?"

"Danielle LeFevre. There is no other mayoral candidate, and there are just three days left to declare."

"Not your problem."

"It's everyone's problem. You know that noise ordinance she's been promoting is going to affect us—which isn't even fair. Her parking permit stuff is outrageous, and she's misallocating funds—you can be sure of that."

"I agree with you. She sucks. But why you?" West asked.

She didn't answer that question directly. "I just can't understand why no one else is running against her."

"They aren't dying to be in charge of a town with less than two thousand people and lord their supposed authority over everyone around them?"

"All right. When you put it like that."

"Danielle isn't your problem. Because she is a small-town mayor, she's just going to do what she's going to do. Spend money that probably should've gone to patch cracks in the sidewalk on silly trips. End up stealing the librarian's fiancé, which I wouldn't even kick up a fuss about except that he has the same name as her brother."

Jessie made a face. "Ugh."

"But hey," West continued, "our ancestors were full-on betrayers and murderers."

"Not *all* of them. Just *one* of them was."

"One of them was a courtesan."

"You say that like it's a bad thing." Jessie Jane grinned widely at her brother.

"No, I didn't. I'm just pointing it out."

"If something is in demand, it's a smart business decision to go into that industry. And I think we know what sells. Always," she pointed out.

"I certainly am not dissing the great and glorious Belle. Not for any reason at all. My point is, we have an eclectic history."

"Sure."

And that history pretty much never included walking the straight and narrow. Oh sure, they were on the up-and-up with the Wild West Show. But Jessie couldn't deny that she had some side hustles that were a little less than scrupulous. On the other hand, she also had a farrier business that was totally scrupulous.

And anyway, regarding gambling, it was her opinion that if people wanted to bet their hard-earned money on horse races, fistfights, and football games, it wasn't her job to talk them out of it. And she made a little bit of cash when she talked them into it.

She was good at explaining a position. Holding it.

If she knew one thing, it was that she was . . . well, one of her friends in high school had said once that she should start a cult. Because for all that she was rough around the edges, she had a way with people.

A hard-earned way.

Not with everybody, though. Flynn Wilder came to mind. He was not charmed by her. Not at all. Annoying, because he was a sexy bastard. Another unclimbable mountain, but one that Jessie had long ago accepted she would never scale. There were a lot of handsome men. If she wanted to hook up, she could just . . . pick one of them. She didn't need to borrow trouble with a Wilder.

But what a spectacle it would be . . .

"You're literally scheming," West said.

"I'm not *scheming*." West continued to treat her to his patented hard glare that many women about town called *sexy,* and she called *annoying*. "Okay. I'm lightly scheming. It's a mild scheme. But it will probably never make it out of the scheming phase."

He lifted his brows. "And if it does?"

"At that point it will become a *plot*," she explained.

"Tell me more."

"If we execute it, then it's a crusade. Maybe even a quest."

"'We'?"

Jessie looked out at the mountains, at the jagged line where the pine trees met the wide blue sky. "Don't worry. I'm not going to involve you in anything. Yet."

"What I would like to involve *you* in is a perfectly executed trick-riding routine where you don't break your neck."

"I can do that."

She urged her horse forward, but she couldn't keep the idea from turning in her head, over and over again.

She had lied to her brother. This was more than just a scheme. More than a plot.

She had a feeling that before the day was out, it was going to become a quest.

And when Jessie Jane Hancock went on a quest, she didn't come back home empty-handed.

Visit our website at
KensingtonBooks.com
to sign up for our newsletters, read more from your favorite authors, see books by series, view reading group guides, and more!

BOOK CLUB
BETWEEN THE CHAPTERS

Become a Part of Our
Between the Chapters Book Club
Community and Join the Conversation

Betweenthechapters.net

Submit your book review for a chance to win exclusive Between the Chapters swag you can't get anywhere else!
https://www.kensingtonbooks.com/pages/review/